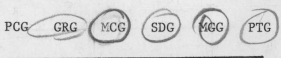

Other books by Shelia E. Lipsey

Into Each Life
Sinsatiable

MY SON'S WIFE

SHELIA E. LIPSEY

URBAN CHRISTIAN

www.urbanchristianonline.net

Urban Books
1199 Straight Path
West Babylon, NY 11704

ISBN- 13: 978-1-60162-971-5
ISBN- 10: 1-60162-971-0

First Printing October 2008
Printed in the United States of America

10 9 8 7 6 5 4 3 2 1

This is a work of fiction. Any references or similarities to actual events, real people, living, or dead, or to real locales are intended to give the novel a sense of reality. Any similarity in other names, characters, places, and incidents is entirely coincidental.

Distributed by Kensington Corp.
Submit Wholesale Orders to:
Kensington Publishing Corp.
C/O Penguin Group (USA) Inc.
Attention: Order Processing
405 Murray Hill Parkway
East Rutherford, NJ 07073-2316
Phone: 1-800-526-0275
Fax: 1-800-227-9604

Dedication

To All Those Who Are Different

Have we not all one father? hath not one God created us?
Why do we deal treacherously every man against his brother?
Malachi 2:10a

Acknowledgements

I honor you, God, for all of your manifold blessings. For loving yourself some Shelia. To you, God, for continually showering me with your unmerited favor, unconditional love, mercy, and grace. To you, God, for ordering my steps. To you, God, for never letting me go, for keeping me cradled safely in your arms. You alone are my rock, my sword, my shield, my buckler. I am grateful, grateful, so grateful, for every good and perfect gift bestowed on me by you. I love you, Lord, because you first loved me. In everything I do, may I always give you the praise, glory, and honor.

Your child,
Shelia

"There is therefore now no condemnation to those who are in Christ Jesus, who do not walk according to the flesh, but according to the Spirit."
Romans 8.1

1

"It's not the tragedies that kill us. It's the messes."
—*Dorothy Parker*

"Frankie, listen. Let's not argue about . . ."

"What do you mean? Don't you think it's a little too late for that? This argument has already started."

Frankie's voice rose higher. Rena took a step backward. She had seen Frankie's volatile temper one too many times. And with less than a week left before she walked down the aisle with Stiles, she didn't want to risk having a bruised face.

"You know that the wedding is already planned and set. The invitations have gone out so even if I wanted to, there's no way I can back out now. Face it, Frankie; I'm going to marry him." Rena chose her words carefully as she moved another step back from Frankie's reach.

"No, I won't face it. What you meant to say is you don't want to call this wedding off. I don't believe this."

"Look, Frankie, listen to me. Please." Rena inched in toward Frankie again like an earthworm trying to find its way back into the dirt from whence it came. "Frankie, believe me when I say this. I love you. You think I don't remember what we've shared since we were fifteen years old? If only things were different. But they aren't. So please try to understand." Rena reached over and gently rubbed the tips of Frankie's quivering fingers. Tears crested in her eyes as she saw the hurt etched across Frankie's face.

"But how can you do this? How can you do this to us, Rena? You don't love Stiles. He's just convenient. You want him because of who he is and what he can provide for you. But love should mean more to you than a nice bank account or being the wife of the adopted son of the senior pastor of some hypocritical church."

"You know it's more to it than that," Rena responded. "Stiles and I have a lot of things in common. So what if he happens to be Pastor Chauncey Graham's son. The thing about it is he and I both love God. He's kind. He's gentle. He's compassionate and he loves me."

Frankie moved in closer and Rena's eye widened as she waited on what she thought was coming next. She cowered and tried to cover her face.

"Please don't do this, Frankie. Try to understand. See things from my perspective."

"Don't worry. I'm not going to hurt you." Frankie stood close to Rena and caressed her face. "Look at you. You're pathetic, Rena. Don't you get it? Maybe Stiles is all of that and a bag of chips to some. But not once have you ever told me that you love him. The two of you have been seeing each other for what, almost eight months, and mostly behind my back? But when I did find out about you two, I thought to myself; maybe you needed to venture out some, then you would come back to me and realize, once and for all, that we were meant to be together." Frankie's voice hardened with each word. "And you'd know that you loved only me."

"You're right. I do love you, Frankie. I love you with all of my heart, but it's a different kind of love."

"No, I don't think so. It's not me who's living the lie. I'm not ashamed of what we've shared. You're the one who has the reservations. But like you said, we've been friends far too long. We love each other. Don't you see, Rena? I am who I am, and you are who you are. "

"I can't believe this, Frankie. I mean look at us." Rena extended her hands, looking at herself and then over at Frankie.

"What's wrong with us? Tell me, Rena."

"For God's sake, Frankie, we're two women! Where do you think we can go and be happy? How can we ever escape the harsh reality of what people will think about us? And don't let me even begin to think about our families and what they would say. Or I should say, what God thinks about us. There's no way I could face my parents, my family, and I certainly couldn't face my church. You, well you're stronger than I am. You always have been. I know you don't believe in the Bible and what God has to say about homosexuality and lesbianism, but I do. I never intended for this to happen between us, but it did. And I'm sorry. I'm so sorry, Frankie."

"Sorry? How can you say that you're sorry after everything we've been through? You're a twenty-five-year-old woman, Rena. You're grown. But you act like you owe something to your parents, the world, and that church you run off to every Sunday. Tell me, if God is so righteous and loving, then why do you keep telling me that he hates what we have together, when all we have is love? What's so wrong with that?" Frankie looked for some connection in Rena's eyes. But for the first time, there was nothing but emptiness.

"I'm going to marry Stiles. I have to. And I hope you'll be at the wedding. I need you to be there." Rena's dark eyes pleaded with her. "It's the only way for us to end this madness. I'm sorry," Rena turned to walk away.

"Rena?"

Rena paused and looked back. "Yes, Frankie?"

"You think you're sorry now. But you don't know what sorry means. Wait until you marry Stiles Graham. Just wait." Frankie's voice trailed off into a whisper.

2

"Nobody has ever measured . . . how much the heart can hold."
—Zelda Fitzgerald

"Pastor, I have everything ready. I picked up your tux while you were at the hospital visiting Elder Campbell."

"Audrey, what would I do without you? If our young people would only listen to God's voice and wait on the mate God has ordained for them, then they could have what we've shared together these past twenty-seven years." A man of short stature, Pastor Chauncey had to lean over to kiss his even shorter first lady. "I love you, Audrey."

"I know you do, Pastor, but it's still good to hear." Audrey could never make rhyme or reason out of why she called her husband 'Pastor' like any other church member. She just did. The couple had met twenty-nine years ago. At the time, Audrey was a young widow with a three-and-a-half-year-old son named Stiles.

Stiles' father had worked as a construction foreman. The day Audrey received the call about that horrible accident changed her and Stiles' life forever. She'd raced to Methodist University Hospital, but by the time she arrived, her husband was dead. She learned later that he had fallen more than 300 feet from a scaffold to his death.

Around the same time, Pastor Chauncey became the pastor of Holy Rock Church. Audrey, a human resources administrative assistant at the time, was invited to the church of barely 100 members by a co-worker. Reserved and quiet, Audrey started to open up a little more each time she heard Pastor's spirited sermons. She and Stiles attended faithfully for several months, before Audrey made the decision to become a member of Holy Rock. She quickly joined a grief recovery group and slowly moved forward with making a life for her and Stiles.

When Audrey and Pastor Chauncey met, he was a bachelor and ladies at the church were vying for his attention. But Chauncey Graham actually had his eye on the beautiful, grieving widow, Audrey, since the first day she had walked into the church. The day of the annual church picnic, he finally made his move and started a conversation with her. Audrey welcomed the conversation and was quite impressed by the ease she felt around Chauncey. Stiles took to the young minister just as quickly as his mother. That day was the beginning of their courtship. After dating for a little over a year and falling madly in love, Pastor Graham asked her to become his wife. Audrey gladly accepted his proposal, and four months later they were united in holy matrimony. Without reservation, Pastor legally adopted Stiles and began raising him as his own. Two years into their God-ordained marriage, Audrey and Chauncey gave Stiles a beautiful baby sister, Francesca. But mostly everyone called her Frankie.

Frankie was furious when Rena told her she was going to marry Stiles. How could she do such a thing? Frankie paced the hardwood floor of her apartment until the shiny waxed glow became dull and brittle. She plopped down on the red microfiber sofa. Wiping the crocodile tears from her oval-shaped face with the back of her hand, she swore out loud. Rena may have been fooling everyone else, but Frankie knew that it was her that Rena truly loved. She lay back against the couch and began to reminisce.

Frankie and Rena's relationship started innocently enough when the girls attended White Station High School. Both of them were reserved and quiet.

Rena Jackson's family, except her two siblings eleven years older, relocated from Andover, Massachusetts when her father's engineering job transferred him to Memphis.

On her first day of class, Rena walked into the tenth grade advance placement History room with a terrified look on her face. At the back of the classroom Rena spotted an empty seat close to a window and hurriedly walked toward it.

Frankie remembered watching intensely as Rena sat down in the seat next to hers. Rena reminded Frankie of a frightened, lost puppy.

Frankie leaned over and whispered, "It's not that bad, honest. None of us bite." Frankie smiled, and Rena returned with a smile of her own. At the end of class, Frankie introduced herself. The two girls struck up a conversation. Frankie offered to sit with her during lunch and Rena was relieved to have found someone to whom she could easily relate. Rena told her about her recent move to Memphis, and Frankie filled her in on the school and on their East Memphis neighborhood.

Much like Rena, Frankie was used to seperating herself from crowds. Her father being a minister made her that much more into herself. But Frankie's brother, Stiles, seemed to soak up the attention he attracted by being a preacher's son. He was one of the most popular guys at school. Stiles was responsible, indirectly, for the two girls meeting and ultimately becoming best friends. It was Stiles who had encouraged his sister to step out of her shell and make friends.

Rena's family members, though none were ministers, were staunch Christians too. The girls discovered they lived and in the same neighborhood.

It didn't take long for Frankie to invite Rena and her family to attend her father's church. Right off the bat, the Jackson family fell in love with Pastor Chauncey's laid back style of preaching. After visiting several churches throughout the city, Rena's parents settled on Holy Rock and became active members. Like Frankie and Rena, Pastor Chauncey and Rena's father, David Jackson, became close friends. David was appointed as one of the deacons of the church while Rena's mother, Meryl Jackson, became a member of the deaconesses.

The closeness of their parents brought Frankie and Rena even closer. If not at church or school, Rena would be over to Frankie's house, or Frankie would be at Rena's house. The two became inseparable. There was nothing they wouldn't share with each other, well almost nothing.

3

At the age of eleven, Francesca Graham's ideal childhood took a drastic turn that would forever change her life. It all started with Francesca's first cousin, sixteen-year-old Fonda, the in-between child of Francesca's Aunt Lucille. If there was any doubt about the existence of middle child syndrome, Fonda dispelled such reservations. Much like a high school bully, whenever Fonda and her family came to Francesca's house, Fonda exerted her frustrations by aggravating Francesca. With each visit, Fonda's bullying escalated to the point where she was down right cruel and vicious. Francesca found out sooner rather than later that there was no use telling her mother or Fonda's mother about Fonda. Fonda's manipulative ways, coupled with the fact she was older, made Francesca appear to be nothing more than a whining little tattle-tale, so they didn't pay any attention to her.

Fonda accused Francesca of being a spoiled brat who got everything she wanted. It wasn't Francesca's fault that Fonda never seemed to quite fit in with anyone, and she definitely couldn't help it if Fonda felt like she had to constantly compete for her parents' attention. But Fonda sure treated her like she was the one to blame. She treated her meaner than a rabid pit bull.

One hot July evening, Pastor and Audrey had a church function to attend. Stiles had plans to spend the weekend with friends at Reelfoot Lake. Francesca listened from around the corner as Audrey suggested to Pastor that they ask Fonda to spend the night to watch Francesca.

Francesca huddled in the corner of the den and listened to Audrey call Aunt Lucille on the phone. She prayed that Fonda wouldn't be able to come, but her prayer wasn't answered this time.

Within an hour, Fonda bolted into the Graham house like she ruled the place. Not even thirty minutes after Pastor and Audrey's departure, Fonda revealed her sick side. Fonda forced Francesca to do unnatural things to her. In return, Fonda did the very same things to her. Francesca begged and pleaded for Fonda to stop, but Fonda acted like she was in another world. Her eyes glared, and obscenities flowed like rushing water from her mouth. After everything was over, Fonda threatened to kill Francesca's tabby cat, Charlie, if she snitched. To make certain she wouldn't blab her mouth, Fonda punched her hard in the gut before picking up Charlie and slinging him back and forth like she was going to throw him against the wall. Francesca's eyes bulged in terror. Laughing wickedly, Fonda released the hissing cat, and turned and walked out of Francesca's bedroom. She violated of little Francesca months, until it miraculously, and Fonda became unusually nice. There were times she even brought kitty treats for Charlie. There were other times when Fonda took the time to show Francesca girly things, like how to put on makeup and how to choose the perfect outfits to wear to school or church. While Francesca's mind couldn't process the reason for the change in Fonda, she was sure glad about it. Soon, memories of the awful things Fonda did erased themselves from Francesca's mind and life as she once knew it returned.

Unfortunately, soon after Fonda and Francesca's relationship changed, Audrey changed radically toward her daughter. Her once kind, loving demeanor toward Francesca evolved into Audrey being impatient and mean. Her whippings, punishment for behavior that was deemed unacceptable, became more frequent. Again, Francesca's young mind couldn't grasp what she had done to make her mother dislike her so. Whatever it was, Francesca grew to resent Audrey to the point that she hated her mother for hating her. A wall began to grow around Francesca's tender heart to shield her from the heartache and pain.

At the age of fifteen, the emotional wall around her heart took root and became stronger. Francesca would soon learn just how much she needed the strength of that wall when Minister Travis D. Jones came into her life.

Minister Travis D. Jones was hired as Holy Rock's youth pastor. When Frankie first saw him, she was smitten by his charm and pleasing looks. She quickly developed a crush on the young minister. She enjoyed spending time with him at church, helping him with youth activities and doing small favors for him like making copies. There was a time when she believed. Whenever she had problems at school, she'd hurry to talk to Minister Travis. Somehow things didn't seem so bad after talking to him. Minister Travis doted on Frankie. He called her his special girl and never referred to her as Frankie, always Francesca.

"I wish Minister Travis liked me as much as he seems to like you," Rena told her one evening after a weekly youth meeting.

"I know you do," Frankie snapped her fingers and laughed. "But it isn't going to happen."

The changes were subtle. Minister Travis always hugged Francesca, but soon his hugs lasted a little longer. Minister Travis always kissed her on the top of her head, so when he began pecking her on the forehead, it was no big deal. Anyone can make a mistake and brush against her, so Francesca dismissed it when Minister Travis brushed up against her more often. When his hands lingered on her body in places that made her feel on edge, Francesca dispelled the thoughts and chalked them up to the dreams she'd had about him. Minister Travis was a good guy who happened to like her. He would never think of doing anything inappropriate.

The night Minister Travis saw her getting ready to leave youth night services without her trusty side kick, Rena, he approached her.

"Francesca, I'd like to talk to you about the youth rally we're holding next month. Do you think you could come to my office for a few minutes?"

For the first time, something about the look on his face, and the urgency in his voice, caused Francesca to search nervously around for some of the other teenagers. Too bad Rena was at home with a bad stomach virus. With Rena by her side, she wouldn't have been uneasy at all.

"No, I can't tonight, Minister Travis." She saw two members of their youth group standing on the other side of the church parking lot waiting on their rides. She called out to them, and walked in their direction. "Safety in numbers," she mumbled to herself, without understanding why. A red Taurus pulled up next to the girls. They waved good-bye to Francesca and hopped inside the car.

Minister Travis bore a satisfied grin as he stood watching the scene.

"Francesca, how about that meeting? It won't take long."

"I . . . I'm waiting on my ride. Daddy told me that since he had to preach at a church across town, my mother would be picking me up tonight.

"I'm your ride," Minister Travis remarked.

"What do you mean?"

"I just spoke with your mother." The satisfied grin returned. "She's not feeling well. It sounds like she may be coming down with that stomach virus that's going around. I believe she said that her blood pressure was up a little too. She's home resting. I told her that I would give you a ride. And you know I can't turn down a request from the first lady, now can I? Come on, let's discuss the rally, and then I'll take you straight home. Promise."

Francesca reluctantly trailed behind Minister Travis. The church was eerily quiet. In silence, she followed him to his office. He closed the oak door behind the two of them and instructed her to have a seat.

True to his word, Minister Travis discussed some of the plans he had come up with for the youth rally. Francesca slowly began to feel at ease again as she listened to the excitement in his voice when he shared his ideas with her. She scolded herself for her stupid reservations.

When Minister Travis stood up, walked over, and sat down beside her, she didn't flinch as he pointed out the various scenes he'd sketched for the rally that was to take place on the church parking lot. She began to give him her feedback on his ideas and threw in some of her own.

"Well, now, what did I tell you?" he said a half an hour later after they finalized some plans. "That wasn't so bad, now was it?"

"No," she answered coyly. "I really need to go now, Minister Travis. I have some homework that's due tomorrow," she added.

"Of course, no problem," he answered. Walking over to the door, he grabbed the brass door handle. Francesca stood beside him. But instead of opening it, Minister Travis stood in front of her and turned the lock on the door. Her heart felt like it was about to jump out of her throat.

"What are you doing? Why are you locking the door?" Her heart pounded against her small chest.

He answered her by placing his hands on her shoulders. Silence followed.

"Please, don't hurt me, Minister Travis," Francesca struggled to free herself from his vice-like grip. Her pleas seemed to only add fuel to his sick flame of desire. Muffling her screams with violent unmentionable acts, he pushed the papers off of his desk with one hand and with the other he forced her to lie back on the cold wooden desk. While he ripped away any barrier to his appointed destination, the impenetrable wall appeared, and Francesca retreated into a world void of feeling. She refused to scream or cry. *Don't cry. Don't you dare cry.*

When he finished satisfying his ugly desire, he kissed her forehead. "Remember, you're my special girl, my very special girl, Francesca. Now come on, let's get you home. I don't want you to miss your homework."

4

*"I do not want the peace which passeth understanding, I want
the understanding which bringeth peace."*
—*Helen Keller*

Frankie was too terrified and ashamed to tell anyone
about that horrible night; not even Rena, her best
friend in the entire world. She believed that somehow it
must have been her fault. Why else would Fonda and
then Minister Travis do the things they did? It had to be
her fault. She was a bad, bad girl. No wonder Audrey
hated her so much.

Frankie thought about telling Daddy, but she couldn't
find the courage to do so. He would be so disappointed
in her for allowing Minister Travis to do what he had
done. And then she would have to tell him about Fonda.
He would see how bad she was too. She couldn't have
both of her parents hating her. What would she have said
to her father anyway? Would she tell him that she didn't
scream because she just wanted it to be over with?
Would she tell him that she didn't fight back because she
was terrified that he would do it to her again and again
and again? Who would take her word over a man of
God? She was dirty and filthy. No wonder God let them
hurt her. God must have hated her too.

Eerily similar to Fonda, after that night, Minister Travis never attempted to harm her again. Quite the contrary, he walked around like nothing had ever happened. There appeared to be an unspoken pact between the two of them and he was assured that what had happened would forever remain their little secret.

Nine months after he raped her, Minister Travis resigned as youth minister at Holy Rock to accept a position at a church on the east coast. Minister Travis was gone and out of Frankie's life for good. Fonda was all grown up and busy with her own life. Part of Frankie was elated, but the other part of her felt awful that some other girl might fall victim to the same horrible things that she had endured. Memories haunted Frankie at night, in place of sleep, but with each day that passed, the wall she'd come to rely on helped her to push the vile thoughts deeper and deeper inside.

"Are we still going to study for the English test this afternoon?" Frankie asked as they boarded the bus after school.

"Yeah. Why don't you go home with me, and we can fix some sandwiches."

"Okay. I'll call home and tell my mother when we get to your house."

An hour passed before they closed their English lit books and fell back on the bed, chattering about the day's events.

Rena placed her arms underneath her head. Frankie moved closer to her and rested her head innocently on Rena's elbow.

Silence filled the room.

"I hate boys!" Frankie sat upright on the side of the bed.

"Where did that come from?" Rena asked with a surprised look on her face. She sat up and positioned herself beside Frankie.

"I don't know. I just know that I hate them. I know it might sound weird to you. And I don't want to freak you out or anything but . . . "

"But, what?" interrupted Rena.

"I think I understand why people sometimes, you know, go the other way." Frankie said slowly, hesitating as she looked at Rena.

"Do you mean, go the other way like being gay or something?" Rena's eyes bulged at the thought as if she was asking herself. "Where is all of this coming from? Why are you talking like this?"

"I'm just being for real, that's all."

"I can't believe you're saying stuff like this. You know better than to even think that way. You won't go to heaven for sure," Rena warned.

"I don't care. Anyway, I can't help the way I feel. And don't you go telling anyone about it either," Frankie retorted.

"I'm not. You know me better than that. But I do think that you've gone off the deep end with this gay talk."

"Forget it then. Anyway, I'd better go." Frankie proceeded to put her books back inside her backpack. She stood up and walked toward Rena's bedroom door. Then, she reached on the dresser and grabbed her purse.

Rena moved back in her bed and crossed both legs Indian style. "Suit yourself. I'll talk to you later."

"See ya."

On the way home, Frankie thought about what she had said. She didn't know what had possessed her to reveal to Rena that she hated boys. It was the first time she had admitted it to herself as well. Before now, every time the thought had tried to enter her mind, she dispelled it with some other thought. But today, lying next to Rena,

she felt different. Was being a lesbian who she really
was? Or was it because of what Fonda had done to her?
But Minister Travis had done the same thing. *What's
wrong with me?* Frankie was confused. On the one hand,
the thought of being with a girl didn't seem wrong. How
could that be? Frankie knew that her father taught from
his pulpit that homosexuality and lesbianism was an
abomination against God. She could hear his thundering
voice as he ministered to his growing congregation about
the sins of the flesh.

Pastor Chauncey had taught at one of his Sunday sermons, "Don't let anybody tell you that the Bible is silent
about homosexuality. The word of God has a lot to say
about it, and it's clear. I don't know what's up with these
young folks today. You can walk up and down the malls,
on the streets, in the department stores, and you can't tell
the girls from the boys, or boys from the girls. It's some
kind of fad — like it's cool to be gay. Well, I'm telling you
that it's a sin and a shame. God is not pleased with the
actions of His people."

Pastor Chauncey preached while Frankie thought, *God
ain't pleased with girls who do unthinkable things to other
girls, and He sure isn't pleased with grown men raping young
girls either—but I don't hear anybody preaching about that.*

In the recesses of her mind, she heard Pastor continue
to preach. "In the book of Romans it says, 'Because of
this, God gave them over to shameful lusts. Even their
women exchanged natural relations for unnatural ones.
In the same way, the men also abandoned natural relations with women and were inflamed with lust for one
another. Men committed indecent acts with other men,
and received in themselves the due penalty for their perversion. Furthermore, since they did not think it worthwhile to retain the knowledge of God, He gave them
over to a depraved mind, to do what ought not to be

done." Pastor's voice rolled like thunder as his eyes roved over the congregation. "I'm telling you people, you need to wake up. Get your houses in order. The Lord is coming back and you better be ready. Judgment day is swiftly approaching. I don't know about you . . ."

Frankie tuned out the remainder of her father's message. If he only knew about her thoughts and desires, what would he think of his precious little Francesca then?

The change in Frankie's personality was subtle. No one said much of anything when she switched from wearing skirts and dresses every day to wearing jeans and casual slacks. Not even the lavishly dressed first lady mumbled a word of discontent.

While Rena was into dressing in the latest fashions, Frankie began insisting that everyone call her Frankie not some of the time, but all of the time. It became so bad that she refused to answer if anyone called her anything other than Frankie. Francesca was gone forever, as far as she was concerned. No more stupid little Francesca who couldn't take care of herself. No more crying herself to sleep at night and no more praying to God, who didn't even come to help her when she was being hurt and abused.

"Frankie, what is up with you? Are you still on that, 'I hate boys' trip?" Rena asked her weeks later when her family was over at Frankie's house grilling.

"Sure am." Frankie swirled her neck from side to side and stood back with both hands on her hips. "And if you have a problem with it, then that's too bad. If I'm your best friend, you should accept me just the way I am."

"I do accept you the way you are." A warning voice whispered in Rena's head. "I've never said anything different have I? Or treated you differently? Right?"

"Yeah, I guess you're right." Frankie relaxed a little and sat down on the couch next to her.

Rena paused. "I've been thinking."

"Thinking about what?" asked Frankie.

"How do you know that you hate boys if you haven't, you know, been with one?" Rena's words trailed off and her shoulders tightened.

"Because I know that I'm not attracted to any of the boys at school, church, or anywhere else. Frankie's fingertips rubbed the soft Italian leather in a circular motion. "But when I see a girl, it's like, well, I get these butterflies inside." She pointed to her stomach.

"Are you serious?" Rena stirred uneasily in her seat. "Uh, then let me ask you something else."

"Go on, ask me then."

"What about me? Are you, you know, attracted to me? I *am* your best friend. And I think I'm rather cute," joked Rena.

When Frankie didn't respond with laughter, Rena stood still, careful not to say anything else.

Biting her bottom lip, Frankie looked away. "I am attracted to you. I just didn't know how to tell you. Remember the day I first told you that?" Frankie looked down at her shoes.

"Yeah," Rena replied.

"I felt it, then but I couldn't tell you. That's why I blurted out that I hated boys. Feeling like I felt lying next to you confirmed it."

"Really?" she asked.

"Yes, really." replied Frankie

In deep thought, Rena finally started talking again. Her next words shocked Frankie.

"You can experiment with me if you want to."

"What did you just say?" Frankie asked, her eyes looming large as light bulbs at Rena's suggestion.

The two girls stood in the family room. Looking around to be certain no one was listening, Rena started to repeat her offer.

"Wait," Frankie insisted. Looking around for herself, she grabbed Rena's hand and led her into her bedroom. "Somebody might walk inside and hear us."

Entering Frankie's bedroom, Rena stopped dead in her tracks. The once dainty room now looked lifeless. Frankie had painted the room from a soft pink tone to a dark blue. Sneakers lined the walls and a stereo system sat in another corner of the bedroom. All of the posters Frankie once proudly displayed all over her wall of her favorite actor, Will Smith, were gone. The dozens of stuffed animals she loved were nowhere in sight.

"Wow, you're really taking this lesbian thing seriously, aren't you? What did your parents say? I can't believe your momma let you do this."

"I'm my own person." Frankie's voice rose.

Rena froze.

"I'm sick of people trying to boss me around. She doesn't care what I do anyway. If it's not anything to do with my father, church, or my brother, then it's not important to her." Frankie's voice trembled.

"I . . . don't know what to say, Frankie. Your momma has always been weird like that. I mean, I'm not checking her or anything."

Frankie shuffled a pair of sneakers and jeans from one side of the room to the other.

"Weird is an understatement. My mother just does not like me. And you know what, Rena?"

"What, Frankie?"

"I'm fine with that."

"Francesca, uh, I meant to say Frankie, you know your mother loves you."

"Look, stop the small talk. What were you talking

about out there?" Frankie closed her bedroom door behind her.

"I said, you can practice with me. If you're really serious, then you need to know for sure if it's for real or if you're just mixed up in the head. I don't know, maybe it's a stupid suggestion. I just don't want you out there trying something and you get in trouble."

"No, no. You might be right. If I can't trust you, who can I trust?"

The two girls never meant to defile their minds and bodies. It just happened. Nervous and unsure, the curious and naïve teenagers stared at each other. Their eyes locked as they moved closer to each other. For a moment, time seemed to stand still, yet the journey into the unknown, into the forbidden, was just beginning.

"Frankie! Rena!" First Lady Graham called. "Where are you two? The food is ready," she yelled.

Frankie was the first one to pop her head out of her bedroom door. "Chill out, we are in my room listening to music and talking, Momma," she answered.

"Well, everyone is outside and you two should be no exception. Come on out here right now," she ordered.

"Sure," Frankie replied with irritation in her voice. She hoped that the wrong they'd just committed wouldn't reveal itself on her and Rena's flushed faces.

It was Saturday, March 18, the day that would forever redefine Francesca Graham and Rena Jackson's relationship.

5

"Each has his past shut in him like the leaves of a book known to him by heart and his friends can only read the title."
—*Virginia Woolf*

Shortly after her fifteenth birthday, Francesca's parents began noticing the change in her. She was more reserved, rarely talked to them, and had acquired new friends. When she was at home, she mostly hung out in her room with her door shut. The Grahams attributed the change to teenage rebellion. However, that theory soon changed when Frankie's grades plummeted. She refused to attend church. It didn't matter that her father was the pastor. It didn't matter if she was grounded for disobedience. It didn't matter if Audrey whipped her or smacked her around. She wasn't going back inside another church, ever again, and no one could make her. She no longer listened to anything they had to say, if it wasn't something she wanted to hear.

Tap, tap, tap.

Frankie ignored the knock on her door.

Tap, tap, tap.

"Who is it? I'm busy," hissed Frankie.

"It's your daddy, sweetheart. We need to talk." Pastor scratched his balding head.

"Not now."

"Francesca, I want to talk to you, sweetheart." A wrinkled brow revealed Pastor's concern.

"How many times do I have to tell y'all not to call me Francesca. Gosh," huffed Frankie, shifting from one leg to another. "Look, I was about to go out with some friends. Can't it wait?" she complained.

"As a matter of fact, it can't, young lady." With a shift of his body, Pastor directed her toward the study. "Now come with me to the study. Your friends will just have to wait."

With folded arms, Frankie followed her father to the study. She plopped down on the sofa, still pouting. Pastor sat down next to her.

"Frances . . . Frankie, I need you to talk to me, sweetheart." Pastor reached over and placed his hand gently on her shoulder. Remaining cold and stiff, Frankie refused to acknowledge him.

"Hey, look at me, baby girl. You know you can talk to me about anything." He moved his hand from her shoulder and tenderly reached under her chin, turning her face toward his.

Sincerity was evident in Pastor's eyes. He was a kind soul, and Frankie loved him so much.

"Daddy, there's nothing wrong with me. I don't know what you want me to say."

"I know you, Frankie. Something is bothering you. You think I haven't noticed the change in you over the past months? Your room, the way you dress, the way you walk around like you're angry at the world. Baby, please tell me how I can help you?" Pastor grasped Frankie's hands and pleaded with his child.

"Okay, so I changed my room, and I like to be more relaxed when it comes to my clothes, so what? Does that make something wrong with me? I don't think so. Even if there was something wrong, you wouldn't understand. Believe me, you wouldn't." Her agitation mounted, and she twisted out of his reach. "I just wish everyone would leave me alone. Let me be me."

"Okay, have it your way, but you're wrong about me. There's nothing you can't tell me. Nothing at all."

Tears formed in her eyes, and Pastor knew beyond a shadow of a doubt, that there was something going on with his child. If only he could reach her. What had happened to make her so cold and isolated? "Talk to me, Frankie."

Frankie quickly wiped her eyes. "I said, there's nothing wrong with me," she yelled without looking at him.

"You're not fooling me. But I'll do as you ask. I'll leave you alone." Pastor stood up, and then reached down and took hold of Frankie's hand to pull her up. When she stood, Pastor embraced her tightly. He felt her body stiffen, and then she surrendered to the comfort he hoped she'd found in his arms.

"I've got to go, Pastor." She moved outside of his embrace.

"I know. Your friends are waiting on you."

"Yeah, they are." Frankie dashed out of the study. On the other side of the closed door, she paused. "If only I could tell you, Daddy," she whispered. Fresh tears gathered while she ran out the door.

Frankie's name was added to the rolls of the juvenile system soon after she turned sixteen. The day that Audrey Graham was called to the school was the ultimate public embarrassment for the Graham family.

Frankie and a small group of girls assaulted a boy who had allegedly teased them about their appearances every day for the last few weeks.

"You girls look more like thuggish boys." Audrey's

tongue mocked with criticism. "This is so humiliating," she cried.

Frankie glared at her mother and rolled her chocolate brown eyes. She expressed no sympathy for anyone. The tears cascading down her mother's cheeks only made her harder.

Frankie heard snickering behind her back. Jerking around, she looked like smoke was about to spout from the top of her head when she saw a couple of girls dressed in juvenile garb, sneering at her.

Audrey continued her tongue lashing while she waited for the intake clerk to bring her release papers to sign.

"No wonder you got teased. Do you realize that you and those, those girls almost killed that poor boy?" Audrey searched in her purse until she found tissue to wipe her eyes. "And here you are, locked up like some wild animal. I don't understand you, Francesca. What on earth has happened to you?"

In a harsh tone, Frankie said, "My name is Frankie." With folded arms and a blank expression, she turned her back toward her mother.

It soon became apparent to Audrey that the one person who could get through to Frankie was Rena. For some reason, she seemed to listen to Rena. Audrey asked her to talk to Frankie about her insolent behavior. She hoped that Rena could find out what was troubling her.

Over the years, Frankie's volatile temper could be fueled by the smallest of things. Soon Rena became privy to it as well. But Rena couldn't find the strength to pull away from her best friend and secret lover.

While Rena attended the local university, Frankie hung out in the streets. She managed to secure jobs, mostly through temporary job assignments. She was able to keep her job as a receptionist at a private doctor's office longer than any other job. To get away from her family, Frankie moved into a small apartment on the other side of town.

Stiles had one semester remaining before he graduated from Duke University with a degree in religion. He planned on continuing his study for his master's in theology at Duke Divinity School because his dream was to, one day, pastor his own church. His father's teachings had inspired him through the years, and he wanted to follow in his footsteps.

Why couldn't his sister's life be more like his? *Why is she so miserable?* Stiles wondered from time to time. Somewhere along the way, Frankie had made a 360-degree turn down a path of self-destruction.

Rena spent as much time as she could with her mixed-up friend. But she had her life to live too. When her father was transferred back to Massachusetts during her freshman year of college, with her parents' blessing, Rena decided not to return with them.

After she received her bachelor's degree in library science, Rena secured a job as a librarian in Marion, Arkansas. She leased a nice apartment. Living in Marion, though it wasn't far from Memphis, gave her some much needed distance from Frankie. Unbeknownst to Frankie, Rena dated guys from time to time. She had to be more than careful whenever she did, because she didn't want to think about the consequences she would have to pay if Frankie discovered her infidelity.

Rena answered her cell phone. "Hello, Mrs. Graham. How are you?"

"I don't know, honey. Have you heard from Francesca lately? We haven't heard from her in over a week. Pastor is worried and so am I. Her cell phone is disconnected

and I've been by her apartment, but there was no answer."

"I talked to her earlier today. She called me at the library. She's fine as far as I know. I told her that I would
pick her up when I get off work. She's going to spend the
weekend with me."

"Oh, thank God. I'll let Pastor know. I don't understand her. I really don't. And you, you're such a sweet
girl. You're really a good friend to Francesca." At times
Audrey simply refused to call her daughter Frankie. It
would be too much like acknowledging that the girl she
gave birth to no longer existed.

Rena began to feel uneasy the more Audrey Graham
talked. *If only she knew the real deal about me and Frankie.
She wouldn't think so well of me then.*

"Mrs. Graham, Frankie will be fine. We just have to
keep praying for her. She's confused about her purpose
in life, that's all," Rena told her.

"I don't know how long it's going to take for her to
find her purpose, if that's what it is. The girl is twenty-
four years old. She's not a child anymore. It's time she
took responsibility for her actions."

"Yes, ma'am. I know what you're saying. And she will.
You'll see."

"I'm glad *you* have faith in her. Well, look, I'm not
going to hold you. But when you pick her up, will you
tell her that her brother will be home this weekend.
We're going to have a welcome home dinner for him this
Sunday at the church. I want her there. She missed out on
his graduation from divinity school because, as you know,
she refused to go with us to North Carolina."

"Yes, I know. But she had to work." Rena made one excuse after another on Frankie's behalf. "She couldn't take
off. You know how that goes."

"If she would hold on to a job and establish some good

work ethics, then she would be able to take off from time to time. I was a second grade teacher for seventeen years before I retired. Before that I worked in human resources, and I've never, and I mean never, gotten fired from a job. As for Pastor, well you know that man won't miss a Sunday or a Thursday from church. All you have to do is say the word 'church,' and he's there. He doesn't care if he's sick or not, he's going to church.

"I know, Mrs. Graham. I know."

Audrey continued to talk, without acknowledging Rena's response. "Even Stiles has the same work ethics. And Francesca, well you know just as well as I do that the girl won't come near a church. I just don't understand it. I know God says He won't put more on us than we can bear, but Lord knows it sure gets hard sometimes, especially when your own child wants nothing to do with God or the church."

Rena listened to Audrey go on and on about Frankie until she couldn't take it anymore. "Well, I'm afraid I have to go now, Mrs. Graham. I need to get back to work. I'll be sure to let Frankie know that Stiles is coming home."

"Thank you, Rena. Oh, you know that I don't have to invite you to be there. You're just like family to us. We'll see you Sunday. And please see if you can get that daughter of mine to call home."

"Yes, ma'am. I will. Bye now," Rena said and closed her cell phone.

Rena glanced at her watch. It was almost 6:30. She finished placing the rest of the books on the shelf before going to her office to grab her purse. She had to drive over to Memphis to pick up Frankie from the Criminal Justice Center. There was no way she was going to tell Mrs. Graham that Frankie was in jail again. This time

Frankie had been caught shoplifting at Macy's department store. Rena was tired of bailing her out. But as usual, Frankie always had some magical way of making Rena feel sorry for her.

Rena drove her orange and black Honda Element across the bridge. She became lost in her thoughts as she imagined what Stiles looked like. It had been almost four years since she'd last seen him. He was always a handsome guy. Medium build, with skin the color of brown sugar and teeth as white as snow. She used to have a crush on him in high school, but he was such a ladies' man then, and anyway he treated her like she was his little sister. When Rena and Frankie started their relationship, she pushed Stiles totally out of her mind. Rena wondered if he planned on moving back to Memphis or if he was just coming to visit.

Rena exited the freeway on to Poplar Avenue. She parked across the street from the Criminal Justice Center. She jumped out and ran inside, being careful to brush her shoulder length, curly brown hair in place with her hands. Her lean figure resembled a fashion model. Her almost white skin and dark eyes added a sense of mystery to her. She was indeed an attractive young woman—the kind that turned men's heads when she walked past.

"I am tired of doing this. Lord, forgive me," she mumbled to herself, knowing full well that although she'd asked for God's forgiveness numerous times, she was not about to break it off with Frankie. She couldn't. She didn't know how.

Rena had to wait two hours for Frankie's release. She had posted her bail the night before, but the criminal justice system took its own sweet time when it came to releasing inmates. When Frankie finally walked out into the jail corridor, Rena breathed a sigh of relief. Frankie looked haggard and exhausted. Her eyes were bloodshot like she hadn't slept in days. Her sleeveless white T-shirt and the baggy jeans were definitely in need of a good washing.

"Hey, there." Frankie said, approaching Rena.

"Hi, yourself. Come on, let's go," Rena told her.

"I need to go by my crib first, you know."

"No, I didn't know, but I should have figured as much." Irritation was apparent in Rena's voice. "Look, you've got to get yourself together. I'm tired of bailing you out of jail. For one thing, I don't have the money, and the other thing is that you're making life harder and harder for yourself, and for me," Rena added. "Not to mention your folks are worried about you," Rena said as they climbed into the truck and headed to Frankie's apartment.

"I know you didn't tell them I was locked up!" Frankie yelled at Rena.

"Of course not." Rena leaned closer to the door. "I'm just saying they're concerned about you, Frankie. You should understand that."

"No, what you're saying is that my mother called you and laid the guilt trip on you again, didn't she?" Frankie stared at her then snatched her seat belt on.

Rena didn't say a word at first. Frankie could almost always tell when Audrey Graham had contacted Rena.

"Yeah, she did. But everything she said is true." Rena chose her words carefully and spoke them calmly. "Anyway, she said that Stiles is coming home. They're having a dinner for him this Sunday at church, and your mother wants you there."

"I don't know about that. They'll want me to dress up and act like I'm just so elated to be at church, when you know that ain't the case."

"Frankie?"

"What?"

"Why do you hate church so much? There was a time you loved it. When we were young, you were the one who was at the church house every chance you got."

"That was back then. Things happen, okay? I don't want to talk about it."

"I hear you, but I still want you to come Sunday. I don't think anyone will be looking at how you're dressed. Everyone will just be glad to see you. Come, please?" Rena pleaded.

"I'll think about it," Frankie responded as she scanned the radio stations in search of her all-time favorite hip-hop music. "Did you check on my place while I was locked up?"

Rena took a deep breath and stared at Frankie. "Don't I always?"

"Thanks. I knew I could count on you."

"You missed my point. I don't have time to check on your stuff every time you decide you want to spend a few days in jail." Rena answered angrily.

They pulled up in front of Frankie's apartment. "Let me run upstairs and grab some clothes. It won't take long. You comin' up with me or what?"

"I guess."

Frankie's studio apartment was tidy. Luckily the apartment had come furnished. It wasn't the best, but it satisfied Frankie, especially since utilities and cable were included in the rent. It worked out great, because she barely could cover her monthly rent, not to mention any additional expenses.

Rena plopped down on the arm of the weathered sofa and waited for Frankie to finish gathering a couple of outfits. "I hope you get something that you can wear on Sunday."

"I didn't say I was going yet, so don't start sweating me about it," Frankie retorted, as she positioned herself in front of Rena.

"For God's sake, we're talking about your brother, not some stranger. You haven't seen him in I-don't-know-when. Somehow, you're always conveniently unavailable," Rena said while raising her hands up to make air quotations.

"I said stop lecturing me!" Frankie yelled.

Rena held her head down, cowering away from Frankie. Knowing how Frankie's temper could change at the drop of a dime, Rena didn't want it to reveal itself today.

"Okay, have it your way. I won't say another word. Do you have what you're taking with you?"

"Yea, let's vamp. Girl, I need a smoke. Stop at the corner store. I need to grab a pack of Black 'n' Milds."

That was another pet peeve of Rena's. Frankie smoked. After months of pleading, Rena had finally managed to convince Frankie not to smoke in her apartment. Frankie didn't like being told what to do, but agreed to smoke only on Rena's patio. But the scent of the cigars and weed lingered in Frankie's clothing and on her breath. Rena tried her best to ignore the stench, but there were times it almost made her sick. Frankie could care less. That was just how she was about everything. *Selfish*, Rena surmised.

What had happened to Frankie over the years? Rena could never quite figure it out. Maybe it was destined for some people to travel down the road of life that seemed carefree and easy, but full of trouble. Frankie was such a person. She had no idea that the road she'd chosen to take led to nowhere fast. Somehow, someway, Rena had begun to realize that the best thing for her to do was to break away from Frankie. But was it possible? And if it was, how?

6

*"Blessed is the man who trusts in the Lord and has made
the Lord his hope and confidence."*
—Jeremiah 17:7

Stiles checked his luggage and proceeded to the boarding gate. Within twenty minutes of arriving, he heard
the agent calling his flight. Boarding the plane, he shuffled to his mid-row seat next to the window. Stiles loved
being in the air, surveying God's wondrous works. There
was nothing more beautiful to him, nothing more mag-
nificent and heavenly than flying through the clouds. It
was his favorite time to meditate about the marvelous
creation of God. He was in awe of his surroundings. He
laid his head against the seat after reading several passages from his Bible. His mind drifted to his family and
home. There were times he thought about how different
his life might have been had his real father been alive.

His mother often told him, "Stiles, you've got the very
best of two good men in you, son. You're a blessed child."

Stiles couldn't wait to get home. It had been a long
time since he'd been to 3290 Pepper Oaks Drive. The
church in Durham, where he was one of three associate
ministers, had taught him a lot. His time in school had
been a tremendous opportunity for him as well. Now he

could go home to Memphis and stand next to his father as associate pastor of Holy Rock and work as the adjunct professor in the religion department at the university. Stiles also had big dreams for Holy Rock ministries. He and his father had made plans for this day, when he was finished with his ministerial training and education.

Three hours and forty-eight minutes later, after an hour layover in Atlanta, Stiles arrived in Memphis. Stepping off the plane, he was exhilarated, energized, and enlivened. It was good to be home.

Proceeding to baggage claim, he felt the tugging of his heart. He couldn't wait to hug his sister. His prayers for her had never ceased. When his mother told him about Frankie's wild ways, he was troubled. Frankie used to be such a dainty little girl who loved to play dress up and get in their mother's makeup. She used to love church so much that Stiles thought she would be called to the ministry with him. But everything had changed in Frankie's life. Well, almost everything. Rena was the constant in Frankie's life. Rena...Rena Jackson. Stiles wondered what she was up to these days. She had been quite a pretty girl with a beaming personality back then.

"Hello, son. Do you need some help with those bags?" he heard the gruff voice looming behind him. Stiles whirled around just in time to land in the massive arms of his father. Pastor embraced his son in a tight, emotional bear hug. Stiles held on to him like he was holding on for dear life.

"Father!" Stiles said and took a step back to look at his father. "It's good to see you." Joy bubbled in his short laugh as his dark brown eyes stared into his father's.

"You too, son. It's good to have you home," Pastor emphasized with a tiny tear glistening in the ridge of his wrinkled left eye. Grabbing hold to one of Stiles' bags, he placed the other hand around his son's shoulder.

Proudly, the two men walked along the airport corridor outside to meet the beaming Memphis sun and sizzling heat.

"Good Lord," Stiles said. "Some things never change, huh, Pastor?"

"You're right, son. This Memphis heat is one of 'em." Both men laughed and chatted until they reached Pastor's metallic blue Deville.

"How have you been?" Stiles asked as they drove along Winchester Boulevard toward Emerald Estates.

"Blessed, son. Blessed and highly favored. The congregation is growing steadily. We have close to 650 members. I'm thinking about adding on to the church."

"That's good to hear," remarked Stiles.

"We've blacktopped the church parking lot. Did I tell you that we purchased the land across the street from the neighborhood store? Remember it had two houses on it?"

"Yes, sir, you told me. Have you decided what you're going to use it for?"

"No, not yet. I was thinking there might be enough space to turn it into a youth center. I'm negotiating with the owners of the store too. I was hoping we could purchase it as well. I could keep it open and that could provide jobs for some of our young people. It could teach them the importance of ownership and show them how to be more responsible. You know we can never have enough ministries and programs for our young people. So much is going on out in the streets. They need a place of refuge; somewhere they can be safe, have good, clean fun, and meet other like-minded kids."

"I totally agree, Pastor. Sounds like I came home just in time. There's a lot of work to be done."

"Yes, there is. The harvest is plentiful but the laborers

are few, son. It's time for us to be about our Father's business."

The Deville turned into Emerald Estates. They turned left onto Pepper Oaks and into the driveway of the elegantly landscaped split-level house. They pushed the remote, and the garage door opened. Pastor maneuvered the luxury vehicle inside the immaculately kept garage.

The side entrance door swung open before Pastor could shut the engine off. Audrey raced out into the garage screaming.

"Oh, baby, you're home," she cried. "My son is home." Tears flowed from her eyes, and ran down her plentiful makeup, undoing it from her face and eyes. She was quite an attractive woman, even without makeup. But Audrey Graham was not the type of lady who would ever look unkempt or unprepared. Her sense of fashion was impeccable. Laden with expensive perfumes, large diamonds on both hands, and two carat diamond studs in the second hold of her ears, she was a sassy and classy woman. She fit the stereotype of a first lady.

Stiles gathered his mother into his arms. His burly frame enveloped her, appearing to swallow her whole. He planted kisses all over the top of her perfectly coiffed hairdo.

"Momma," he said repeatedly. "You are a vision of loveliness." He hugged her again before walking inside the house. Just as he entered into the kitchen, he stopped.

"What is it, Stiles?" Audrey asked as Pastor looked on.

"It's . . . it's just good to be home. That's all. Good to be home." This time he gathered Pastor underneath one of his arms and Audrey underneath the other. The three of them walked through the kitchen into the family room.

"Sit down, honey. I'll fix you and Pastor an ice cold glass of tea with lemon. I know it's hot outside. You're

probably thirsty and hungry too, aren't you, sweetheart?"

"Mom, a glass of your delicious iced tea will suit me
just fine. I'm really not all that hungry right now."

"What about you, Pastor?" Audrey asked as she
walked into the kitchen to pour her two favorite men
glasses of tea.

"I'll take a light sandwich, honey," he answered.

"All right, darling," she replied as she stood at the
kitchen island looking out over the family room. Audrey
smiled and prepared the sandwich.

Moments later, Audrey brought out the tray with the
iced tea, fresh-cut lemon slices, a Dagwood-style deli
sandwich on sourdough bread with low-fat baked chips.

"Mom, looks like you haven't lost your touch in the
kitchen."

"I can vouch for that, son," Pastor interjected.

Audrey smiled and took a seat next to Stiles. She
rubbed through his hair like she used to do when he was
a little boy. It felt good to have him home again. Her
prayers had been answered. Since he left for college, he'd
promised time and time again to return home. But there
was always something that persuaded him to change his
mind. She realized that Pastor needed his son in the pulpit of Holy Rock, working right alongside him. Pastor
would never admit it, but Audrey knew him better than
anyone.

When Stiles first told his father that he had been called
into the ministry, Pastor was speechless, because it was
an answered prayer—to have his children work in the
ministry. He hadn't given up hope for Francesca. He understood that sometimes God allowed His children to
travel pathways that others may not understand, including the person going down the pathway. But no matter
what happened in life, whether it was good or whether it

was bad, Pastor believed God was in control of every facet of life, and that Frankie was not excluded.

He and Audrey never openly discussed Frankie's way of life, but from the way she dressed and the fact that she didn't show the least bit of interest in boys, Pastor suspected that Frankie was practicing a homosexual lifestyle. He wasn't pleased with it, but he didn't bash her or condemn her either. He continually lifted her up in prayer and believed that one day God would remove the scales from her eyes and she would own up to her mistakes. For him, sin was just that—sin. He often reminded his congregation that every human being was far from perfect, including him.

"Is Francesca coming over?" Stiles finally asked between the chatter.

"Honey, I don't know. But if I were you, I wouldn't count on it," Audrey said.

"Audrey, I wouldn't give up on our daughter just yet. You know that young lady, she's full of surprises. If she knows her brother is home, she'll show up sooner or later."

Audrey furrowed her eyebrows. "Humph."

Stiles laughed it off. He could tell that there was something much more going on that his parents obviously were not willing to talk about. His mother had kept him informed about Frankie and her constant trouble with the law over the years. But what else could it be? Had his rebellious sister become involved in something way over her head? He was determined to find out. But not tonight. All he wanted to do was take a shower and climb into bed for a good night's sleep.

"Mom, Dad, I've had a really long day."

"You don't have to say another word," Pastor spoke up. "Your mother and I know that you're tired. You go on and get yourself some rest. We'll talk to you later."

"Pastor's right, baby. If you want me to fix you a bite to eat, just holler, okay?"

Stiles leaned over and kissed his mother on her cheek before he stood up and started down the hallway toward the room he used to call his own.

"Good night, you guys." Stiles stopped midway in the hallway. Turning around he said, "Oh, if Francesca comes by or calls, let me know. If I'm asleep, just wake me up."

"Sure," answered Audrey, with a hint of doubt in her voice.

Audrey waited several minutes before she reached over on the side of the sofa for the cordless phone. Walking into the kitchen, she dialed Rena's cell phone. Pastor peeped around the corner and watched as Audrey paced back and forth on the ceramic tiled floor.

"Rena, why don't you answer your cell phone?" Audrey said out loud. Pastor stepped from behind the small wall that divided the den from the kitchen.

"Francesca will call or come by. Be patient, dear."

Audrey ignored Pastor, something she rarely did. She mashed the button on the cordless phone and hurriedly began to dial Rena at home. After four rings, Rena picked up.

"Hello," Rena answered

"Rena?"

"Yes, ma'am?"

"Honey, have you seen Frankie? We still haven't heard from her. Stiles is at home, and he's been asking about his sister. I tell you, that child is going to be the death of me yet."

"Don't worry, Mrs. Graham. Frankie's here. She's asleep. She wasn't feeling well so I picked her up from her apartment when I got off work. She took something for her headache. Now she's out cold. I don't think she remembered what time Stiles was supposed to arrive."

Audrey listened to Rena. She was skeptical. She wondered if Frankie had been in jail again; it seemed to be her home away from home. Was Rena covering up for her?

Frankie could manipulate people into doing and saying things they wouldn't ordinarily do or say. Rena, for some reason, seemed to be more prone to it than anyone.

"Listen to me, Rena."

"Yes, Mrs. Graham?"

"When Frankie wakes up, tell her that her brother is here," Audrey emphasized in a less than pleasing voice. "Tell her that we expect to see her here first thing tomorrow morning."

"Yes, ma'am, I'll be sure to bring her over there. You have my word on that, Mrs. Graham. I can't wait to see Stiles myself."

"Honey, I know Frankie is my daughter, but I'm telling you, that girl is taking advantage of your kindness, not to mention your friendship. Sometimes, sweetheart, you just have to let folks go. You should be somewhere spending time with a nice young man. Someone who will appreciate you for you. But I tell you, as long as you let my daughter use you, then you won't have time for anyone in your life. Do you hear me, Rena?" Audrey stopped and sighed loudly.

"But Mrs. Graham, I can't push her out of my life that easily," Rena reluctantly explained. She hated getting into these kinds of discussions with Mrs. Graham.

"Just think about what I said, Rena. Pastor and I will see you two tomorrow morning. Good night."

"Good night, Mrs. Graham." Rena hung the phone up

and stared at it. She walked into the bedroom. Frankie was curled up in the queen-sized bed with her head underneath the vintage rose comforter, asleep.

When they had arrived at Rena's apartment, Frankie took a hot bath while Rena fixed turkey burgers and garden salad. Frankie wolfed down the food like she hadn't eaten in days. She probably hadn't.

Whenever she was carted off to jail, Frankie was sure to lose a few pounds because she refused to eat the poison they dished out, as she described it. Rena had told her that Stiles would be arriving today, but Frankie refused to call her parents to find out the details. Instead after she finished eating, she told Rena she was going to crash. And that she did. As soon as her head hit the down pillow, she was asleep. Rena knew better than to wake her. Frankie could be mean as a witch when her sleep was interrupted. So Rena stood in the bedroom door for a few seconds and then turned to leave. She went into the sitting room.

"I wonder what's up with Stiles," she said to no one. "Who would have ever thought that boy would grow up to be a preacher?" Rena wondered and then laughed. "I'll see what he's all about tomorrow," she spoke out as she picked up a novel by one of her favorite authors. She read until she drifted off to sleep.

1

"To see what's in front of one's nose requires a
constant struggle."
—George Orwell

"Frankie, are you ready?" Rena asked impatiently.
"Almost. I'm trying to do something to this hair of
mine. I have to look good for my brother, you know,"
Frankie said and giggled.

"Your hair looks fine. All you needed was a good
shampoo."

"No, all I need is a good hair cut," Frankie countered.
"These twists are nappy. But I guess they'll do for now,"
she said, surveying her head in the full-length mirror on
the back of Rena's closet door.

Frankie meticulously looked over her outfit. She wore
a pair of loose fit signature jeans with a spice-orange
short-sleeved polo shirt. Her low quarter boots were
black with a splash of orange in the design that set off her
outfit. The only jewelry she wore was a small gold loop
earring in her left ear. Walking over to the nightstand,
she picked up her wallet and placed it in her back pocket.

"Let's get outta here," she ordered Rena.

Rena grabbed her purse. She looked the total opposite
of Frankie with a chic indigo knot skirt and tiered ruffles

that fell graciously along her knees. A flutter-sleeve V-neck top complimented the skirt and enhanced her perfectly smooth, baby soft skin. A dash of her favorite perfume confirmed that she was indeed a woman and proud of it. The two girls hopped into the car and headed across the bridge to Memphis.

The beat of Rena's heart quickened as they neared Emerald Estates. Frankie hadn't said much of anything during the twenty-two-and-a-half-minute drive from Marion to Memphis.

"Don't be nervous, Frankie. It's Stiles, remember? Not some stranger. This is your brother." Rena reminded her as she drove up in the driveway of the Graham household.

"I know, but I'm still jittery. I don't know why. I just am is all."

"Everything will be fine. Come on, let's go inside."

They walked up the walkway and pressed the doorbell. Seconds later the red oak door swung open. Stiles stood on the other side.

Rena gasped.

Frankie stood next to Rena. Goosebumps broke out on her arms as she eyed her brother. She hadn't known she would be this happy to see him.

Stiles eyed both of the women. He opened the iron security door and stepped out on the porch, grabbing his sister and twirling her around in the air.

"Boy, put me down," she squealed.

For the first time in a long time, Rena saw Frankie act like the Frankie she had once known, happy and carefree.

Stiles planted sloppy kisses all over Frankie's face before releasing her. Then he walked over to where Rena stood. He grabbed her into his massive arms and squeezed her tightly.

"Girl, look at you. Don't you look good? You're all grown up now," he complimented Rena.

He kissed her on the forehead and held onto her hands, looking her up and down with a big smile plastered across his bearded face.

Frankie interrupted. "I don't know what you two are going to do, but I'm getting out of this scorching heat." Frankie wiped sweat from her forehead, pushed the door open, and went inside.

"You got that right," Stiles agreed. "Come on, Rena," he said and tugged her by the hand. The three of them went inside.

Audrey and Pastor both smiled when they saw Frankie walk into the kitchen with Rena and Stiles. Audrey had paced the floor nervously most of the morning, hoping and praying that Rena could get Frankie to come.

Audrey had prepared a feast for the occasion. The table was set perfectly, with fresh-cut white and yellow roses from her garden. Bacon, eggs, sausage, home-made waffles, buttered grits, buttermilk biscuits and a bowl of fresh fruit sat on the dining room table.

Pastor felt proud to ask his son to bless the food, and Stiles was more than honored to do so. Frankie felt somewhat uncomfortable listening to her brother pray. It had been a long time since she'd had anything to say to God. But she didn't make her feelings known to anyone. She glanced around the table at everyone while Stiles prayed.

As the family sat around the table for the first time in years, things appeared normal in the Graham household. There was much talking, laughing, reminiscing, and definitely lots of eating. Just like they used to do, Frankie and Stiles jokingly argued over who would wash the dishes and who would dry them. They decided to toss a coin. Stiles called heads and Frankie called tails. Stiles ended up having to wash, which made Frankie burst out in laughter. Rena cleared the dishes off of the table and Mrs. Graham placed the leftover food in plastic containers.

Pastor went into the family room and sat contently in front of the television, sipping on a steaming hot cup of decaf coffee. He mouthed a "thank you" to God for everything turning out so well. He loved to see Audrey happy. Being troubled about Francesca was hard for her. The fact that Audrey believed her daughter was a lesbian made things that much worse. Audrey told him that members of the church whispered and gossiped about Frankie all of the time. It had made its way back to Audrey that some of the members had seen Frankie out in the streets and malls with women who looked gay. One of the Holy Rock members worked at the Criminal Justice Center and had been Frankie's pre-trial counselor. Pastor understood the embarrassment it caused the first lady.

He tried everything in his might to soothe Audrey's nerves and keep her from worrying. He explained to his wife that when a child, especially a child who has been raised to know God, rebels and chooses instead to walk in darkness rather than the light, there is nothing to do except turn that child over to God. But Audrey didn't want to do that. She wanted so badly to solve Frankie's problems herself.

The weight of the family's problems, coupled with being the shepherd of Holy Rock, sometimes bothered Pastor so much that he started having anxiety attacks. From time to time his heart fluttered and a cold sweat would come over him. He did well to hide it from Audrey. She didn't need anything else to add to her list of worries. God would take care of him. *No need to claim sickness of any kind.*

* * *

By the time the kids finished cleaning the kitchen, it was close to noon. They sat around for about an hour or so before Frankie stood up.

"We had a good time, but I think it's time for us to push."

Rena stood up next to her with her head slightly downward, as if she was hiding something.

"I hate to see you all leave so early," said Pastor. "Come on over here and give me a hug."

Pastor hugged the girls but remained seated.

Stiles and Audrey followed them to the front door. Pastor could hear his wife in the front reminding them about church tomorrow. Stiles was going to deliver the morning message. Afterward they were going to have dinner at the church. Pastor didn't hear a response from Frankie. He only heard Rena say that she and Frankie would be there. For Audrey's sake, Pastor sure hoped Frankie showed up.

Stiles and Audrey returned to the family room after Frankie and Rena left.

"Mom, Dad, thanks for a wonderful feast. I enjoyed it," Stiles stated.

"Baby, now you know there's no need to thank us. You're our son, and we're proud of you. I know you wanted to see your sister. Since she didn't have the common sense to come by last night, I knew she had to come and see her brother this morning," Audrey said.

"Now, honey. There's no need to drudge over yesterday. We had a good time today. Francesca came and that's all that matters," Pastor said.

"Daddy's right, Mom. I wasn't expecting Frankie to drop everything just to come to see me. I am here to stay you know. Plus, you said that Rena told you last night that Frankie wasn't feeling too well. Like Dad said, what counts is now. It was good seeing my sister. And Rena, that young lady looks awesome." Stiles chuckled.

"She is a nice girl. Always has been," remarked Pastor.

Audrey raised an eyebrow and added, "And she's quite available."

"Mom, no," Stiles laughed and held up a finger, waving it back and forth. "Don't you even go there. The last thing I need is you to try to set me up with Rena. She's like another sister."

"Stiles Jennings Graham." Audrey gleaned. "It's too late to try to convince me that you weren't looking at Rena with a more than sisterly eye. Didn't you notice it too, Pastor?" she asked and looked directly at Pastor.

"This time, Son, I have to take your mother's side. It sure looked like you had an extra sparkle in your eye."

"Well, maybe," his mouth curved into an unconscious smile. "Shoot, I couldn't help it. The girl is beautiful. But before I say anything else, I'm going to the study. Since you asked me to preach, I don't want to disappoint you. I want to go over my message for tomorrow."

"Sure, you do that, but I already know you're going to set the church on fire. Isn't that right, sweetie?"

"Yes, that's right, Pastor. I believe our son is certain to do just that."

"I had a good time, didn't you?" Rena asked Frankie as she drove away from the Grahams'.

"Yeah, I have to admit that I had a great time. It was good to see Stiles. He's still crazy as ever." Frankie remarked. "I'm glad Momma didn't ruin it."

"What do you mean?"

"She can be so judgmental and condemning. That's all. And you know it. I was waiting for her to start in on me. I wasn't having it today."

"Well, she didn't 'start in on you,' as you put it," Rena

replied and glanced over at Frankie. "So there's no need to go there or even think about that. I'm glad you're going to come to church tomorrow. It's been like forever since you stepped foot in Holy Rock," Rena commented.

"What have you been doing? Keeping count or something? Anyway, I didn't say that I was going—you did."

"So you're not coming?" Rena looked over at her again before quickly dropping her lashes to hide the hurt.

"I didn't say that either. Just drop me off at my apartment. I have to take care of some things."

"Do you want me to wait on you?"

"No, that won't be necessary. I've got to do a couple of things, and if I do decide to go, I need to find something to wear."

"Oh, Frankie," Rena said excitedly. "I knew you wouldn't let Stiles down. I knew you wouldn't."

"Hey, wait a minute. I'm not doing this for Stiles. I'm doing it for you. It's the least I can do for you. You're always there for me." Frankie reached over and grabbed Rena's free hand. "Sometimes I know you think that I don't appreciate you, but I do."

"I'm glad to hear that. All I want is what's best for you. I know you've been through some tough times over the years, and I know you don't want to have anything to do with the church or God right now. But if you'll just come tomorrow, give it a chance, then I believe you'll start to feel better about your life."

"Maybe you're right. It's hard out here in these streets. But it can be hard in the church too. You know how Christian folks do. They're always condemning each other. Always judging and pointing fingers. Accusing and chastising people. I don't want to hear it, and I don't want to see the stares and listen to the whispers. I might just go off. Then Daddy's congregation will really have something to talk about."

"You're not going for those people. They have to answer to God for themselves. So don't even let that get next to you. Anyway, it might not be like that at all," Rena told her.

"We'll see," Frankie said.

When they pulled up at Frankie's place, she leaned over and gave Rena a light peck on the cheek before climbing out of the car.

"I'm going to pick you up at around 10:30 tomorrow morning, so be ready."

"Cool." Frankie told her. "I'll call you later on tonight."

"Okay." Rena waited until Frankie disappeared inside the building. Then she turned the car around and drove off with a smile of satisfaction on her face.

8

Rena dialed Frankie's number for the fourth time. There was still no answer. It was well after midnight. Rena hadn't heard from Frankie since she'd dropped her off at the apartment earlier that afternoon. She checked her cell phone to make sure Frankie hadn't tried to call, but there were no missed calls.

"Why would she lie to me?" Rena asked herself. "If she didn't want to go to church, she should have just said it. Well, if that's the way she wants to play, then so be it. I'm sick of her games."

Rena got on her knees and said a short prayer, asking God to do the usual things like taking care of her parents, her sister and brother, the Grahams and those who were sick or grieving. She said a special prayer for Stiles that his sermon would be a good one. Before she said "Amen," she asked God to take care of Frankie wherever she was and to keep her safe and in His care. Climbing between the pastel sheets, she wondered where Frankie could be and who she could be with until her eyelids drooped and she answered the call of sleep.

* * *

The next morning, the alarm clock woke Rena at 8:30. She turned over sleepily and pushed the button to turn it off. Reaching for her cell phone, she looked to see if Frankie had called. No such luck. She then searched for the cordless phone and found it underneath the covers. No calls. Dialing Frankie's number, she climbed out of the bed and walked into the bathroom with the phone up to her ear.

"Dang, Frankie, you're pissing me off!" Rena screamed into the receiver when Frankie still didn't answer. "I don't have time for your mess this morning."

Rena slammed the phone down on the vanity. She walked over to the tub, turned on the water on full force, reached for the scented bath beads, and she poured some underneath the warm running water. While the tub filled, she brushed her teeth.

Rena finished her bath, dried off and walked to the closet in her birthday suit to peruse the clothes. Settling on a dove grey strapless dress with the matching jacket, she laid the outfit across her unmade bed. She pulled out her underwear set from her dresser and an unopened package of sheer pantyhose. After putting on her underwear and hose, she opened the hall closet where she kept her dozens of shoes. Rena searched through the closet until she located her grey leather sandals with the wrap-around ankle strap. Once she finished dressing, she called Frankie again. The buzz in her ear infuriated her that much more. She looked at the clock. Ten minutes to ten. Without bothering to eat, Rena picked up her purse and cell phone and headed out the door.

She made it to Frankie's in record time. Racing up the stairs, she didn't stop until she reached Frankie's door. Just as she opened her clutch purse, she huffed loudly

when she realized she had left the key to the apartment
in her other purse at home. She beat on the door for several minutes and called out Frankie's name. No one answered other than one of Frankie's neighbors who cracked
the door and told Rena that Frankie left with some chick
the night before. The neighbor sneered when he told
Rena what he'd seen. Rena gave him a less than pleased
stare before she stormed away and back down the stairs.

Rena went back to her car and sat quietly inside for
several minutes with the air conditioning running. She
had to cool off inside and outside. It was time to gather
her thoughts. She pondered over who Frankie could
have left with. Now instead of anger, Rena grew somewhat concerned. It was one thing for Frankie not to be at
home, but it was another for Rena not to have received at
least one call from her by now. The only times that oc-
curred was when Frankie managed to get herself in trouble, or locked up.

Rena leaned her head against the head rest as she held
onto the steering wheel with both hands. If Frankie was
in trouble again, Rena was finished. She couldn't keep
rescuing her. Rena sat in the car for fifteen minutes before
leaving and heading for church. She was not about to
miss Stiles' sermon. She would have to deal with Frankie
later, that was for sure, but for now her mind was on
Stiles Graham.

Rena walked into the sanctuary and claimed a seat on
the third row. The first lady walked up beside her.

"She isn't coming, is she?" Audrey asked Rena.

"No, ma'am. I don't think so. I think she . . ."

"Stop right there. Don't do it, Rena. Don't make up another excuse for that ungrateful child of mine. How
could she do this?"

"Mrs. Graham, I'm so sorry. I wish there was something I could say."

"Rena, maybe you'll let go now," Audrey whispered. "This is the last straw for me, and you need to move on with your life too. People are already talking about you, associating you with Francesca's ungodly ways. Some of them are even calling you—Well, I don't want to say it in God's house," Audrey said and placed her freshly manicured hands over her lips.

"No need to, Mrs. Graham. I don't care what other people say. Frankie's my friend, my best friend and I won't turn my back on her. I can't." Rena said. "I'm worried about her. I haven't heard from her since I dropped her off at her apartment yesterday afternoon."

"You know and I know that she's fine, wherever she is. She always is. I wouldn't be surprised if she's laid up somewhere with God knows who just so she wouldn't have to be here. But I tell you, Rena, I'm through with her. I'm giving her over to Jesus. I won't send myself to an early grave worrying about Francesca. Friend or no friend, move on, Rena. You're too smart, too beautiful, and too intelligent. You have a lot going for you. It's time you start living your own life and concentrating on yourself. Do you hear me, young lady?"

"Yes, ma'am. I hear you. And you're right. It is time for me to let go." Rena slowly agreed.

"By the way, you look lovely this morning."

"Thank you, First Lady."

"We'll talk later. I'm going to go and greet some of the members. I don't know what I'm going to tell Stiles," Audrey remarked, and then turned and walked away.

Eleven o'clock Sunday morning worship service started. The praise team encouraged the congregation to join them in singing Donnie McClurkin's, "I Call Him Faithful." After a prayer by one of the deacons and two songs by the choir, Stiles walked up to the pulpit. The congregation stood and applauded.

Stiles stood tall in the pulpit. His black tailored suit, crisp white shirt and patterned tie added a spiritual aura to his already dashing, handsome build. Rena swallowed hard as her eyes transfixed on him.

Stiles took his place in the pulpit and scanned the congregation. When his eyes stopped on Rena, his heart quickened. She was simply ravishing. He cleared his throat before taking his eyes off of her. He scanned the sanctuary further. Not seeing Francesca, he concluded that she had not come to hear his message. *I won't allow the enemy to steal my joy; I'm here to do what you have called me to do, Lord.*

Before taking his text, Stiles prayed. "Father, thank you for this opportunity to speak your word. I ask you to anoint every word that proceeds from my mouth. Amen. What kind of fruit is growing in your garden? Turn your Bibles to the fifth chapter of Galatians, verse 22 and following. Reading from the New Living Translation, you'll find these words:

"But when the Holy Spirit controls our lives, He will produce this kind of fruit in us: love, joy, peace, patience, kindness, goodness, faithfulness, gentleness, and self-control.

"The word of God is true, people. The word of God in this passage of scripture calls the character that we, as children of God, should produce fruit." Stiles looked at his mother. At that moment he felt a magnetic pull of his spirit to her. "There's a story I read not too long ago about a Special Olympics team. There were nine contestants, all physically or mentally disabled, assembled at the starting line for the 100-yard dash. At the sound of the gun, they all started out, not exactly in a mad dash, but with delight to run the race to the finish and win. All, that is, except one little boy who stumbled on the asphalt, tumbled over a couple of times, and began to cry. The other eight heard the boy cry. They slowed down and looked back." Stiles looked over his shoulder. "Then they all turned around and went back until they reached the crying boy; every one of them. One girl with Down's Syndrome bent down and kissed him and said: 'This will make it better.' Then all nine linked arms and walked together to the finish line. Everyone in the stadium stood, and the cheering went on for several minutes."

"Hallelujah, Praise God," several members shouted one after another. "Preach, boy, preach," someone else called out.

Audrey's eyes gleamed with tears. A smile spread across Rena's face. Pastor stood on his feet and shouted across the pulpit behind Stiles.

Nothing seemed to faze Stiles. He kept on preaching. His message was simple and clear.

"I shared that story just to make you understand that it's not about you or me. The life we live should be all about God, about helping someone who's down and fallen by the wayside." Stiles pointed a finger upward. "It's not about whether you win the race or not, it's about who you help to win. Sometimes that means you have to change your direction in order to save someone else. Sometimes, people, you have to go to the places you don't want to go in order to pull someone out of the dungeon. What kind of fruit are you growing in your hearts for God? What are you doing to further God's kingdom?"

Stiles appeared to be at ease. He was truly where he was supposed to be, in the house of God. "In Galatians 5:19-21," Stiles bellowed, "it tells what happens when you follow the desires of your sinful nature. Some of you don't want to hear what I'm saying, but I'm still going to tell you what's true. Follow the commandments of the Lord Jesus Christ. Stop being stuck up and self-centered. Stop pointing fingers at everybody but yourself. The next time you encounter someone whose behavior frustrates your patience, think about what that person's life experience may be and give them a little extra love and attention. You never know what's going on in another person's life. Both hands were positioned on his waist and his body reared back. "If you want to spend eternity with Jesus, you better hear me." After several more minutes of preaching, Stiles closed out his sermon by offering Christ to anyone in the congregation who did not know God as his or her personal Lord and Savior.

Audrey raised her hands in joy, and clapped them in the air and began yelling, "Amen. Come to Jesus!"

Pastor Chauncey and the deacons stood up and extended their hands toward the congregation, calling the unsaved to come to God. Several people walked down the aisle and the church thundered an applause as each of them came forward.

Rena's eyes glistened with tears, too. She looked in her purse and pulled out a tissue to catch the tears before they fell.

At the close of the service, members formed a line to greet Stiles and tell him how much they enjoyed his message. Rena was one of them. When she finally made it up to him, she hugged him tightly while grasping his hand inside of hers.

"Stiles, I'm so proud of you. Your message was outstanding. I'll remember it always."

"That's good to hear, Rena. The word of God never returns to us void." He smiled. "Are you going to stay for the church banquet?"

"Yes, I'm headed to the Fellowship Hall now."

"Good. Oh, by the way, looks like my sister pulled a fast one on us, huh?"

"Yeah, looks like she did," Rena answered before walking away.

The banquet went off without a hitch. The kitchen ministry had prepared so much food that it was nearly impossible to taste it all. Stiles and his family were seated at the head table. Members stopped to welcome him back home. It was almost three o'clock when the last members left, including the pastor and his family.

"Rena, thank you for coming," Stiles told her as he walked her outside to her car.

"No need to thank me," she replied. "I wouldn't have missed this for anything in the world. I'm sorry that Frankie didn't show up. You know I'm worried about her."

"So am I. But from what Momma tells me, this is her M.O. Is that true?"

"Basically. But usually she would have called me by now. I hope she hasn't gone and gotten herself into trouble again. She's good for doing that."

"I heard that too. I'm praying for my sister. And I'm praying for you too. From what I hear, you're being drawn into this with Frankie. Racing to her rescue, always getting her out of jail, helping her to maintain a place to live. You know you can't keep doing that, Rena. You're only enabling her."

"I know that. But why can't people understand that Frankie's my friend, my very best friend. Like I told your mother, I can't just leave her out there to face God-knows-what all alone."

"You're some kind of friend. Look, I know you have work tomorrow, but after you get off, do you think you'd like to go to dinner with me? No strings attached. I'd just like to get out for a while, refamiliarize myself with the city."

"I wish I could, but tomorrow is my late night at the library."

"Oh, I see. Which library is that?"

"Marion Public Library, in Arkansas. I don't know if I mentioned it yesterday, but I live in Arkansas."

"No, you happened to leave that bit of information out. I don't think we had much time to talk about anything. We were too busy eating," Stiles laughed.

"Yeah, you're right about that. Tuesday will be fine."

"I beg your pardon?" Stiles replied.

"Tuesday evening will be fine for dinner. That is, if you don't have any plans. I get off early on Tuesdays."

"Hey, gee, that sounds great. I'll come to Marion. Give me your phone number, I'll call you tomorrow, and you can tell me how to find you."

"Sure."

Stiles pulled out his cell phone and added her number to his contacts list as she dictated it to him. She, in turn, added his number to hers as well.

"Look, I guess I'd better be going. I have to get across the bridge and prepare myself for work tomorrow."

"Okay. Oh, by the way, I don't think I told you that you look lovely today."

Rena blushed before turning away and saying, "Thank you, Stiles. Bye."

He walked over to the driver's side of the Honda, opened the door for her, and waited until she climbed inside.

Rena took one last glimpse at him before starting the truck and pulling off. On the way home, her thoughts were on Stiles Graham. Not once did she think about Frankie.

9

*"Worry is a total waste of time. It doesn't change anything. All it
does is taint your mind and steal your joy."*
—*Unknown*

Rena scanned the computer for the new shipment of
library books that was scheduled to arrive today, but
it was hard to remain focused. She still hadn't heard from
Frankie. She went into the break room and called Frankie's
apartment for the umpteenth time, and for the umpteenth
time there was no answer. She began to perform the ritual that had become way too common whenever Frankie
pulled a disappearing act. She called the hospitals in
Memphis. She knew all the numbers because she had
called them so many times over the years. After confirm-
ing there was no Francesca or Frankie Graham, Rena
went back to the front desk and logged onto Internet Ex-
plorer. She went to the Shelby County Jail Information
website. Putting in Frankie's name, she was surprised
when the system said, 'No information." Now Rena was
really worried.

Frankie wasn't in jail, and she wasn't at her apartment.
She wasn't in the hospital. Where could she be? Rena
called Frankie's job, not expecting her to be there, and
she was right. The man who answered the phone in-

formed her that Francesca Graham no longer worked there.

"Rena, excuse me," her co-worker, Irma, said, sticking her head in the break room, "but you have a phone call on line two. Do you want to take it?"

"Yes, of course. Thanks, Irma."

"No problem."

Rena rushed to the phone, hoping to hear Frankie on the other end.

It was UPS, and Rena didn't know whether to be overjoyed that it wasn't bad news about Frankie or sad that it wasn't Frankie on the other end. She listened as the UPS employee explained the reason for her late shipment.

When she finished talking, Rena began organizing books that needed to go back on the shelves and others that needed to be placed on the sale rack in the front lobby of the library.

She and Irma went to Pizza Hut for lunch. Irma's jokes allowed Rena to relax and release her stress. Irma was hilarious. Rena didn't understand why she worked at the library instead of on somebody's stage performing comedy.

When they made it back from lunch, Rena jumped right back into her work. Her cell phone's ring startled her. She looked at the number.

"Hello."

"Hello, Rena. Did I catch you at a bad time?"

"No, not really. I just returned from lunch." She felt a sense of calmness when she heard Stiles' soothing voice.

"I won't hold you. I wanted to know if you've heard anything from my sister."

"No. I wish I could tell you that I have. I've checked the hospitals and even the jail. But there's nothing. I don't know where she could be. Frankie is known to disappear into oblivion from time to time, but there's just something that has me rattled this time around. I can't imagine that she would purposely miss hearing your first sermon, whether she despises church or not. She loves you too much to disappoint you."

"And you're sure that you don't have any clue where she could be?"

"None."

"Okay, look I'll call you later tonight."

"Sure, that'll be fine. And if I happen to hear from her, I'll call you.

"Thanks, Rena. Bye for now."

Rena closed her cell phone and returned to the project she had started before lunch.

It was going on ten o'clock when Rena unlocked the door to her apartment. She kicked off her shoes, dropped her purse on the living room table, and went straight to the kitchen to grab a cold bottle of water. The first sip of the ice cold liquid cooled her off immensely. The phone rang just as she was about to take another gulp. Walking into the living room, she lifted the cordless phone from the base unit.

"Hello."

"You must be just getting home." Frankie asked like she hadn't been AWOL since Saturday afternoon.

"Where the . . . are you?" Rena swore. She hated to swear but it was times like these that Frankie brought out the worst in her.

"Chill, will you? I'm with a couple of my girls. I would have called earlier, but we went out of town, and you know I have a Cricket which means no long distance."

"I've been worried sick about you! I've called the hospitals, jail, your *former job*." Rena tried to indicate to Frankie that she knew she had been terminated yet again. "Your parents are worried, not to mention Stiles." Rena continued to voice her anger.

"Stiles? What does he have to do with this? I'm a grown woman, Rena. I don't need Stiles, my folks, you, or anyone else all up in my business. I was just calling to tell you that I'm home. I didn't have time to tell you that I was going to ride to Jackson, Mississippi with some friends. One of my girls had to go down there to handle some business, and she wanted some company. That's all. Anyway, I'm back."

Rena was quiet. "Don't you have to be in court tomorrow?" Rena spoke up, without addressing anything Frankie said.

"Yeah, I'll be there. I'm hoping the judge will let me walk. Are you going to pick me up?"

"Not unless you call your parents, and let them know you're safe."

Frankie was quiet.

"Frankie, did you hear what I said?"

"Yeah, I heard you. Look I'm tired. I'm going to crash. I'll see you in the morning."

"Whatever." Rena retorted and pushed the end button on the phone.

The phone rang again.

"Look, Frankie, I meant what I said." Rena yelled into the phone without looking at the caller ID.

"You've heard from Frankie?"

"I'm sorry. I thought you were Frankie. Yes, we just hung up. She said she went to Jackson, Mississippi with some friends at the spur of the moment. I told her to call and let you guys know she was back."

"Hold on a sec, Rena. Someone's on the other end." Stiles told her.

Rena waited for more than a minute, and Stiles did not return to the phone. Rena decided to hang up. She went into her bedroom and stepped out of her clothes before going into the bathroom to run her bath water. No sooner had she started the water and added her bubble bath did the phone ring again. She picked up the phone that was laying on her nightstand next to the bed.

"Hello, Stiles," Rena said when she saw the Graham's number pop up on the ID box.

"Hey, sorry about that. I didn't mean to leave you on hold, but that was Frankie on the other end," he apologized.

"Oh, I thought it was an angry girlfriend you left back in North Carolina," Rena joked.

Stiles was shocked by Rena's assumption, but in a pleasant way, he figured she was fishing. "No. That was definitely not the case. One thing I don't have is a girlfriend. Getting my doctorate was my girlfriend. It was no easy feat, you know."

"I'm sure it wasn't." Changing the subject back to Frankie, Rena asked, "What did Frankie say?"

"We just had a rather heated conversation. That girl is not going to be the death of my parents. I told her that too. All this running around, in and out of jail, has got to stop." Stiles ripped out the words impatiently. He was highly upset.

"What was her reaction?"

"She didn't like what I said, but I said it anyway. She ended the conversation by hanging up in my face. But that's cool. I said what I needed to say. And I meant every word of it too. Anyway, now that I know my little sister is safe, I'll get to the reason for my call earlier this evening."

"Oh, I thought Frankie was the reason for your call. Hold on for a minute." Rena rushed into the bathroom to turn off the water before it spilled onto the floor.

When she returned to the phone, Stiles asked her, "Is everything okay?"

"Sure. I forgot I was running my bath water, that's all. But I caught it in time. Now what were you saying?"

"I called to see if we're still on for dinner tomorrow."

"Of course we are. There's this nice cozy restaurant in West Memphis called Ron's. The food is delicious."

"Ron's it is. How does seven sound?"

"Seven is perfect."

"Do you want me to pick you up?"

"No, that won't be necessary. I live about seven minutes from Ron's. I'll meet you there."

"Okay, that'll work."

Before ending the conversation, Rena gave him directions to the restaurant. Climbing into her lukewarm bath, she laid her head back against the Jacuzzi tub, closed her eyes, and cleared her mind of Frankie and her antics. She replaced them with pleasant thoughts of Stiles that made her smile.

The following morning, Rena made the trip over the bridge. Frankie was due in court at 9:30. It was exactly 8:45 when she pulled up in front of Frankie's apartment. Rena turned off the engine and climbed out of the car. Before she could make it to the stairwell, Frankie came bouncing down the steps. Frankie reached out to hug Rena, but Rena was cold.

"Aren't you going to speak to me this morning? You still mad?" Frankie asked Rena.

"Good morning," Rena replied nonchalantly.

Rena wished there was somebody she could talk to about the relationship she was trapped in with Frankie. But who would listen to her without condemning her? There wasn't a single person she trusted when it came to her involvement with Frankie. It was a good thing her parents were no longer living in the city. Thank God for small miracles! Her two oldest siblings seemed more like distant relatives. With one in Rhode Island and the other in Seattle, she rarely saw or talked to them. She didn't have many friends outside of work because she didn't want anyone to suspect anything. There were times she considered seeing a psychologist, but she always managed to talk herself out of it. Rena believed that she was definitely going up a creek without a paddle.

Breaking the stiff silence, Rena asked, "What do you think is going to happen in court? The last time you were there the judge told you that he didn't want to see you back in his courtroom."

"They all say that. My lawyer told me that the most I'll get is a year, maybe two, of probation."

"I hope your lawyer knows what she's talking about. I've paid her enough. And if you're going to continue to spend more time in court than on a job, then I'm letting you know that you need to get those girls who you rode out of town with to take care of you. I'm not going to do this anymore. I've told you that before. But this time I mean it, Frankie."

"Rena, stop getting your panties all up in a wad. I didn't know you were jealous," Frankie said, grinning.

"Jealous!" Rena made a sharp right turn onto Poplar Avenue and gave Frankie a wicked stare. "Jealousy is the least thing on my mind. You're breaking me financially and mentally. I can't keep this up. Worrying whether you're all right, or if you're locked up, or somewhere hurt."

"I'm sorry. I really am. I promise things will be different. I know I've said it before, and I know you don't believe me. But you'll see. When I walk out of that courtroom today, I want you to drop me off at the unemployment office. I'm going to find a job, and this time I'm going to keep it. You have my word on that."

A sigh pierced Rena's pink lips. She looked over at Frankie and smiled slightly.

Frankie stood before the court, hands clasped behind her back; legs parted like the police had ordered her to spread eagle against a car. The judge knew Frankie all too well. She had several arrests on her rap sheet. Theft of property under $500, fraud, shoplifting, simple assault, and today she was being sentenced on a charge of writing bad checks. When the judge sentenced her to serve eleven months and twenty-nine days in the penal farm, with one year of probation, to begin immediately, Rena's mouth dropped open. Frankie slowly turned around to meet her gaze. A teardrop trickled down Frankie's oval shaped face as the deputy led her away.

Rena rushed around Wal-Mart to purchase toiletries and other items Frankie was allowed to have. The list was quite limited but detailed. She bought six packages of plain white women's T-shirts, crew socks, and cotton panties. Frankie was allowed to have one eight-ounce bottle of clear shampoo in a clear bottle, one hair brush and a plastic comb. When she arrived back at the penal farm with the items, a guard told her they would be dispensed to Frankie once she was processed into the system. From past experience, Rena understood that could take as long as two days. She wouldn't be able to visit Frankie for at least four or five days.

Leaving the penal farm, Rena set out for home. On her way across the bridge, she phoned the Grahams. Audrey picked up the phone on the first ring.

"Hello," Audrey said loudly in the phone.

"Mrs. Graham, it's Rena."

"Hi, how are you? I'm glad you called. Stiles told me about Frankie. I tell you, I don't know what we're going to do about her. I just don't know. It's time we do more than talk about tough love. I told Pastor that it's time to start practicing what he preaches. We have to learn how to let go and let God, child."

"Yes, ma'am," Rena agreed, afraid to tell her what she'd called to tell her.

"Do you know she went clean off on her brother? She even had the nerve to hang up in his face. Something has to be done." Audrey didn't rest between words. Rena didn't have a chance to answer before Audrey blurted something else out. "Where is she? You tell her that I want to talk to her," demanded Audrey.

"That's what I was calling about." Rena fidgeted with her cell phone, almost dropping it on her lap. She looked at the muddy river as she crossed the Memphis-Arkansas Bridge.

"What is it?"

"She's is in jail."

"Jail? Not again." Audrey cried into the phone. "Lord, we're going to be the main topic of discussion at Holy Rock. Lord, have mercy. For how long?"

"Eleven months and twenty nine days, I'm afraid. She'll have to serve at least seven or eight months of that before they consider releasing her."

Rena listened to the commotion on the other end of the phone. The next voice she heard was Pastor's. Rena repeated to him what she'd already explained to Audrey.

"Lord, have mercy on my child," Pastor prayed before the phone went dead.

10

"The Almighty has his own purposes."
—Abraham Lincoln

Rena was glad to be at dinner with Stiles. It helped to take her mind off of how upset the Grahams had been when she told them about Frankie.

"How's your food?" Rena asked.

"Delicious." Stiles wiped his mouth on the cloth napkin and spread it back in his lap. "Southern cooking like this is one of the main things I missed about being away from home."

"I'm glad you like it. Ron's has been around for a long time. I'm surprised you haven't heard of it."

"It's probably because I never came to Arkansas. There was nothing over here that interested me."

"I see." Rena noticed how both water glasses were so close. She lifted her glass, careful not to let her fingers touch his. A swallow of her lemon water cleared her throat.

"What made you decide to move here?" Stiles twirled his spaghetti onto his fork.

"I like the small town atmosphere. And I can go right

across the bridge to the big city whenever I want to."
Rena laughed.

"I guess you make a good point."

"It's proved to be one of the better decisions I've made
in my life. I used to try to convince your sister to move
over here, but she's too much of a city girl."

"You know something? I don't know what to say
about Francesca. The girl must be crazy."

"Why do you say that?"

"You mean you have to ask? Frankie is so caught up in
the world that she's sinking lower and lower. I don't
know what happened in her life, but she's mixed up,
confused. All of this in and out of jail, smarting off to
Momma, messing around with women, not wanting to
have anything to do with God or the church. Need I say
more?"

Without warning, Rena blurted, "I don't know if your
parents told you or not, but Frankie is in jail. She was
sentenced to eleven months and twenty-nine days for
third-degree assault."

"What?" he yelled. "When did this happen? You said
she was fine."

"It happened earlier today. We expected her to beat the
case, but because of her criminal record, the judge gave
her jail time. He warned her before this charge that if she
came before him again, he was going to lock her up, and
he did.

Stiles ran his hand over his head. "That girl is going to
drive this family crazy." He stopped and looked around
like he was in a foreign land. Then he asked Rena when
he could go and visit her. Rena told him the visiting
hours and days.

"Are you okay?" Rena reached across the table and
grabbed his arm.

"I'm fine." His expression was like someone who had been struck in the face. "It's just hard for me to accept that my sister's violent nature landed her behind bars."

"Listen, who are we to judge anybody, Stiles?" Rena swallowed hard, lifted her chin and boldly met his gaze. "I admit that Frankie has some issues, some serious issues. But I will not turn my back on her, and neither should you."

"I wasn't suggesting that you or I turn our backs on her. If anything, I want to help her. You think I like seeing her going through whatever it is she's going through? Shutting her family out? You think her alternative lifestyle doesn't bother me?" For an instant, his glance sharpened.

"Okay, if I'm wrong, I apologize." Rena bit her bottom lip and looked away. "But all I hear is what a terrible person she is. And how Frankie shouldn't be doing this and Frankie shouldn't be doing that. Doesn't anyone see that something happened to make her the way she is? I have no idea what it was, but the Francesca we used to know disappeared a long time ago and this, this Frankie person appeared. But the Francesca I know is still inside. That's the part that no one sees—the good in her. She's kind, sensitive, and smart as a whip." Rena tossed her cloth napkin to the side. She felt her composure was under attack. "I don't want to explain Frankie's behavior to you or anyone anymore. No matter how she alienates people, she's still my friend. And another thing, who are we to talk about her lifestyle?"

The look on Stiles's face was one of shock. "Look, why don't we change the subject?"

"I think that would be a great idea," she answered. "I've decided to sublet Frankie's apartment. Do you think you might be interested?" Rena asked him.

"I don't know. I did tell Pastor I was going to start

searching around for a place. Maintaining her apartment might be a good idea. I'll pray on it and get back to you in a couple of days."

"Good."

For the next hour, the two of them talked about everything, until Rena no longer felt like she was putting on an act to make time pass. It felt good to be out with a man who offered stimulating conversation, which made her feel relaxed. Stiles could be quite the gentleman.

Stiles smiled.

"What are you smiling about?" Rena asked.

"I'm smiling because I'm thankful to be here with you, Rena—a beautiful, intelligent, Christian woman."

Rena awkwardly cleared her throat and stirred uneasily in her chair. *Humph, if only you knew.*

When they finished dinner, Stiles walked Rena to her car.

"I'll follow you home." Stiles offered.

"No, that won't be necessary."

Stiles showed no sign of relenting. "I'm not leaving you alone." His voice was smooth but insistent.

"Really," Rena shook her head. "It isn't necessary. I'll be home in seven minutes. But thanks anyway."

"Are you sure?"

"I'm sure."

His eyes pierced the distance between them. "I enjoyed your company."

"Me too. It felt good to get out and relax for a while."

"I'm glad I was the one to make that happen tonight. Maybe we can do it again sometime."

Rena looked at him, and then diverted her eyes toward the busy street.

"Did I say something wrong?" His voice almost broke to a whisper.

"No. No you didn't. It's just . . ." *He noticed my uneasiness.*

Stiles interrupted. "Oh, I'm sorry. I didn't think to ask if you had a boyfriend. A woman as attractive as you, I'm sure you have one," he said without giving her a chance to answer.

Rena blushed. "Quite the contrary. "

"Well, well, well. Looks like the two of us have something else in common," Stiles laughed.

"What else do we have in common?"

"Spaghetti and meatballs of course," he joked.

Rena allowed her gentle laugh to ripple through the air until tears gathered in her eyes.

Stiles brushed a lock of her hair away from her face. In the heat of the night, stars sparkled and a gentle breeze blew. He cautiously moved closer to Rena.

Rena stood still, like time had stopped just for her. The look in his eyes aroused her. At the same time, it made her nervous. Just as he leaned over to kiss her, Rena moved away slightly.

"Thanks for a wonderful evening," she told him, opening the door to her Honda, avoiding his kiss.

"The pleasure was indeed all mine."

On the way home, Rena thought about her evening with Stiles. There had been no one in her life except for Frankie. Whenever men approached her, and they did quite often, she denied their invitations for dates. The men from church ogled over her beauty but could not understand why Rena Jackson was not in the market for a man. Many of the men gave up. Still others considered her a challenge. There were times she felt an attraction to men but there was no way she was going to try to turn two wrongs into a right. The last thing she needed was to

become involved with anyone else. Frankie had been
enough, and Frankie was almost about to destroy her.

Frankie was in a cell block with eight other women.
She sat on her steel cold bunk with her feet propped up,
oblivious to the idle chatter and petty arguments between some of the other inmates. This would be the first
time she had to do a stretch this long. She'd done a week,
ten days tops, but a year behind bars? Frankie had been
totally shaken by the judge's sentence.

Glancing around at her surroundings, she felt isolated,
alone and forsaken. An unexplainable emptiness enveloped her. For the first time in a long time, she was
alone to face her fears. *Where are you God? You're so
mighty, so big, so powerful. Where are you? Why did you leave
me all alone? How could you ever say you loved me? If you
loved me, you wouldn't have let me be hurt. You wouldn't. But
you did.*

She turned over just as the deputy jailer came into the
cell block and yelled, "Lights out."

Frankie didn't have to prepare for the lights to go out.
It was already dark inside her mind, her heart, and her
spirit.

11

"Love is not weakness. It is strong. Only the sacrament of marriage can contain it."
—*Boris Pasternak*

Frankie had been locked up for almost two months, and Audrey refused to visit her. It was far too humiliating for her. How could she take the chance of running into any of her church members? How would she be able to visit with her child through a window? Not Audrey, she couldn't entertain the thought of Francesca being a common criminal. When Pastor or Stiles visited Frankie, all Audrey sent was her love.

Stiles informed Rena that Frankie had faced eviction when he moved into her apartment. Rena was livid. All of the times she'd given Frankie money to help her out on the rent——what had she done with it?

"She's not going to convince me that she isn't using," Rena exclaimed to Stiles when he told her he'd paid all of the back rent on the apartment.

"You really think Francesca is using hard drugs?" Stiles stiffened before looking up from putting the receipt in his wallet.

"I know she was before she got locked up. Maybe this stint behind bars will force her to get clean and sober."

"I'm going to pray that God delivers Francesca."

"That's what she needs."

"Yeah, I know, and I believe God has set everything in motion for my sister."

"I pray that you're right. Let's change the subject. It's too depressing." Rena twiddled with her hair and held the phone between her ear and her shoulder.

"Some good news, hmm, let me see if I can think of something that might make you feel somewhat better." Pausing for only a second or two, Stiles began, "Pastor told me that he's bringing me on as the full-time associate pastor.

Rena was excited by his news. "That's great. When did this happen?"

"Yesterday. I guess I proved to him and to God that I was ready for the job. It's not a huge salary, but it's a nice one. God is good. The adjunct professorship at the university offsets whatever else I might need. So I can't help but be grateful."

"I know that's right," Rena agreed.

Rena's visits to the Grahams became more frequent as her friendship with Stiles intensified. Several times after she left the jail from visiting Frankie, Rena drove to Emerald Estates to spend time with Audrey. Audrey focused her attention on Rena for the mother-daughter relationship she lacked with Frankie.

"Pastor," Audrey said one evening as they prepared for bed. "What do you think about Stiles and Rena?"

"Stiles and Rena? What are you talking about?"

"You know. What if Stiles and Rena were, you know, to get together?"

"Rena's a fine young lady. I believe Stiles likes her a lot, and she likes him too. But it's none of our business, and it's not our place to do anything to get them together. What we should be doing, if anything, is praying for our children and for their future mates."

Pastor pulled back the covers and sat on the side of the bed, waiting on his wife to finish putting on her night gown. When she finished, he reached his hand out to her and guided her around to the side of the bed where he sat. Together they knelt to pray.

"Pastor," Audrey said when they had finished praying and climbed in the bed.

"Yes, dear."

"What do you think is going to happen to Francesca?"

"Honey, she's in God's hands. And as long as I know that, I know she's going to be all right."

"You went to visit her today," she stated. "How . . . how is she?" Audrey turned on her side and propped herself up on one elbow.

Pastor lay on his side and looked at his wife. She was as lovely as the first day he'd laid eyes on her. Her radiance hadn't diminished with the years.

"Frankie is fine, honey." He rubbed his wife's cheek with the back of his wrinkling hand. "I think she would be even better if you would go with me the next time." He said the words tentatively as if testing the idea.

"I can't do it, Pastor." Her face clouded with uneasiness as she searched for a plausible answer. "I can't stand the thought of seeing my child behind bars."

"Are you sure that's all it is? Or, is it because you're ashamed of her and embarrassed that the pastor and first lady's daughter is in jail?"

Audrey didn't respond. She eased back on the pillow, and then turned over on her side to turn off the lamp. "Goodnight, Pastor."

"Goodnight, Audrey. I love you."

"I love you too, Pastor."

"Audrey," he called out her name. Placing his hand on her side, he moved his body close to hers.

Audrey turned over to face him. Pastor stroked the side of her face some more and kissed her lips. Propping himself up on one elbow, his hand explored the soft lines of her back, her waist, her hips. His kisses were tender and enticing.

"You're the love of my life." Audrey whispered. "I can't see myself living without you." Audrey yielded her body, her mind, and her soul to the man she loved.

The years had brought them closer, and her very touch sent sparkles of passions rippling through his body. Just watching her sometimes could get him aroused. The scent of her sweet body and the softness of her skin ignited wave after wave of desire in him. He expressed his satisfaction as they became one. The warmth of her femininity caused him to moan with pleasure.

"Audrey." He called her name, his voice pleading, his hands demanding.

"Yes, yes, Chauncey, I'm yours," she curled into the curve of his body. "I'm all yours," she cried out in sheer ecstasy. "All . . . yours."

It was flesh against flesh, man against woman, husband against wife.

12

"The ear tests words as the tongue tastes food."
—*The Bible*

Audrey was more than thrilled when Rena called and asked her if she wanted to go to the new open air mall in Horn Lake, Mississippi. Audrey absolutely loved shopping. Eager to maintain her snazzy wardrobe, anytime an opportunity to shop presented itself, she was eager to do it.

The two ladies spent the first part of the morning stopping at almost every store in the mall. The ladies easily enjoyed the mild September day. The beginning of fall could be felt in the air. The mild wind gathered golden leaves and pushed them through the mall while the two ladies laughed and talked like mother and daughter.

Audrey purchased a two-piece teal suit from Anne Klein. At Jones of New York, she brought several pieces of costume jewelry. Several hours passed before they stopped to have lunch at Mac's Seafood Restaurant.

Audrey sipped on her diet Sprite with cherry. "Rena?"

"Yes, ma'am?"

"Thank you for calling me this morning. You don't

know how much it means to have you concerned about my well-being. Francesca should appreciate your friendship more than she does." Audrey looked out at the people passing by. Stains of scarlet appeared on her cheeks. She took a deep breath. "All I can say is that Francesca is just totally confused. I don't know what else to make of her. I just don't know."

Rena didn't comment. It was the same old, same old whenever Audrey brought up Frankie. She set her coffee mug back on the table then picked up her fork to slice a piece of the vanilla bean cheesecake.

"Mmm," Rena said and placed a generous portion inside her mouth. "Mrs. Graham, you haven't eaten any of yours. It tastes absolutely heavenly."

"Now, haven't I asked you to call me Audrey? After all, you're just like a daughter to me. God knows you've been part of our family since you were what? Fourteen? Fifteen years old?"

"It takes some getting used to, that's all. But, Audrey, I know you have a hard time understanding Frankie. I mean, we all do. But she's just different, that's all. She's really a good person." Rena, once again, came to her defense.

"I guess you're right. I pray when she gets out of jail this time," Audrey said with emphasis, "she'll turn her life around. There was a time you couldn't keep that child away from church. Now, you can't keep her away from jail." Audrey shook her head in disgust.

"Rena, tell me. What exactly happened with Frankie? Who did she assault and why?"

"I don't know all the details," Rena lied.

There was no way Rena was going to tell Audrey that Frankie jumped on some female who called herself confronting Frankie about another female. Rena would never divulge what she knew to anyone in the Graham family, not even Stiles. If they wanted to know anything, they'd have to hear it from Frankie.

Rena stopped daydreaming and tuned back in to Audrey.

"I understand that you don't want to tell Frankie's business. So I won't bother you about it anymore." Audrey took another small bite of cheesecake before pushing the remaining dessert away from her. "Are you ready to go and find a dress and shoes for church?"

"I think so. As much as I've eaten, I hope I haven't gained a pound while sitting here," Rena laughed while getting up from the table.

Audrey laughed. "I want to find something chic. Let's go back to that first store we looked in. I think I saw something that might just be what I'm looking for."

"I'm right behind you," remarked Rena. The two ladies left the restaurant. At that moment, Audrey Graham couldn't have been happier.

It was almost 4:30 in the afternoon when the ladies left the mall with an armful of shopping bags filled with clothes, shoes, and jewelry. On the way back to Emerald Estates, in her midnight blue Altima, Audrey skillfully maneuvered the conversation toward the subject of Stiles.

"Rena, since Frankie is obviously not a topic of conversation you want to indulge in, tell me what you think about Stiles." Audrey slanted her eyes at Rena's for a brief second before refocusing on the road.

"Stiles is a nice man, but then again, he always has been. He's going to be good for Holy Rock." Rena admitted with a smile on her face.

"My Stiles is quite a man. But I mean, what do the two of you have going on?"

"Audrey, are you trying to insinuate that Stiles and I are involved?" Rena queried and diverted her eyes away from Audrey. "What would make you think that?"

"Child, it's apparent the two of you like each other. Take it from someone who knows. I know my Stiles, and I know you quite well too, my dear. Y'all are smitten with each other. There's no denying it."

Rena saw the slight smile that covered Audrey's face.

Audrey remained quiet. It was just what Audrey had longed for. Rena would be the perfect wife for Stiles. And if there was anyway she could help them to realize it, then she was going to do it. Pastor wouldn't have to know a thing. Not one thing.

On Rena's way from Emerald Estates, her cell phone rang. It was Stiles.

"Hey, you," he said when he heard her voice.

"Hey, yourself," Rena responded.

"Are you still hanging out with my mother?"

"No, as a matter of fact, I left about five minutes ago."

"Why don't you stop by the apartment? That is, if you don't have anything else scheduled. I'd like for you to critique my message for Thursday night."

"Oh, you're going to preach Thursday night, huh?"

"Yep, Pastor said he wanted me to get as much training as possible. I only hope that I can be as great a preacher as he is some day. The man knows how to deliver the word of God."

"He sure does. But honestly, from the times I've heard you, I don't think you're going to have a problem following in his footsteps."

Stiles blushed over the phone. "So, are you going to come over? I promise it won't take long. That's another thing Pastor is teaching me. He says I should keep my messages short and simple. He said it doesn't take all night long to tell people what thus says the Lord."

"I heard that." Rena grinned as she spoke. "Expect me there in, oh say, about fifteen minutes."

"All right. I'll see you then."

Rena closed her flip phone and headed to Frankie's apartment.

Exactly sixteen minutes later, she pulled into the apartment's parking area. This would be the first time she'd been there since Stiles had moved into the unit a month ago.

She knocked on the door, and Stiles answered almost immediately. When she stepped inside the apartment she was amazed at the transformation. Stiles had totally redecorated the apartment. What used to be a drab, dull, lifeless apartment was now a bright, cheery space filled with live plants, a new chocolate sectional, with scented candles lit throughout the living room and kitchen. Rena slowly walked around, enchanted by what she saw.

"So, I take it you like my decorating skills," Stiles said with his hands clasped behind his back as he walked behind Rena.

"I don't know what to say. This place looks like a totally different apartment." Rena continued to walk around, going down the hallway before stopping and turning around. "May I?" Rena looked at him and then refocused her eyes in front of her.

"You may," he answered.

She walked to the bedroom. What used to be decorated bedding in mix-matched items from the thrift store was now color-coordinated in vibrant shades of purple. Curtains, comforter, and an area rug all made the room look like a space right off of HGTV.

"I must say that I'm quite impressed."

"You have no idea how that makes me feel," he said in an almost inaudible, endearing whisper that made Rena's stomach flutter.

She turned around, stepped away from the bedroom, and went back into the living room. "Another talent you've kept hidden from me, huh? Tell me, what other secrets are you keeping?"

'I promise that whatever they are, when revealed, you'll be just as pleased. Can I get you something to drink?" he offered.

"Just a glass of water, please." She needed something to put in her hands and her mouth. She felt like she was being a tease.

Stiles went into the kitchen and returned with a glass of water for Rena and a soda for himself.

"I can't seem to get enough of these," Stiles told her as he raised the glass of cola up to his thin, curved lips.

"I used to be that way about colas too. But I finally weaned myself off of them. Now I try to drink more water." Rena took a swallow of the ice cold water.

"Stiles, this apartment is just, simply. I don't know what to call it. Simply fabulous." Rena glanced around again as she took a seat on the sectional. "Thank you, again my lady." He bowed as if he was acknowledging credit for a great performance.

Stiles took a seat on one of the bar stools at the kitchen island.

"Did you and my mother enjoy your shopping spree? And did you leave anything for the other shoppers?" he teased.

"The answer is yes and yes," replied Rena.

"That's good. I'm sure my mother had a great time. She loves to shop. Plus, being out with you, I'm sure did her a world of good. It's the kind of stuff she'd love to do with Frankie, but, well you know how that goes."

"Yeah, I know." Rena flipped the subject quickly. "Now what about this sermon you want me to hear? I'm going to warn you. I'm a tough critic. No holds barred."

"Uh oh. I just may have gotten myself in trouble. I thought you would be easy prey. Now you're telling me that you're not going to give me a break." Stiles chuckled loudly. Rena loved to hear him laugh.

Stiles walked over to a small desk, in the corner of the living room, next to the window. It was a desk that Frankie already had that she kept cluttered with unopened bills, papers, and junk. Now the only thing on it was a tabletop lamp, a manila folder, and a pen and pencil holder. Stiles picked up the folder and walked back toward the kitchen. He stood in front of Rena, he opened the folder, and began his message. The more he read, the less he had to read. He got off the stool and walked around with his notes in hand, barely looking at them.

Rena sat on the sectional and listened intently at the handsome preacher standing before her. He looked so confident, so self-assured. The words he spoke touched her deeply. She thought of Frankie as Stiles talked about the forgiveness and the love of God. She thought about her own faults and shortcomings, of the mistakes and wrong turns she'd made throughout her life. She listened as Stiles talked like he was standing before a sanctuary full of people.

"There is therefore no condemnation in Christ Jesus," Stiles said in closing.

Rena was in awe of the man before her. Something stirred within her spirit. A feeling she'd never felt before. The words drew her into him more and more. Stiles Graham had captivated her heart in more ways than one.

When he finished, sweat poured from his face. He sat down next to Rena. The message had drained him. She had seen the same thing happen to Pastor when he preached. She stood up and went into the bathroom. Returning with a cold towel, she wiped the sweat off of his face. Rena went into the kitchen, poured a glass of orange juice, and took it to Stiles.

"Here, drink this. It'll help place some of the nutrients back into your system."

Reaching for the glass, he looked up into her eyes, and they locked. She quickly dropped her head.

"Thanks," he whispered and sipped the juice.

"That was a powerful word. You allowed God to speak through you tonight."

"Rena, when I'm speaking the word of God, I can't explain the joy within my spirit. It's like I can't stop. I have to tell anybody who'll listen about God's love." Drops of moisture still clung to his forehead. His whole face spread into a smile.

Rena watched his lips as they puckered when he talked. His hands moved around as he used them to describe various points about his message. She was mesmerized by him, drawn into him by his gentle spirit. His desire for God's word and the eagerness he had to please the Lord. Rena looked at him. For the first time, there were no shadows across her heart. A bottomless peace and satisfaction filled her spirit and she realized that Stiles Graham was the man for her.

13

"In jealousy there is more of self-love than love."
—*F. de la Rochefoucauld*

The night Rena listened to Stiles's sermon marked the turning point in their relationship. She began to let her guard down. Rena couldn't deny that she enjoyed being with him. For once, she felt good about going out in public with Stiles. No more stares and whispers from people when they saw her and Frankie together. Rena felt uncomfortable when Frankie insisted that she accompany her to places frequented by homosexuals. Rena didn't want to be associated with them because as far as she was concerned, she wasn't gay. She was Frankie's best friend, and that was all. Being with Stiles had changed all of that. She was happy, carefree and on top of the world.

Rena relaxed on the sofa, next to Stiles. It felt good and right, for once, to have someone other than Frankie at her apartment. She and Stiles exchanged friendly banter while they waited on the pizza and buffalo wings Rena had ordered. They planned to spend the evening watching DVDs. She loved that Stiles filled her days with good conversation and her nights with dinner, movies, and his sermons.

When the food arrived, they prepared to enjoy their time together. With their shoes off and sitting back on her couch, they waited for the first movie to start.

"If this isn't a good one, remember you picked it out." Rena nudged Stiles in the side. He grunted.

"Uh, you're the one who picked it. I got this one." Stiles waved *The Pursuit of Happyness* under her nose.

"No, you didn't," she challenged in a joking tone.

They chit-chatted back and forth until the previews ended and the movie started. Stiles slid closer to Rena, and wrapped his arm around her shoulder.

She tensed.

"I'm not going to hurt you. I promise," he whispered in her ear. "I just want to be close to you, that's all."

"I know. It's not you. It's me, Stiles."

"Come on, lighten up. Let's enjoy the movie."

Rena did as he said. She laid her head against his arm. Stiles smiled with pleasure, but their romantic moment was cut short by the shrill ring of the phone.

Rena raised her head, straightened and reached for the phone on the table in front of her.

The recorded voice said, "This is a collect call from an inmate of a correctional facility. Press one to accept the call. Press two to reject the call."

Rena pressed one and waited. Placing her hand over the phone, she whispered, "It's Frankie."

"What's up?" Frankie asked her in a not-so-pleasant tone.

"Nothing, I've just been working hard. How are you doing?"

"Obviously you don't care how I am. You haven't been to see me at all this week. What's up with that?"

"I told you, I've been working hard, and with that comes long hours. I shouldn't have to tell you that. Things have really been hectic this week. But I'll be there Monday. I promise."

Rena looked back over her shoulder at Stiles, who observed how tense she'd become after talking to Frankie for less than thirty seconds.

"I guess you forget that I know you better than anyone, Rena. You don't sound right. Tell me what's really going on with you! For the past few weeks, you've been acting weird. I just haven't said anything. But I've been listening, and I've been watching you. There's something different in your voice. And you look, I don't know, guilty or something when I do see you. You wouldn't be messing around on me?"

"Girl, please. I don't have time for this. You know good and well that it's nothing like that."

"Oh, it's like that, huh? Now you don't wanna to talk to me. Is somebody there?"

Out of nowhere, Stiles spoke up, right on cue as if he'd heard what Frankie said. "Tell my little sister her big brother says, hello."

"Who is that?" Frankie screamed, and a stream of expletives spilled from her mouth like a waterfall.

"Stiles. He said to tell you hello. We were just sitting here watching a couple of DVDs."

"What's he doin' over there?"

"You have two minutes . . ." the recorded voice said.

"Answer me, Rena! What is my brother doing over there?"

Words wedged in Rena's throat. She couldn't say anything with Stiles sitting next to her, practically breathing down her throat, and Frankie on the other end cussing her out.

"Frankie, the phone is going to cut off. Look, I'll be there Monday after work. I promise. Now wait, say hello to Stiles before your time runs out."

"Don't . . ." Frankie was about to tell her not to put Stiles on the phone. But the next voice she heard was her brother.

"Hey, sis. You okay?"

"What kind of question is that? I'm locked up, in case you forgot. So no, I'm not okay," she snapped. "Seems like if you were so concerned, you'd be paying me a visit or something. But I see you already paying visits. You and Rena got something going on, huh?"

"Not yet, but believe me," he said and grinned. "It's not because I'm not trying." He winked at Rena while he talked to his sister.

Ohmigod, she must have asked him something about me and him.

Frankie was fuming. She was about to tell him that Rena belonged to her but the phone went dead.

"Hello. Hello." Hearing the dial tone, he hung up. "Boy, did she sound bent out of shape," Stiles said. He went to the kitchen to get some pizza.

"She's just tired of being behind bars. Plus, I didn't get a chance to visit her this week. I should have made time to go and see her."

He walked back into the room where Rena sat trembling and almost in tears.

"Rena, you can't run to the jail every visiting day. Don't get me wrong, I love my sister. But she got herself into this mess. You do the crime; you have to do the time. That's just how it works. Sometimes we tend to think that when we go to God and ask Him for forgiveness that everything is squashed. Well, God does forgive, and He does forget. But we still have to pay the consequences for the sins that we commit. It's the same with Frankie. We all love her, but the fact still remains, she broke the law and she has to pay for what she did. But we can't do time with her, Rena, and that's exactly what you're doing. You've been a true friend to my sister for all these years, and I commend you for that, for sticking by her. But now," Stiles set the pizza on the table and knelt down in front of Rena.

Rena's hands were shaking as he took them inside of his and gently massaged them back and forth.

"But now," Stiles repeated. "You need to take time for yourself."

Rena looked at him. "I know everything you said is right. But I can't seem to break away from her. She's counted on me all of these years. I know you all don't understand, but it's like me and Frankie are joined at the hip. I can't turn my back on her." She flung out her hands in despair.

Stiles gently used one hand to caress Rena's face. Her eyes automatically closed at the first stroke of his touch. He moved in closer to her, his lips scathed hers. Rena's body released a soft gasp as the warmth of his tongue parted her lips. Stiles moved his hands over her shoulders and brought her down toward his body. The space between them was sealed when Rena wrapped her arms around him.

Stiles held her trembling body, reveling in the softness of her skin and the fragrant aroma of her body. When he pulled away from her, their faces were flushed. He kissed Rena lightly on the lips again before standing up and reclaiming his seat next to her.

"How about some pizza?" He picked the plate up and passed it to her. Rena grabbed a piece, and looked away, then picked up her glass of tea and took a swallow.

Stiles and Rena enjoyed the rest of the evening watching DVDs. The last one was a suspense thriller. Both of them enjoyed trying to figure out who the killer was. By the time they finished watching both movies, there was one slice of pizza left and a couple of buffalo wings.

Stretching, Stiles said, "I enjoyed myself tonight."

"So did I."

"I guess I better get ready to head back across the bridge," he told her, standing up. "Are we still on for tomorrow?"

"Yes, I'm still going to the scholarship prayer brunch with you."

"Great, I'll pick you up tomorrow morning, say around nine-thirty?"

"Nine-thirty will be fine." Rena walked him to the door.

Stiles turned around and faced her again. He leaned over and kissed her on the tip of her tiny pointed nose before moving to her waiting lips.

"Good night." His voice simmered with barely checked passion.

Rena opened the door. "Good night, Stiles. Drive safely."

"I will." Stiles jetted down the walkway, climbed in his car, and sped off. Rena watched him until he was out of sight before closing the door.

She locked the door then leaned against it, closed her eyes, and traced her lips with her fingers.

Rena walked back into the living room in a trance and began clearing the table. When she finished, she settled into the deep cushions, caressing the spot where Stiles had sat minutes earlier. Without saying her prayers, Rena fell asleep with thoughts of Stiles dancing in her head.

14

"Love seeketh not itself to please, nor for itself hath any care,
but for another gives its ease, and builds a heaven in
hell's despair."
—William Blake

The following morning, First Lady Audrey's eyes sparkled when she saw Stiles and Rena walking into the brunch together. Neither of them would admit it, but Audrey didn't need anyone to tell her that Stiles and Rena were in love. She recognized love when she saw it.

After enjoying the brunch, Rena and Stiles agreed to accept Audrey's invitation to come to the house.

"Do you think they suspect there's something between us?"

"I wouldn't think so. We haven't said or done anything for them to assume that there is."

Rena said a silent prayer. *God, you know that I'm uneasy about the relationship between me and Stiles. One part of me wants to see how far a relationship with Stiles can go. The other part of me is terrified of what Frankie will do if she even suspects that me and Stiles are involved. Help me, God. I've got to figure out a way to get things right in my life. I'm tired of betraying you, myself, and those I love. I need a way out. I know your Word says that you won't allow us to be tempted without giving us a way of escape. Lord, I need a way of escape.*

"You all right over there?" he asked Rena as he drove down I-240 toward Emerald Estates.

"Yes, I'm fine," replied Rena, mere seconds after finishing her prayer.

"I was thinking." He chuckled with happy memory.

"Think about what?" Rena grinned.

"About how thankful I am that God brought you into my life. I mean, we share the same Christian values, we both love our families, and our families love us. We certainly love God."

Rena looked at Stiles. He seemed to be peering at her intently. "Where is all of this coming from?"

"What I'm trying to tell you, Rena. Okay, listen. We've been seeing each other for what, three months or so?"

"Uh, huh," responded Rena.

"Rena, I'm just going to come out and say it."

Rena's head tilted back and she laughed. "Boy, will you just say what it is you have to say?"

Stiles felt like his throat was closing up. He removed one hand from the steering wheel and grabbed hold of Rena's delicate hand. Pulling it toward his lips, he kissed it lightly over and over. "Rena, I love you. That's what I've been trying to tell you. I love you, girl." He looked at her with a steady gaze.

"I . . . don't know what to say, Stiles."

"You don't have to say anything. The look on your face says it all." Stiles focused his eyes on the car ahead of him with a broad smile plastered across his face.

Stiles approached Emerald Estates. Rena turned and smiled at him again before leaning over and kissing him on the cheek.

"What was that for?"

"I felt like doing it, that's all. You bring out the best in me, Stiles." Rena's cheeks turned crimson.

Arriving at Emerald Estates, Stiles pulled up in the circular driveway. Turning off the ignition, he jumped out of the car and went to the other side to open the door for Rena. Taking hold of her hand, he helped her exit the car. Hand in hand, they went up the walkway to the front door. Stiles rang the doorbell, and Audrey came to the door with her robe on.

"Come on in. I was just changing out of that dress. Pastor is in the study. I'll be back out in a minute. "

"No problem, Mom," Stiles told her. "I think I'll go in and speak to him."

"Okay, sweetheart. Rena, darling. Why don't you go in the kitchen and pour us some tea. I'll be done in just a sec," Audrey told her as she disappeared into the bedroom.

"Yes, ma'am."

Looking around to make sure Audrey was gone, Stiles pulled Rena toward him and kissed her quickly before turning and going to Pastor's study.

Audrey came out of the bedroom with the phone up to her ear. She laid the cordless phone down on the chair in the family room.

"Are you all right?" asked Rena as she brought two glasses of iced tea into the family room.

"I guess." Audrey met Rena, reached for one of the glasses, and practically emptied it. "That was Frankie," she finally said when she put the glass down. "I refused to accept her call. I can't keep doing it. Pastor and I aren't rich, and we can't afford to have a $450 phone bill every month because of her. Those calls are way too high. If she would get her life in order, she wouldn't have to be calling us with one sob story after another. All that girl does is make empty promises and keep up mess. Always talking about how she's going to get her life together this time. There's always something when it comes to that child. I'm sick of listening to one excuse after another."

Rena remained silent. She sat in the chair and slowly sipped some of the tea. The beverage, as well as the conversation, chilled her insides.

"Pastor is supposed to go and visit her this week. Maybe he can get through to her. But I can't do it. She'll have my blood pressure sky high. I already have to deal with the members at the church whispering about her. You know how that must look. Pastor's daughter is locked up in jail, not to mention the other thing."

Rena popped her head up quickly. "What other thing?" she asked, afraid of the answer.

"You know what I'm talking about," she huffed, as she focused some of her anger toward Rena. "I know we don't talk about it around here, but that doesn't make it go away." Audrey paced across the stained concrete floor.

"What is it, Audrey?"

"Frankie is gay. You know it. I know it. Shucks, practically everybody knows it. Pastor doesn't want to accept it. But I know it's true. I don't care what he says."

"What makes you think she's gay?" Rena squinted her eyes like she was totally unaware of what Audrey meant.

"Don't play dumb with me, Rena. You know better than anyone else that I hate to be patronized. All you're trying to do is keep it hush-hush. But it's too late for that. Every one knows that Pastor and I have a lesbian for a daughter. It's humiliating." Audrey cried, putting a hand to her mouth.

"Audrey, I mean, if she is a lesbian, then that's her. Frankie has her own life to lead. I'm the last person who can judge another individual."

Audrey stopped pacing and sat down on the couch near Rena. "You're right about that. But I get so angry. I don't understand why Frankie does the things she does."

"We all have something we're ashamed of. Everybody

falls short. That's what the Word of God says. We all sin and fall short of the glory of God."

Audrey moved closer to the chair where Rena sat. She took hold of one of Rena's hands. "That's why I love you so much. You're such a sweet-spirited young lady. So forgiving. So understanding. No wonder Stiles is crazy about you," Audrey told her.

Rena gasped. "What on earth makes you say that?"

"Child, you know that boy loves you. Why, I see it every time you're around him. And when you're not around him, it's like everything that comes out of his mouth is something about you. The boy is hooked. And I think you feel the same way, don't you?"

"I don't know." She shrugged her shoulders slightly.

"Oh, yes you do. Don't play coy with me."

Rena decided to confide in Audrey. She was dying to tell someone. She flashed a huge smile. "You're right. I do like Stiles. I like him a lot. I think I might even be falling in love with him," Rena whispered and looked around to make sure there was no one in the room but the two of them.

Audrey squealed. "I knew it! I knew it!" She still held onto Rena's hand and began raising it up and down in the air.

"You're going to be my daughter-in-law. Watch what I tell you."

"Audrey, wait, I think you're going way too far." Rena tried to retrieve her hand. "Who said anything about marriage?"

"Mark my words, Rena Jackson. You *are* going to be my son's wife."

"Son, tell me something."

"What is it, Pastor?" Stiles asked as the two men sat in the study that brimmed over with what Stiles imagined had to be almost every biblical book and Bible concordance there was.

"What do you think is going on with your sister? I want to know what I should expect when I go to the prison. The last time I tried to visit her, she refused to see me. Frankie has me baffled. But even a man of God gets confused sometimes. You know, we're not perfect. We're called to carry out God's message, to bring in the lost sheep. Sometimes I ask the good Lord, how can I be an effective shepherd when I can't reach my own daughter?"

Stiles listened intently.

"God knows what He's doing. I don't doubt Him one iota. I just wish I could do something, anything, to help my child. She's hurting and has so much rage built up inside of her. It all started when she was a teenager. I know that much. But what could have happened to make her change like that? Your momma wants me to believe that Frankie is gay. I'm no fool, son. I know your momma's probably right. But I don't want to claim that for my baby girl." Pastor rubbed his hands back and forth over his thinning gray hair. Staring out of the picture window, he raised his eyes skyward as if expecting God to usher down a stream of answers right then and there.

"Pastor, I worry about her too. All I know is what I've been taught since I was a little boy. You taught me that God doesn't make mistakes. You told me no matter what, to keep the faith and keep on trusting. Everything will work out. There's nothing too hard for God. Isn't that what you've always said, Pastor?"

Pastor turned around and looked proudly at Stiles. "You're going to make a great pastor. God has truly blessed me. I have two wonderful children, a lovely wife and a great congregation. The Lord has really bestowed

His favor upon my life. So why am I sitting here allowing the devil to have me worrying and fretting? You're right, Son. God has everything already worked out. So enough of that kind of talk for me. Tell me something." Pastor said, flipping the subject to something cheerier. "What's going on with you and that young lady out there who your mother is probably grilling for answers as we speak?" Pastor quipped, slapping his hand on his knee.

"Rena? What can I say about her?" He turned up his smile a notch. "The girl is all of that. I'm in love with her."

"Is that right?" A flash of satisfaction crossed Pastor's face.

"Yes, sir. I can't explain it. I just know it, that's all. I've prayed about the situation, and I've asked God to guide and direct me. I want to be with whomever God wants me to be with. Pastor, I believe with all of my heart that Rena is supposed to be my wife." Stiles' eyes glowed as he talked about her.

Pastor saw a look of love spread across his face with every word his son said. "How does she feel about you?" asked Pastor.

"I really can't say. I know that she worries about Frankie so much that she can't seem to concentrate on her own life. The two of them are so close. But to me, Frankie seems to take advantage of Rena's friendship. She hassles her all the time, and I think she's being selfish."

"I hear what you're saying. But you can't allow your sister to hinder you from doing what you know God has placed on your heart to do. If Rena is the woman for you, then you should tell her. The two of you can work this out with Frankie. Maybe after you talk to Rena, the two of you can go and visit Frankie together. Once Frankie sees how happy the two of you are, she'll understand."

"Yeah, maybe she will. I love you, Dad." Stiles stood and walked over to his father. Pastor rose from the chair too, and father and son embraced one another.

When Stiles and Rena prepared to leave, Pastor and Audrey walked outside with them. They chatted for a few more minutes before Stiles and Rena got in the car and drove off. Audrey and Pastor stood in the driveway with their arms encircling one another's waist. Audrey smiled as she thought to herself, *it's only a matter of time, Rena, before you become my son's wife.*

15

"There is no disguise which can hide love for long where it exists, or simulate it where it does not."
—La Rochefoucauld

Stiles and Rena arrived at East Women's Facility a little after four-thirty. After being thoroughly probed by a less-than-friendly guard, they were directed to the visiting area. Nervously, Rena sat down in the one chair positioned in front of the dirty window while Stiles stood directly behind her. It took almost forty-five minutes before Frankie, along with some of the other inmates who had visitors, was escorted into the cramped visiting area.

When she approached the window, Frankie stood frozen instead of pulling out the chair.

Rena watched as Frankie's eyes slanted and narrowed like a serpent's, when she saw Stiles next to her. She sensed the barely-controlled power that was coiled in Frankie's body. *Dang, she looks like she can spring through that glass and choke the life out of me. I've made a mistake bringing Stiles with me.* Rena felt a momentary wave of panic before she remembered that Frankie was behind bars and unable to reach her.

Trying to avoid looking Frankie in the eye, Rena

shifted her gaze toward Stiles. "Look who's here. We thought we'd surprise you," she tried to say lightly.

"Definitely did that." Frankie yanked the chair and plopped down. "I guess the joke's on me," she retorted sarcastically.

"How are you, Sis?" Stiles asked bending down to speak through the circular microphone built into the glass.

She shrugged dismissively before focusing back on Rena.

"So, what's the happy occasion, Rena?"

Frankie's eyebrows raised and her stare sent shivers up and down Rena's spine. Stiles couldn't help but notice the look his sister gave Rena. Before Rena could answer, Stiles knelt down next to her and placed one arm around her shoulders.

"We wanted to come together, Sis. Rena and I want to let you know that we're going to stick by you, and we're praying for you everyday. When you get out of this place, we're going to do whatever we can to help you. I've been taking good care of your apartment. I even added a few touches to it that I think you might like." Stiles giggled.

"Hardly," Frankie mumbled. "I didn't get an answer, Rena," Frankie emphasized. "What's the occasion? Looks like you two are playing the happy couple or something."

"Uh, I don't know what you're talking about, Frankie. I told you."

Again, Stiles butted in. "Look, Frankie. What's up with the third degree?

Rena watched and listened. She saw Frankie's jaws clinch. Stiles gritted his teeth and inched as close as he could to the window that separated him from his sister. "Look," he pointed at her. "I don't know what your problem is, but I'm sick of feeding it. I don't know why you're trying to put Rena on some kind of guilt trip when she's the one who sticks by your trifling tail."

Frankie's jaws puffed out so big she looked like a blow fish. Before she could make a come back to his stinging remarks, he spoke up again.

"We came here . . ."

Rena squeezed his arm to try to stop him from saying what she knew we was about to say, but he ignored her.

"We came here because we wanted you to be the first to know about the two of us. But you're too busy thinking about yourself, as usual," he blasted at her.

"And what exactly is it you want me to know, brother?" Frankie responded sharply.

Stiles placed his arm around Rena's shoulder and kissed her hair. "We're in love, Sis."

Rena remained speechless, shielding her own surprise at Stiles' remarks. She forced her lips to part in a curved, stiff smile. *He loves me? My God, he loves me?*

"Is that so?" Frankie remarked angrily.

"Yes, Stiles is right." Rena reached up and grabbed the tips of his fingers and tried to make light of what she believed was about to become an unpleasant situation. "I've fallen in love with my best friend's quirky brother."

Stiles' grip tightened around her shoulder when he heard Rena admit that she loved him too. Frankie jumped up and startled the rest of the inmates. The guard rushed over next to her and pushed her shoulder down so hard that she almost fell to the floor. With a string of expletives gushing out of her mouth, Frankie demanded that the guard take her back to the pod.

As the guard led her away, Rena shivered when she saw the vile, evil stare from Frankie's bloodshot eyes.

Stiles couldn't move. "Where did all of that come from? She acted like a mad woman." Stiles turned toward Rena. "What's wrong with that girl?"

"I . . . I don't know. Frankie can be like that sometimes. You don't know her like I do. None of you do," Rena said, standing up with tears flooding her eyes. "Let's get out of here." Without waiting on him to respond, she rushed out of the visiting area.

"I want to go home. I need to be alone for a while."

So much had transpired so quickly that Stiles didn't rebuff her demands. He went to the church to talk to Pastor about his sister's odd behavior.

Listening to his son, Pastor replied, "Stiles, people in prison often experience loneliness and isolation. The two of you remind Francesca of how she's made a mess of her life. It's normal. Seeing you and her best friend happy and in love was too much for Frankie at the time."

"Maybe you're right, Pastor. But if she would understand how much Rena and I care about her, then she wouldn't have to feel the way she does."

"Give her some time, Son. Let me talk to her. I'm going to visit her and a few other inmates tomorrow morning. She'll be fine. You'll see."

Stiles left the church and headed home. He called Rena a couple of more times but she still didn't answer her phone.

"Rena, it's Stiles. I'm on my way home. I thought I'd try reaching you again, but I guess you're already sleeping. I'll call you tomorrow. I love you. Good night." *I guess she needs some time to sort things out too, after Frankie's behavior. After Pastor talks to Frankie, maybe things will be better for everybody,* Stiles thought.

Rena lay across the bed and listened to Stiles' message. Falling down on her knees beside her bed, she prayed. "Lord, I can't talk to Stiles. Not after the way things went with Frankie. What do I do? I feel like I'm backed up in a corner without a way of getting out. Help me get out of this mess, please." When she finished her prayer, she climbed between the bed cover and fell asleep.

The next morning, unable to convince Audrey to go with him, Pastor drove alone to Jail East Women's Facility, arriving there in time for morning visiting hours.

Pastor walked in and sat down in front of the plate glass window. Unspoken pain glowed in his eyes when he saw his frazzled daughter enter through the narrow corridor. She sat down in the rickety chair in front of the glass partition.

"Hey, Pastor." Her eyes glistened and tears formed.

He pressed his hand against the window. She matched hers against his.

"Hello, sweetheart. How are you?"

"My life is so messed up. I'm always screwin' up. I make one bad decision afta anotha. Everyone I'm 'roun' ends up mis'rable. I can't keep a job. I'm in and outta jail all the time. My own motha can't stand me."

"Francesca, baby that's not true. Your mother loves you. We all love you."

"I love you too. Being a disappointment to you was never on my list of things to do in life, I swear."

"Remember, you shouldn't swear." His smile deepened into laughter.

"Oh, yeah, forgot." She smiled back at him. "Pastor, rememba when I was a lil girl and you took me places with you?"

Pastor nodded his head.

"It would be just me and you. What happened to those days? Why do things got to be like they are now?"

"Frankie, life is made up of a series of events and situations. Sometimes they're unfortunate and are caused by the decisions we make. Other times, it's not of our own doing, things just happen. But the important thing to remember is that life is for living, baby. Sure, sometimes we choose the wrong path, but honey, you can't beat up on yourself for the mistakes you've made. If I took an inventory of all the things I've done wrong or beat up on myself for all the bad decisions I made, honey, I would be crazy. But I refuse to do that. I'm human. You're human. We all make mistakes. In the book of Philippians chapter three, Paul says, 'I do not consider myself yet to have taken hold of it. But one thing I do, forgetting what is behind and straining toward what is ahead.' Honey, that's what you have to do. Stop clinging to the mistakes of your past. Serve your time here, and move on from this place. As for your brother and your best friend, you have to find it in your heart to be happy for them instead of angry. They love each other, and that's a good thing, sweetheart."

"Yea, I guess."

The guard yelled, "Visiting hours are over. Return to your cells."

Frankie stood up and pressed the palm of her hand against the glass. Pastor laid his palm against the glass to match hers.

"Bye, sweetheart. Stay strong, and remember that you are loved."

Frankie tilted her head and leaned it against the window. She mouthed the words, "good-bye" to Pastor and then walked away.

Lying in her bunk that night, Frankie thought about the things Pastor and she had talked about. She smiled when she thought of his way of soothing her troubled spirit. When she drifted off to sleep, she was awakened by the same, terrible nightmares. Screaming out loud, the only response she heard were the yells from the other inmates for her to shut up.

* * *

Three days after her and Stiles' visit, Rena went alone to see Frankie, who refused to see her. Rena, though hurt, still left money for Frankie so she would be able to buy toiletries, snacks, and magazines. Frankie hadn't called either, something she used to do almost every day.

Rena told Stiles about Frankie's refusal to see her.

"Take my word for it, Frankie will come around," he tried to reassure Rena.

"I hope so. We've been friends far too long for it to end because of our relationship," Rena countered.

Deep down inside Rena wanted to tell him that it wasn't the friendship she was afraid of losing. It was the fear that was nestled inside about what Frankie would do once she was released from prison.

16

*"The story of a love is not important—what is important is that
one is capable of love. It is perhaps the only glimpse we are
permitted of eternity."*
—Helen Hayes

Audrey couldn't have been better since learning that
Stiles and Rena were in love. Stiles had confided in
her and Pastor that he was going to ask Rena to marry
him.

Stiles told his parents of his plans to visit Mr. and Mrs.
Jackson. He wanted to do things in the proper manner.
Although Rena had already told her parents about their
love, she had no idea that he wanted her to become his
wife.

Two days before he was supposed to fly to Andover,
Stiles told Rena that he had to go out of town on business.

"Son, I'm proud of you for going about this the right
way."

"Thank you, Pastor." Stiles' smile broadened at his father's approval.

"It's right to seek the blessing of a woman's parents
before you ask her to become your wife. They'll respect
you for it."

"I wouldn't feel right if Mr. and Mrs. Jackson didn't

know my intentions. I not only want their blessing, but I want them to know that I love Rena," explained Stiles.

When he arrived in Andover, the Jackson family greeted Stiles with open arms. Mr. Jackson had gained a tremendous amount of respect for Stiles Graham. Nowadays, there weren't many men who asked for a daughter's hand in marriage. But Stiles wasn't like many men. He had been raised to be respectable, to treat others the way he wanted to be treated. Stiles assured Mr. Jackson that he intended to spend the rest of his life showing Rena just how much he loved her.

Two days later, Stiles returned to Memphis with the full blessing of Rena's parents. If Rena accepted his proposal, he would be sitting on top of the world.

No sooner than his plane touched down and he retrieved his bag, Stiles hurried outside to wait on Rena to pick him up. It wasn't long before he saw her driving into the airport pick-up area. He dashed toward the car, threw his bag in the back seat, and jumped inside. His lips found hers, and he embraced her with fervor.

"I'm glad to see you too," remarked Rena as he released her lips.

"I can't help that I missed you." That irresistible grin danced at the corners of his mouth.

Pulling away from the curb, Rena stole a look at him and smiled. "How was your trip?"

"Better than I could ever expect."

She viewed him a bit curiously, and shrugged her shoulders offhandedly. "You never said what it was about."

"I had to tie up some loose ends, that's all." He reached over and caressed Rena's thigh without her putting up a fuss.

She loved the feel of his touch. She never dreamed a man's hands would feel so warm and so gentle.

* * *

The next afternoon, Stiles called Rena. Everything was planned, and he hoped tomorrow night would be perfect.

"How's the girl of my dreams?"

Rena blushed over the phone and returned with her own quirky response. "Absolutely wonderful, now that she's talking to the man of her dreams."

"Ah ha, so you do know how to get to my soft spot? Am I going to see you later?"

"Do you want to see me?"

"I can't think of anything I'd like better."

"What time?"

"Well, I have a few members to visit this afternoon and a minister's meeting. After that, I'm free. What about sevenish?" remarked Stiles.

Rena laughed lightly into the phone. "Sevenish, it is. Bye, sweetheart."

"I'll see you tonight." He ended the call and returned to church business.

Pastor walked into his son's office.

"How is everything coming along with the development of the men's ministry?" Pastor inquired.

"I believe it's going to be a positive ministry, Pastor. We met last week, and we're going to meet again Saturday morning. I've been getting some great cooperation from our men. We've had some productive brainstorming sessions. Once we put everything together, I believe we're going to have a powerful Men's Ministry."

"Good, Son. Real good." Pastor patted Stiles on his shoulder. "Would you like to come to dinner this evening? Your mother is preparing your favorite: carrot soufflé."

"That sounds good, but I have to pass tonight. I'm supposed to pick up Rena at seven."

"You know she's always welcome at Emerald Estates. I

know Audrey wouldn't mind. She's still swooning over the fact that you and Rena are in love and that she's going to be your wife." Pastor chuckled lightheartedly.

"Tell you what. Let me check with her. If she doesn't have special plans for us, then we'll stop by. But if we don't, tell Mom to set aside some of her delicious soufflé for her son."

Pastor threw back his head and chuckled again. "Will do." He turned around and walked toward the door, still talking. "I'm going to my office to study some more for Sunday's message. We'll talk later."

"Sure thing, Pastor."

At seven-fifteen Stiles arrived at Rena's apartment. Before he could ring the doorbell, she opened the door and ushered him inside.

"Hello, beautiful." He kissed her fervently on the lips, as his hand positioned perfectly around the coif of her neck.

Rena accepted his kiss eagerly.

"Don't you think we need to be leaving?" Rena asked, putting space between them.

"Just where are we going, anyway?" Stiles viewed her curiously.

"It's such a beautiful evening, I thought we should do something outside," suggested Rena.

Stiles cuffed his chin with his left hand. "Let's see. What can we do?" He paced across the floor a couple of times. "Hey, I know. There's a Redbirds game tonight."

"I'd like that. Let me grab my purse and phone. I'll be right back."

Stiles couldn't pass up the opportunity. He followed her.

"What are you doing?"

He answered by walking up on her and pulling her

into his arms. His kisses ravished her body and sent shivers up and down her spine. It was hard for her to pull away because she didn't want him to stop.

"Stiles," whispered Rena. "We have to go. We need to go." Her words turned into soft moans.

Stiles was quickly losing control until his spirit jolted him. He pulled away from Rena. "You're right. Let's get out of here before there's no turning back." His breathing was heavy and other parts throbbed with desire.

Driving back across the bridge after the game, Rena and Stiles enjoyed each other's company. Their constant chatter proved that they had much in common. Being around Stiles, there was never boredom. Hating to compare him to Frankie, she tried not to think of the friction that often arose between them whenever they were together. There was always something that the two of them disagreed over. But with Stiles, everything went smoothly. She hated to admit it, but it felt good not having Frankie around. Not that she wanted her to be in jail, but knowing that she wasn't free to wreak havoc in her life, at least for now, made Rena's life that much easier.

Excitement dripped from Stiles' voice. "I made reservations for the two of us for tomorrow night at Chez Philippe."

Rena's eyes glowed as the joy of excitement bubbled forth. "Oh, Stiles, did you? I hear that it's top of the line."

"Nothing but the best for my girl."

17

Stiles was a man of elegant taste. The eighteen karat white gold engagement ring with a two carat round bezel set diamond revealed his exquisite taste even more. Encircled by ten glittering round diamonds, when he showed it to his mother, she almost fainted. It was absolutely stunning.

When Stiles arrived to pick Rena up, he was in awe of her beauty. The rose print organza silk dress accented her milk-colored skin. Stiles loved her even more at that moment. The wintry February evening gave Stiles a welcome excuse to cuddle against the woman he hoped would soon become his wife.

With her arms folded, Rena huddled underneath her wool and cotton waist-length jacket. Stiles opened his stylish wool flannel trench and cradled it against her coat, providing extra warmth for Rena's thin frame.

When they arrived at Chez Philippe, they checked their coats. The hostess led them to their table. Stiles noticed that Rena's brows were drawn together in an agonized expression. He placed the menu on the table. "Would you like me to order for the both of us?"

"Yes, please." Rena laid the menu down and sighed with relief.

Stiles chose the braised shrimp and turnip salad with fresh thyme for the appetizer accompanied by a glass of white wine. With the engagement ring tucked safely away inside his pant pocket, he waited patiently for the perfect time. They talked about everything from high school to college. The environment was relaxing and upscale.

"So this is the famous Peabody's Chez Philippe. The food is delicious," Rena praised him then pointed out the beautiful restaurant decor. It felt sensational to be treated like she was the only woman in the world. Stiles was able to bring out the very best in her. For the first time in her twenty-five years, Rena admitted to herself that she was someone special. She'd never really thought about her feelings about herself before. But sitting across the table from Stiles, listening to him compliment her and pamper her, was the best feeling in the world. She felt worthy of love and not the rollercoaster treatment she'd grown used to from Frankie.

Frankie, oh my goodness. Frankie would explode if she could see me now. As soon as her mind ventured to Frankie, Rena dispelled the thoughts. Shaking off thoughts of Frankie was becoming easier. Tonight was no different. Nothing was going to ruin her evening, not even Frankie.

Stiles raised his glass. "To us."

Rena raised her glass and echoed, "To us," and smiled. As he made a toast to their future, he discreetly reached inside the pocket of his black designer's suit, using his fingers to caress the tiny gold box. Pulling it out as they both set their glasses down, with one swoop Stiles stood, then knelt down on one knee next to Rena, and tenderly took hold of her hand.

"What in the world are you doing?" She looked around to see if any one noticed the tall figure bending down before her. Trying to shield her embarrassment proved to be rather difficult.

Stiles didn't bother to say a word. He allowed his baby brown eyes to do all the talking. Rena was transfixed. Everything appeared to be moving in slow motion as she eyed the gold box in his hand.

This can't be. Oh, my God, it can't be. She watched in utter stillness as Stiles cautiously opened the box and said the four most life-changing words a man could ever say to his woman, "Will you marry me?"

Her tears that sparkled in the dim restaurant chandelier as brilliantly as the diamond Stiles held in his hand. She leaned over and wrapped her arms around Stiles' neck, rising only slightly so she could place butterfly kisses over his face.

"I hope this means you're saying yes to my marriage proposal."

"Yes, yes, yes," was Rena's response.

Several people in the restaurant "oohed" and "aahed" when Stiles placed the sparkling engagement ring on Rena's finger. Rena's eyes scanned the diamond. Then she looked into Stiles' eyes with appreciation for being appreciated.

"My God, this is beautiful, Stiles." The cry of relief that she had been holding broke from her lips. Rena raised her tear-filled eyes, caught his eyes, and held the moment in time.

Stiles, still on bended knee, used his thumb to delicately wipe a tear from her cheek. "You got me on my knee, girl." He had to find some humor so he wouldn't get emotional.

"I plan on using the rest of my life to see that you're just as happy as you are right now, love of my life."

A bottle of wine was placed on their table, compliments of Chez Philippe. They picked up the bottle and left. Stiles drove to the park on the river. The icy breeze coming from the Mississippi forced Rena to find warm refuge underneath Stiles's arms. While cuddling in the car, she examined her ring over and over again.

"I love you so much, Stiles."

"I love you too." He kissed her forehead then his lips traveled ever so slowly toward hers. Caressing her shoulders with his hands, his kiss became more passionate. The intensity built up inside of Stiles was ready to explode. His breathing became heavy and he pulled Rena so close against his body that it was hard to tell that they were indeed two.

Rena felt the pounding of his heart as it beat against her bosom. Welcoming his kisses, she returned his passion with her own heightened desire for him. Suddenly, thoughts of Frankie penetrated the moment, and she pulled back from Stiles.

"What is it?" he asked her.

"Nothing really. It's just that we don't need things to get out of control."

What is Frankie going to say when she finds out me and Stiles are going to get married?

"Rena, Rena." Stiles called her name.

"Yes."

"I said I'm sorry. I didn't mean to come off so strong. I respect the fact that you want to wait until our wedding night."

"That's right. I know that you aren't a virgin, but I am. And I plan to remain one until my wedding day," Rena trembled from the coldness that invaded the car.

"Come on, let's get out of here." Stiles cranked the car and turned up the heat. "You're shivering."

Stiles couldn't help but honor Rena's wishes. She was

definitely right about his past. In high school, girls swarmed him like bees on honey. He kept them at arms' length, but when he went off to college, well, that was an entirely different story. The life of freedom, great parties and girls from everywhere was more than he could stand. It was much easier to allow his sexual desires to overrule his moral teachings. No restrictions, except those he put on himself.

Being a pastor's son, and majoring in religion, didn't deter him from leading a wild lifestyle. If he had had his way, he probably wouldn't have gone to college in the first place, and he certainly wouldn't have majored in religion.

At the end of his sophomore year, Stiles realized he wasn't living the kind of life he'd been taught to live. Partying wasn't so much fun anymore. He became more focused and started attending a small church off campus, and replaced partying with studying. His grades improved and his "different chick every night routine" ceased. The more he returned to following what his parents had taught him, the stronger he became in his walk of faith. By his senior year of college, Stiles accepted his call to the ministry and made plans to continue his education at Duke Divinity School.

On the drive home, Stiles and Rena discussed their impending marriage. Stiles wanted to get married right away, but Rena wanted a big wedding. They agreed on an August wedding.

When he dropped her off, Rena immediately rushed to the phone to call her parents with the exciting news. She was even more amazed when her mother told her that Stiles had flown to Andover to ask her father for her hand in marriage. Rena couldn't believe it. The man who had captured her heart was a gem. After talking to her parents for a while, Rena hung the phone up and ran a hot bath. The ringing phone startled her just as she was about to step in the hot bubble bath.

The familiar sound of the operator on the other end sent a cold chill through her body as she accepted the call.

"Where have you been?"

"I . . . I went out to dinner. How are you? Is everything all right?"

Ignoring Rena's questions, Frankie continued with her probe. "You were with Stiles, weren't you? And don't even think about lying."

Sighing heavily, Rena wished she hadn't bothered to pick up the phone. But it was too late for that. *Should I tell her about Stiles' proposal? I don't know what to do.*

"I know you hear me talkin' to you," Frankie yelled into the phone. "I *said*, you were with Stiles tonight, weren't you?"

"Okay, I was with Stiles! Is that what you wanted to hear?" Rena screamed back as her nostrils flared with fury. She couldn't and wouldn't take it anymore. Enough was enough. She was sick and tired of Frankie's temper.

"I shudda known you couldn't be trusted. You're nothing but a good-for-nothing, two-bit slut. Who do you think you're fooling, Rena? How long do you think it'll be before everyone knows about you and me? Huh?" Frankie threatened as curses fell from her mouth.

"I'm sick of this, Frankie. I can't take your accusations and threats anymore. Do whatever you wish," Rena bluffed. "I want to be happy for once in my life. I have an open relationship, one that every one can know about. One that I don't have to be ashamed of. Can't you understand that? All of these years we've been living the unthinkable. Well, I can't do it anymore. I won't do it anymore."

"What?" Frankie's voice rose in fury. "You think all of

a sudden you're above me or something, just because my brother comes along and feeds you a bunch of bull? Well, think again, 'cause the only thing about you is that you try to hide your sins. You pretend like you're so perfect." Frankie was breathless with rage. "You're one of those folks who sit up in church on Sunday, but outside of the church, you're doing nothing but living a lie."

Rena's tears flowed. Listening to Frankie, she became so furious she could hardly speak, but Frankie was right. Who was she fooling? Certainly not God.

"I don't think I'm better than you. I just know that I don't want this anymore. I never meant for that day ten years ago to turn out to be like this. It was only meant to be an experiment, not some sick, unnatural relationship.

"Is that what you think of us—sick?" Frankie's voice softened. Hurt replaced anger as she listened to Rena.

"Look, I don't want to hurt you, Frankie. I would never intentionally do such a thing. But I can't keep this up." Without thinking about her next sentence, Rena blurted out. "Stiles asked me to marry him. And I said, yes. I love him, and he loves me. I have the engagement ring to prove it. We're getting married in August." Rena swallowed hard. "I'm sorry."

Frankie held the phone to her ear. Numbness rushed over her body. The operator's timing was perfect. "You have exactly two minutes before this call will end."

"Frankie, are you there?" Rena asked.

Frozen, Frankie hung up the phone. All of these years, it had been her and Rena. Now their relationship had been severed by her own brother. Another piece of her heart had been ripped apart.

Rena held the phone to her ear as the dial tone buzzed. Relief and sadness swooped through her. Looking down at her finger, she gazed at the huge diamond Stiles had placed on her finger. She smiled.

18

"Love is like war: easy to begin, but hard to end."
—*Unknown*

Audrey, Rena, and Rena's mother, Meryl, began making plans for the wedding. The three women were in a constant state of euphoria.

Rena hadn't heard from Frankie since the night she told her about Stiles' proposal. She had tried to visit her, but Frankie had removed her name from the visitor's list. Planning a wedding, however, quickly alleviated any sad thoughts about Frankie.

Audrey was having the time of her life. Helping out with the wedding made her feel that much closer to her future daughter-in-law. Something told her that she would never have such an opportunity like this with her own daughter. A twinge of disappointment ripped through her.

Almost every weekend, and sometimes during the week, Audrey and Rena were running around gathering information about the wedding. Meryl made plans to fly down a couple of weekends leading up to the wedding to help Rena with her dress and cake.

The days turned into months. Rena could hardly believe that it was already June, and in ten short days Frankie would be getting out of jail. Frankie had been locked up almost nine months.

There were times she wanted to confess to Stiles about her and Frankie, but she could never bring herself to do it. Now she could only hope and pray that Frankie would not expose her. Their friendship over the years had to count for something; at least Rena sure hoped it did.

Audrey was totally against going to the jail to pick up her daughter. Pastor convinced her that it was the least she could do since she hadn't seen her in close to nine months. But Audrey didn't see things through rose-colored glasses. Suppose someone recognized her, which was more than likely to happen. Pastor told her to not allow other people to make her feel inferior, but Audrey couldn't seem to do that.

She rushed inside the jail, her printed scarf draped over the lower portion of her face. The pomegranate A-line jersey dress flew in the wind with her every hurried step. Once inside, Audrey waited almost an hour before she saw Frankie being led out by a guard.

"Audrey, hello," Frankie said dryly. "How did Daddy talk you into coming?"

"Francesca, please. Don't start. Come on, let's get out of this filthy place," Audrey commanded and swiftly turned on her heels and headed to the exit. Stepping outside, Audrey inhaled the fresh air like she had been the one behind bars for almost a year.

Frankie followed her mother to the car and barely got her leg in before Audrey gunned the accelerator, burning rubber and leaving a trail of dust so thick she couldn't see the inmates standing outside in the recreation area.

As they approached the security gate, it seemed that Audrey was headed straight for the guard. He must have thought so too. He screamed in Spanish, jumped on top of the security car, and held on for his life.

Frankie glared at her mother. "You're going to kill somebody."

"Shut up!" Audrey glared back at her rebellious daughter. "I hope you never put me and Pastor through this again. It's embarrassing to have the Pastor's daughter locked up like a common criminal."

"Mother, when are you going to realize that I am a common criminal? Oh, and in case you haven't noticed, I'm also a lesbian." Frankie said with a smirk on her face, clearly taunting her mother.

Audrey almost lost control of the car. Glaring at Frankie, Audrey said, "How dare you make light of such a despicable thing!" she scolded her. "When are you going to grow up? You are not a lesbian, and you are not a criminal. You're doing this to hurt me and Pastor for some reason. I don't know why, but I tell you that you'd better stop it, Francesca. Stop it right now."

Frankie flippantly threw up her hand. "Whatever, Mother. Just drop me off at my apartment."

The remainder of the twenty-five minute trip was driven with the radio blaring gospel tunes. That way, Frankie guessed, her mother wouldn't have to think of anything else to say to her. It was fine by Frankie because there was little she had to say to her mother anyway.

When Audrey pulled up in front of the apartment, she didn't bother turning off the engine. "Frankie, your brother and Rena are getting married. The wedding is the first of August. Being that you and Rena are best friends, she expects you to be her maid of honor."

Frankie swished her head around like a fierce windstorm. "Oh, no. I'm not going to do any such thing."

"Francesca Graham, you are not going to disappoint Rena. She's stuck by you all of these years. You will not hurt her. I won't have it. You hear me. And you will not humiliate your brother, or any of us, anymore with your selfishness and stupidity," Audrey retorted, pointing a freshly polished finger at her.

Frankie opened the door, stepped out of the car and slammed the door behind her. Rushing upstairs, she stood in front of her apartment, furious at what her mother just told her. *I can't believe Rena expects me to be her maid of honor. The nerve of that . . .* Frankie dug deep down inside her jean pocket for her key. It was one of the few things she'd had on her when she went to jail. Turning the key and stepping inside, she couldn't believe the scene before her. Her apartment was totally transformed. She agreed with Rena's decision to let Stiles live there while she was locked up, but she didn't expect him to change everything. Resentment formed in the base of her chest. She was startled by the voice behind her.

"Welcome home, sis," Stiles said from behind, grabbing Frankie around the waist and lifting her off the ground.

Frankie turned around in a tail spin. "What is all of this?" she asked, using her hands to point.

"You like it?" he asked cheerily.

"No, I don't like it," Frankie answered roughly. "I told you that you could stay here while I was locked up. That didn't include throwing my stuff out and replacing it with all of this, this fancy get up," she gestured in a sweeping motion with one arm. "Then you got the nerve to put Bibles and stuff all over my place?" Frankie stated harshly, as she zeroed in on a Bible laying on the sofa and another one on the counter connecting the kitchen to the living room.

"You need some Jesus in your life," Stiles teased, ignoring his sister's obvious discontent with the changes he made. "Anyway, I put your stuff in storage. I was going to get it out before you got out of jail, but I wanted you to see how I fixed up the place. I thought you might want to keep it like this."

"I don't. I want my stuff."

"Why are you so uptight? You just got out of the slammer. I would think you would be on cloud nine, you know." Stiles paused and gazed at her speculatively. "Say, me and Rena want to take you to dinner. We have something to tell you."

"I heard already. You're getting married. Rena didn't tell you that she already let the cat out of the bag?" She tilted her head and eyed him with cold triumph.

"Uh no, she didn't."

"Figures," Frankie mumbled. "Look, I can't go to dinner. I got other plans. You two lovebirds go on without me."

"Come on now, sis. Rena's going to be disappointed. She's looking forward to seeing you."

"I bet she is. Where is she anyway?" Frankie scanned the room.

"Work."

"Umph. Anyway, like I said, I got plans. Now, if you don't mind, I'd like to be left alone."

"Sure." He shrugged dismissively. "I understand. If it's no trouble, I want to leave my belongings here another day or two. That'll give me time to get your things back to you. You think you can manage to do that for your big brother?" Stiles asked and stepped forward to hug Frankie.

Moving quickly out of his reach, Frankie told him, "Yeah, but it better not be more than two days or I'm selling this junk and keeping the cheddar."

Stiles frowned in exasperation. "I guess I'll be leaving. Call me on my cell phone if you need me."

As soon as Stiles left, Frankie kicked off her shoes and dived for the couch. "Might as well take advantage of it while I got it." She twisted and turned until she found a comfortable position. "Dang, there's no place like home," she said, just before her eyes refused to stay open any longer.

"Why do you think she didn't want to go to dinner with us?" asked Rena, fully aware of the reason.

"She said she already had plans. Look," His eyes furrowed in a frown. "We can't worry about Frankie. If she gets a kick out of being mad at God-knows-who or what, so be it. God has to work on her."

"I didn't mean to get you upset," Rena said softly, her eyes narrowing.

"I can't be bothered with her mess any longer, Rena." Stiles let out a loud, audible breath. "I love my sister, and I care about what happens to her. But I have to give her over to God. I pray for her deliverance every day. And I also pray that God will continue to keep her safe wherever her feet trod. But I won't take on her burdens and allow myself to become stagnated by worry. And neither should you." Stiles reached across the table and took hold of Rena's hand. "You've been at Francesca's beck and call every since I can remember. Now I want you at my beck and call," he smiled tenderly.

Rena moved from the kitchen table. She grabbled hold of Stiles' hand as he stood, then kissed him.

He returned her kiss with one of his own. "It's getting harder and harder for me to be a good boy," Stiles said hoarsely as he looked into her eyes.

"I'm not going to let you slip up. Don't worry," she reassured him. "We only have a couple of months. Until then, take plenty of cold showers," she laughed.

"Come on, then. Let's get out of here and go get something to eat. We might as well take in a movie, too, since my sister doesn't want to join us. How about it?"

They left Rena's apartment and drove to downtown Memphis. They walked along Beale Street. Pigeons pecked at specks of food on the ground, and horses pulled white carriages at full trots. The night was still young. The diverse crowd of people moved in circles down the street enjoying the night. They decided to eat at the Hard Rock Café. Afterwards, they walked to Muvico and enjoyed a comedy. By the time the movie ended, it was past midnight.

"I wish I could say that we could go to my place, but as you know, I no longer have a place," Stiles said jokingly.

"Don't worry. It won't be long before we're married and have our own place. I need to get home anyway; I have a busy day tomorrow." Rena clasped her arm inside the curve of his as they walked out of Peabody Place Mall into the parking garage. On the way home, Rena laid her head on Stiles' shoulder and drifted off into a light sleep. It wasn't until he pulled up to her apartment that she opened her eyes.

"You're home, sleepy head," he whispered and kissed her hair.

"Already?" She sat up, yawned and rubbed her eyes. She shook her head to knock the sleep away.

He walked her to the door and waited patiently while she scrambled through her purse in search of her keys. "Would you like me to come inside?" He grinned mischievously when she unlocked the door.

"You and I both know that wouldn't be such a good idea. You'd better go. Emerald Estates is calling you. Be safe, sweetheart," Rena leaned over and kissed his warm lips before fully opening the door to go inside.

Stiles waited until he saw the light in her bedroom before driving away.

Rena fell backward on her bed and sighed. A smile spread on her face as she thought of Stiles's kiss. Kicking off her shoes and clothes and slipping into her PJs, she crawled into bed. Saying her prayers in the bed, she prayed for Frankie to come around and accept her relationship with Stiles. She was so exhausted that she didn't hear the key turn in the front door.

The next morning, Rena woke up to the blare of her alarm clock. Stretching and yawning loudly, she ambled to the bathroom and started her daily ritual. Stepping underneath the warm spray of water awakened her. As she lathered her body, she became transfixed with thoughts of her wedding day. It was the chance for a new beginning. She wondered how it would be to be with a man for the first time. Technically, she was still a virgin, or was she? She often wondered about that. Did living a life of homosexuality mean that she was no longer the innocent woman she wanted Stiles to believe she was? The more she thought about it, the harder she scrubbed her delicate flesh. With each thought of the sickening acts she'd committed with Frankie, the harder she scrubbed. Her skin turned redder with each stroke of the washcloth against it. She tried desperately to scrub the stench of sin off of her. Maybe she could scrub until everything that dishonored God was washed away. Tears streamed from her eyes. Her body heaved at the thought of all she'd done wrong throughout her young life. "God," she cried out. "Forgive me."

A thunderous crash caused Rena to stand dead still underneath the streaming water. The deafening sound of a second thud almost caused her to lose her balance. *Oh my God, someone has broken into my apartment.* She was terrified. She turned off the shower but remained inside and listened. It sounded like someone throwing things around in the living room. Then Rena heard someone cursing. As she listened, too petrified to move, she began to recognize the voice. Round after round of expletives freely poured from Frankie's mouth.

Rena didn't know what to do. She quietly and quickly stepped out of the shower, grabbed a towel and began drying off. She slowly tip-toed into her bedroom, only to meet Frankie's evil stare.

"What are you doing here?" asked Rena, trying to conceal her fear.

"Don't I get a hug, a 'how you doin', baby' or something?"

Rena continued putting on her clothes. She wanted to be prepared to make a run for it just in case Frankie tried to do her harm.

"Don't look so stunned. I do have a key, remember?"

Rena chewed on her lower lip. Without responding, she walked slowly past Frankie into the living room. "What is wrong with you?" Rena yelled, turning to look at Frankie. "Look at this place. You trashed my living room and kitchen. Why did you do this?" she asked with disbelief in her voice.

"What you gonna do 'bout it? Call the police? Go on. Do whatcha gotta do." Frankie's face was a glowering mask of rage. "You didn't even have the decency to call me and say, hello Frankie. I'm glad you home, Frankie. No, you send your boy to my apartment talkin' 'bout taking me out to dinner. B, you have me messed up. Don't try and pretend like what you doing is all good, because it ain't."

"Frankie, please don't do this to me." Rena pleaded

with her. "My life will be ruined if anyone finds out about me and you."

"Is that all you're concerned about? Yourself? You're just like Audrey. All she ever thinks about is what the church folk are sayin' or what sista so-and-so thinks about her. Some First Lady, not to mention mother, she is, huh? I don't know why I didn't see it before. You don't care 'bout me. All you care about is yoself, just like Audrey. You're selfish and cruel. I hate the day I ever met you." With that said, Frankie turned abruptly and stormed out of the apartment, leaving the door wide open.

Rena rushed behind her, closing and locking the door just in case Frankie had second thoughts about coming back. She ran to the picture window just in time to spot Frankie getting into a blue Mustang. Rena watched until the car was no longer in sight. Returning to check the locks again, she slid against the door, slowly crumbling to the floor as she tearfully surveyed her trashed apartment. With her head resting in her hands, they caught the tears as they fell. She crawled over some of the trash until she reached the phone. Picking it up, she called in to work to let them know she wouldn't be coming in.

Rena searched the yellow pages for a cleaning service. There was no way she would be able to get the apartment back to normal without help. She found an agency that could send someone over within the hour. Rena lay across the sofa and sobbed. What if Frankie was on her way to tell Stiles and his family about them? What was she going to do? Her hands trembled, sweat formed on her brow and inside the palms of her hands. She decided to call Stiles.

No answer.

The clock in the kitchen was torn from the wall so Rena went into her bedroom and looked at the alarm clock. It was already after nine. Stiles was teaching his Old Testament class at the university. Rena then called Audrey. When she answered, Rena sighed in relief.

"Good morning, Audrey. How are you?"

"Honey, I'm blessed and highly favored," replied Audrey, her southern drawl kicking in.

"Shouldn't you be at work?"

"Yes, ma'am. But I . . . I'm not feeling very well this morning. I think I'm coming down with a cold or something. I'm going to stay home," lied Rena.

"Is there anything I can do for you?"

"No, I'll be fine. Have you heard from Frankie?"

"Heaven's no. Why? Has she gone and done something else? The child just got out of jail. I tell you, if she's already gotten in trouble again, I am not going to let Pastor run to her aid this time. I just won't do it."

"No, it's nothing like that. I wanted to tell you that Frankie's not going to be my maid of honor. She said she can't see herself in anyone's wedding, even if it is mine, so I'm going to ask my co-worker, Irma."

"I hope you see for yourself what I'm talking about. That child is so stupid and selfish," Audrey said in a bitter tone. "Anyway, I think asking your co-worker is a good idea. Of course, she'll have to get measured for her dress right away. We don't have much time, you know. If she can't do it, you shouldn't worry about it. I've attended many weddings, and some had a maid of honor and matron of honor, and some only had one or the other. As a matter of fact, when Pastor and I got married, my sister, Lucille, stood as my maid of honor, and I had one bridesmaid." Audrey laughed lightly into the phone.

Rena chuckled. "That's good to know. Well, look, I'm not going to hold you."

"Okay, darling. Take care of that cold, and call me if you need me."

* * *

Contrary to what Rena expected, she hadn't seen or heard from Frankie since the morning of her rampage. Rena was relieved on one hand and worried on the other. She called Frankie's apartment several times, but there was never an answer. Surveying her own apartment, Rena couldn't tell that a couple of weeks ago, it had looked like Hurricane Katrina had swept through it. She was thankful that the cleaning service performed such a spectacular job. The items that Frankie had broken could be replaced over time; she couldn't say the same about Frankie's heart.

No news is good news for some people, but when it came to Frankie, any news coming from her could mean the beginning of the end for Rena.

19

"I never felt true love until I was with you, and I never felt true sadness until you left me."
—Anonymous

"Hey, sweetheart," Stiles said tenderly. "Do you want to see your fiancé' this evening after work?"

"I do, but unfortunately I can't. I have a staff meeting. By the time we finish, it'll be late, and I still need to go home and work on the wedding."

Stiles pretended to pout in a whiny voice. "But I want to see my lovely bride-to-be," he said in a little boy's voice.

"I want to see you too. What if I make it up to you tomorrow, after midweek Bible study? I'll take you downtown to Cheesecake Corner," Rena offered.

"You got yourself a deal. I've wanted to go back to that spot for the longest time. That guy can whip up a mean cheesecake. Can I get the chocolate chip cheesecake this time?" he asked, the child's voice returning.

Answering him in a loving, motherly tone, Rena told him, "You sure can. But only if you're a good boy and let Mommy get off this phone and get back to work," she played along.

"You got it. Love you."

"Love you too. Bye now," Rena hung up the phone.

The next evening, at Wednesday night service, Pastor taught from Matthew chapter 28. "People, you'd better get your lives in order. No one knows the day or hour when God is going to return. But rest assured, Jesus is coming back. You might be able to fool the person sitting next to you. You might be able to fool me. But you can't fool God. Matthew 23 verse 28 talks about hypocrites. The Pharisees, you see, strutted around the city like they were so special. They wanted everyone to believe that they were pure and holy. Some of you do the same thing today. The Bible says, 'In the same way, on the outside you appear to people as righteous but on the inside you are full of hypocrisy and wickedness.' I'm telling you, God sees inside your closet," Pastor said as he moved back and forth across the long span of the pulpit.

On the front row, sitting next to Audrey, Rena twitched in her seat, consumed by Pastor's words and her own thoughts. *How can I blame Frankie for being wrong when I'm just as much to blame? She isn't afraid to own up to who she is. She doesn't care what people say or think about her. Here I am, sitting in here pretending to be righteous when I'm really a hypocrite.*

Members of the congregation shouted, "amen" and "praise God." Others stood on their feet and waved their hands in the air. Stiles stood in the pulpit behind his father and patted him on the back as a show of agreement.

Just like she promised him, after midweek service, Rena took Stiles to Cheesecake Corner. They enjoyed a hefty slice of chocolate chip cheesecake and a cup of piping hot coffee.

"Stiles, I can't wait to become your wife." Rena watched him as he took another bite of the scrumptious delicacy.

"I'm going to be the best wife I can be," she said grinning.

"I believe you." Stiles reached across the small, octagon table and squeezed the tips of Rena's slender fingers. "I'm going to spend the rest of my life showing you just how much you mean to me." Stiles wiped his mouth with the back of his hand.

"Stiles?"

Stuffing another piece of the cheesecake in his mouth, he responded, "Huh?"

"Frankie doesn't want to be in the wedding, so I asked my sister if she would be my maid of honor.

"Honey, that's understandable. You can't keep holding out just in case Frankie decides she wants to drop the attitude and be in the wedding. As much as I hate the fact that she refuses to be part of our day, there's nothing either of us can do to change that. Only Frankie can do that. And right now, she's somewhere that only God knows."

"I just wish she wasn't so bitter, that's all."

"Yeah, me too. But I know I haven't done anything to make her feel the way she does, neither have my parents, and you most definitely haven't. Whatever issues Francesca's dealing with are between her and God. Until she wants help, there's not a single thing we can do. So stop worrying about her. She's taken care of herself all this time. And, trust me, she'll keep on doing it. All you have to worry about is taking care of me."

Smiling back at him, love for Stiles Graham flowed through her veins. How she lived the kind of life she'd lived before Stiles, she didn't comprehend, but no way would she ever walk along that destructive path again. Watching him closely, Rena vowed to herself, *from this moment on, it will be me and Stiles. No one will ever come between us, not even you, Francesca Graham. Not ever.*

* * *

Pastor sat in the family room overlooking the kitchen, while Audrey made him a steaming cup of peach tea. A warm cup of tea seemed to soothe his voice after he preached. Reaching for the remote, he surfed the cable channels.

"Pastor, Rena is going to make a lovely bride. That girl knows she loves our son. I can tell."

"I agree with you," Pastor said with satisfaction in his eyes. "All I want is for them to be happy, to love each other and spend the rest of their lives as one. I had a talk with him; he assured me this is what he wants. He loves her." Pastor commented and flipped the subject as hurriedly as he did the channels. "By the way, have you heard from Francesca? I'm really worried about her." Leaning forward, he put the remote on the coffee table, looked at his wife and sighed heavily.

Audrey rubbed her hands on a paper towel. "Believe me. She's fine. I didn't say anything to you or anyone else because I was too mad."

Pastor walked into the kitchen, and planted himself at the marble top island. "Mad about what? Have you seen her?"

Audrey put the cup of tea in his hands. "No, but I did go by her apartment day before yesterday. I knocked on the door and some manly-looking woman answered. It was so disgusting, Pastor." Audrey's lips turned up and she threw the back of her hand on her tilted head in a fainting motion.

Pastor dispelled his wife's diva antics. "What did the woman say?"

"Well, I asked her who she was and she had the nerve to ask me who I was! Can you believe the nerve of some folk? She needed to be in somebody's church trying to get saved, and then maybe then she wouldn't be parading around as something she's not. People like her are going to hell in a hand basket."

"Audrey, please. What did the woman say?" Pastor asked again, this time with a pinch of aggravation in his voice.

"I asked her if Frankie was there and she told me that Frankie had rode to St. Louis for a couple of days with one of their mutual friends. I tried to step inside and look around, but she wouldn't budge. She told me she would tell Frankie that I came by. Before I could say anything else, she closed the door in my face. You see the kind of people our daughter deals with? As much as we spent raising her in the church, telling her about God, and look what she does. She's made us the laughing stock of the church. People everywhere know about Pastor Graham and First Lady Graham's wayward gay daughter. Pastor, I can't take it. I just can't take it anymore. That's why my blood pressure is always up. That child is worrying me to death."

Pastor walked up to his wife, pulled her toward him, and kissed her full on her thin lips. Using his hands, he explored the familiar curvatures of her body. Placing a cavalcade of kisses along her neck line and shoulders, he used his hands to knead her sensitive points. Verbal conversation between them was a thing of the past as Audrey gave way to her husband's passion. Pastor was an expert lover who would do anything to please his first lady.

"Let's go to our room. You're all mine tonight," said Pastor as a gasp pierced Audrey's lips. Holding onto her waist, he led her to their private sanctuary.

The woman who Audrey saw at Frankie's apartment was named Kansas. Frankie met her one night at Incognito, a club frequented by gays and lesbians. Like Frankie,

Kansas was an outcast. She had two children of whom she lost custody due to neglect. Her parents were raising the kids and Kansas was awarded limited, supervised visitation rights. Without a stable living arrangement, she slept at Frankie's from time to time.

"What did my mother want?" asked Frankie.

"I don't know. She didn't say," remarked Kansas with a frown. "I see what you mean about her. She come here trippin', tryna push her way up in here. But I stood my ground, and didn't move a muscle."

"That's the way she is." Frankie pulled a soda from the fridge and popped the top. "Always tryin' to be up in my business. I've told her, more than once, to stay outta my life," Frankie said angrily. "It's like she can't rest, 'less she's making my life mis'rable." Frankie pranced to and fro across the barren tiled floor, smoking a joint, laced with cocaine. "This is what I'm worried 'bout," Frankie said to Kansas as she sucked on the joint. This is the bomb."

"Gimme some of that," Kansas reached for the joint and took a hard pull on it and started coughing like she was choking to death.

Frankie took the joint back and started talking about Audrey again. "Always tryin' to tell me I'm going down a road of destruction." She inhaled. "If it is," Frankie laughed loudly, "I tell you what, I ain't ready to get off.

Kansas turned and walked toward the door. "You somethin' else, girl," she said. "I'm outta here for a minute. I'll be back later." She closed the door behind her

Early Saturday morning, Audrey and Rena went shopping for food, supplies, and decorations for the annual Independence Day barbeque Audrey hosted for her church family and neighborhood friends. They had exactly one week to finalize what Audrey considered to be the event of the year. This year's barbeque, however, was going to be a little bit different from the previous ones. Audrey planned to couple Independence Day with a wedding shower. Meryl would be arriving to help arrange things too. Rena was so excited. She and Audrey were going to the airport later that evening to meet her mother's flight.

The two ladies spent hours going from store to store. Audrey insisted on decorating in the wedding colors of pearl white and sage green rather than traditional red, white, and blue. The lanai at Emerald Estates was large enough for several round tables that Audrey planned to cover with sage green tabletops and a blume box filled with colorful fresh flowers to match. By the time they'd completed their shopping excursions, and ordered the blume boxes from the florist, they barely had time to drop off their collection of goodies at Audrey's house before striking out for the airport.

Rena waited with anticipation for her mother inside the airport, while Audrey manned the car. When she saw the splash of honey blonde hair peaking through the flurry of people, Rena waved her hands and ran in until she reached her mother.

They embraced each other tightly.

"Don't you look radiant," her mother said after pushing her back and inspecting Rena's oval face.

"Momma, I'm so glad to see you." Rena's tear-smothered voice shook with joy. How long are you going to be here?" Trails of questions further revealed Rena's happiness. "You said you might stay until after the wedding. Are you, Momma? How's Daddy? When is he coming?"

"Honey, please. Calm down." Meryl laughed and hugged her daughter again. "There's plenty of time to answer all of your questions. Right now I just want to look at my precious baby. It seems like ages since the last time I saw you."

"I know, Momma. I've missed you and Daddy too. But you're here now and you can help me with my wedding and everything," her voice rose in surprise. Rena retrieved the luggage, and locked her free hand with her mother's.

"Where did you park?" Meryl looked around the busy airport.

"Audrey brought me. She's outside waiting on us."

"Well, come on. We don't want to keep her waiting. You know how the airport authorities are these days. I hope they haven't already made her move."

The day of the barbeque, laughter and love permeated the air. Though it was July, one of the hottest months of the summer in Memphis, the weather was perfect. The temperature hovered around 80 degrees with a gentle breeze that scattered the backyard with the scents of the dozens of flowers. Invited guests filled the lanai and overflowed into the landscaped grounds. The fragrances of roses were mixed with the tantalizing smell of barbeque tenderloin, steaks, burgers, chicken, and grilled vegetables. While some people were busy talking, others enjoyed the delicious taste of southern home cooking.

Audrey was in her element. She took full advantage of the opportunity to entertain and show off as she walked around making sure everything was in place and that the guests were well taken care of. Organizing the loads of gifts for Stiles and Rena, Audrey gloried in all of the attention, smiles and laughter.

Audrey clasped her hands together like a child and grinned. There was no doubt in her mind that after today, the talk around the neighborhood and at Holy Rock would be centered on the grand Fourth of July bash she'd thrown in honor of her darling Stiles and her soon to be daughter-in-law.

Pastor had no problem giving the reins to Audrey. He understood her need for attention and for perfection at this event. She hadn't always been that way though. When he first met her, she was rather shy, almost withdrawn. But soon after their marriage, the church began to expand and Audrey quickly climbed out of her shell. She loved being the First Lady, with the members doting on her and treating her like she was royalty. Initially, Pastor didn't quite know how to accept the change in his wife's demeanor. But it didn't take long for him to become accustomed to her desire to be the center of attention. He loved his wife dearly; for Pastor there was no one else who he could ever remotely love more than his Audrey.

The phone rang just as Audrey and Rena closed the door to the last of the guests. Stiles rushed to answer it. "Hello, Graham residence," he spoke articulately into the phone. His face turned ashen as he listened to the voice on the other end. Pastor stood close by watching the peculiar look on his son's face.

"What is it, Son?" he asked, moving in closer to where Stiles stood.

"Yes, we'll be right there. Thank you. Thank you very much." Stiles hung up the phone and stood motionless. "That was the hospital. Frankie's been in an accident." Holding his hand to his forehead, Stiles continued. "She's . . . she's at The Med, in the trauma unit."

"Oh, my God," Pastor yelled, his voice like an echo from an empty tomb. Audrey, Rena, and Meryl rushed into the family room when they heard the urgency in Pastor's voice.

Stiles remained silent with the phone still in his hand.

"What is it? asked Audrey, her breath caught in her lungs. "Who was that on the phone?"

Pastor walked over to where his wife stood, and took hold of her hand. He didn't give his son time to explain the call. "Audrey, honey. Frankie's been in a car accident."

"Oh my God, is she all right?" Audrey's voice broke miserably into a scream. "Tell me my child is all right." She found her voice again.

Rena went to Stiles. She peeled the receiver from his hand, her eyes brimmed with tears. Meryl helped Pastor comfort Audrey.

Holding his wife underneath the grip of his arm, they listened to Stiles repeat what the nurse had told him.

Stiles took a deep breath and tried to relax. "She's in stable condition. We need to get to the hospital."

When the family arrived at the trauma unit, Rena immediately recognized Kansas. She looked fatigued. With eyes the color of blood, the woman glared wickedly at Frankie's family. Rena pretended not to notice Kansas. She couldn't bring herself to look at her face-to-face. The two of them had run into each other a time or two before when she popped up over to Frankie's apartment. Neither Kansas nor Rena liked each other. Rena was no fool, she knew Kansas had feelings for Frankie but Frankie always refused to reciprocate, or so Rena thought. Maybe Kansas finally got what she wanted. Now that Rena was involved with Stiles, the door had certainly creaked open for Kansas to slip through.

Rena prayed silently, hoping that Kansas wouldn't say anything to her. Her prayers certainly had been answered so far because Kansas turned and walked away.

Pastor walked up to the nurses' station and inquired about Francesca's whereabouts.

"Sir, your daughter is still being X-rayed and evaluated." Her voice was kind and sympathetic. She stood and walked from behind the desk. "If you'll follow me, I'll take you all to the waiting room. The doctor will come and talk to you as soon as he can."

"Thank you, ma'am," replied Pastor.

With her head bowed down, Audrey sobbed as they went into the waiting room.

Kansas was already in the waiting room sitting next to three other ladies and a man that Rena recognized as some of Frankie's friends. Rena clung to Stiles as if he could protect her from her horrid past.

The doctor walked in some fifty minutes later and asked for the Graham family. Kansas' ears perked up and she listened to what he told the family.

Rena, Stiles, Pastor, Audrey, and Meryl huddled together.

"What happened to my baby?" Audrey cried.

"Ma'am," the doctor answered. His piercing green eyes drifted from person to person. "It appears that Miss Graham was a back seat passenger in a car. The driver lost control of the vehicle, veered off the road and down an embankment."

Rena gasped, and her tears gushed from her baby doll eyes.

Stiles slammed his fist in the palm of his hand.

"Is she going to be all right?" asked Meryl.

"Miss Graham was thrown from the back of the car, out of the rear window. She wasn't wearing a seatbelt. She sustained some pretty serious lacerations on her arms. It's a miracle that she came out with minor bruises and scratches on her face, but she fractured both legs and her right ankle. We also had to insert a breathing tube because she has a collapsed lung. The tube should relieve some of the pressure off of her lungs."

Audrey's hands flew up to her mouth. "Noooo," she cried harder. Pastor kissed her forehead and wrapped his trembling arm around her shoulder.

"Doctor, tell us. What's my sister's prognosis?" Stiles asked.

Kansas stood against the wall. She listened silently to the doctor.

"Her injuries are extensive, but we do have her stabilized. I expect her to make a full recovery. But it's going to take some time."

"I want to see her," Audrey insisted.

"Can we?" asked Stiles.

"Now is not a good time, I'm afraid. I just gave orders for her to be transferred to critical care, and she's heavily sedated. "Tomorrow might be a better time," he explained.

"Thank you, thank you so much, doctor," Pastor said.

After the doctor left, Kansas walked over to where Frankie's family was seated.

They all looked up.

Pastor spoke up. "Yes, young lady, can I help you?" he asked.

"I'm a friend of Frankie's. I was in the car too," Kansas mumbled nervously while scanning her bruised and scratched body.

"Thank God, my child." Pastor stood and embraced Kansas. Her body stiffened at this touch.

"They released me after checking me over, but Frankie and one of our other friends wasn't so lucky. I heard what the doctor said. I was wondering if I could go with y'all to see her? They won't tell me, or any of us nothin'," said Kansas as she looked over her shoulder at the rest of Frankie's friends. "They say it's 'cause we ain't immediate family."

"That's right and I don't think it would be a good idea anyway," Audrey abruptly spoke up, with a look of total disdain. She stood and looped her arm inside of Pastor's. "Francesca," Audrey emphasized her name, "doesn't need to be upset. If you heard the doctor, then you know she's in critical condition, and no one can see her tonight anyway. We'll be glad to tell her you were here."

Rena refused to lock eyes with Kansas, afraid that her secret would be revealed by the look in her eyes.

Stiles didn't utter a word.

"Kansas, it's nice of you to be concerned about Francesca. And I'm certainly glad you came out of the accident all right. That's truly a blessing from God. I tell you what," Pastor said meekly, "why don't I take your number and call you when we hear something? There's no reason for you to hang around here. You may not be scratched up but I know you're going to be sore in the morning. It'd be a good idea for you to go home and get some rest. I promise to call you," Pastor said humbly.

"Thanks, but no thanks," Kansas retorted loudly, and glared at Audrey and Rena too. "You know what? I see why Frankie don't want to be 'round y'all. You're all a bunch of . . ." The people with Kansas rushed to her side and guided her away from Frankie's family, but not before Kansas screamed at Rena, pointing a two-inch crooked nail, "And you, Miss Thang, sitting there like you the loving bride to be. You make me sick to my stomach."

Stiles pounced up like a starving lion after its prey, but Pastor reached out in time and grabbed hold of his arm, pulling him back down in the chair.

"Let her go, Son. Let her go." The strength in his father's arm and the compassion in his eyes made Stiles relent.

The security guard grabbed Kansas. She shook his hands off her. "Turn me loose." She seethed with mounting rage. She straightened her clothes and huffed down the hall toward the elevator.

Frankie was in the hospital almost three weeks. Somewhat apprehensive, Rena went to see her for the first time by herself. She opened the door and saw Frankie sleeping. Rena stood next to the bed and watched her.

"She looks like the Francesca I remember from school, not the angry, uptight woman she is now," whispered Rena.

Frankie stirred in her sleep. Her eyes slowly opened, and she saw Rena hovering over her. "What are you doing here?" Frankie's anger couldn't be restrained. "How many times do I have to tell you that I don't want you here, or Stiles?"

Rena rolled her eyes toward heaven. "I had to come. I wasn't about to let you lay up here without checking on you. Are you feeling better?" Rena asked her.

"Like you really care."

Rena pursed her lips and shifted from one leg to the other. "Come on, Frankie. Let's not go there. You're my best friend. Of course I care."

Ignoring Rena's response, Frankie asked, "Why aren't you at work?"

"I turned in my resignation last week. I'm going to start working in Memphis at the Benjamin Hooks Library after the wedding."

"Humph, is that right?" Frankie mumbled and turned her head away.

Rena ignored her. "You never answered me. How do you feel today?" Rena reached for Frankie's hand but she quickly snatched it away.

Turning to face Rena again with raised brows she complained, "I'm tired of this place. I'm ready to get out of here."

"You will soon. Audrey said the doctor thinks you'll be able to go home in a day or two. She's busy fixing up your room at Emerald Estates so you'll be comfortable."

"I'm not going back there. No way." Frankie rebuffed, trying to ease herself upright in the hospital bed.

Holding her down, Rena responded, "Don't get yourself upset. Anyway, what choice do you have? You need to have someone take care of you until you're feeling better. Look at your legs!" You can't walk with casts on both of your legs, not to mention the wounds on your arms and hands." Rena pointed, looking down at Frankie's legs.

Frankie's right leg was encased in traction and the other leg was positioned in a bent angle in the cast. Her left hand was wrapped in bandages and the bruises were still quite evident on her neck and forehead.

"I don't need Audrey's sympathy," Frankie growled. "All she wants to do is make herself look good. She wants people to tell her that she's such a good mother, taking her daughter in and nursing her back to health. Well, I won't give her the satisfaction of using me. I can manage at my own place."

"How do you suppose you're going to do that, Frankie? First of all, you won't be able to get up the stairs to your apartment in your condition. And if you think you can rely on Kansas to help you out, then you're crazy. You and I both know she won't hang around too long; she's not exactly the nurturing kind." Rena watched Frankie's expression change from a frown to a blank look.

As much as Frankie hated to admit it, Rena was right. Kansas wasn't about to stick around and play the good samaritan to her.

"That's not for you to worry about. I have more friends than Kansas anyway. You just concentrate on your little wedding and this charade with my brother." Frankie waved Rena off. "Look, I'm tired. Will you just go?"

Rena looked hurt. "Frankie, I'm praying for things to be better between us. Maybe you need more time, then we can be friends again like we used to minus all of the baggage." When Frankie didn't respond, Rena walked away. "I'll check on you tomorrow." Upon reaching the door, Rena stopped briefly and said, "Audrey asked me to tell you that she'll be out here later this afternoon."

Frankie spoke up. "Why did she have to send the mes-

sage by you? The phone is right there," Frankie looked at
the hospital phone sitting on the table next to her bed.

"Get some rest," Rena said, ignoring Frankie's snide
remarks. And with that, she left.

The elevator doors opened and Rena walked in. She
almost bumped into Kansas stepping off of the elevator.

Kansas gave her an evil eye of jealousy, not bothering
to say one word to her. She pushed past her and walked
in the direction of Frankie's room.

"I hate to be the bearer of bad news. You laid up in
here all bandaged up and everything."

"What is it? It can't be no worse than everything that's
already happening."

"When I got up this afternoon, an eviction notice was
hung on the door. That punk landlord said he's gonna sit
your stuff on the curb in two days.

"What do you expect me to do about it?" Frankie gritted her teeth and yelled. "There's nothing I can do about
it in here. This place is like being in jail."

"I'm tryna see what I can come up wit. But I had to tell
you."

"Yeah, I know that. But still, I don't have any money,
no job, and I sure ain't about to ask Rena, my daddy, and
none of them for anything. They're spending all of their
money on that big fancy wedding. I tell you what I want
you to do."

"What?"

"Go back to the apartment and get all of my stuff. Take
it to Emerald Estates. Tell my momma that I told you to
bring it there. Since she talkin' about she wants to take
care of me, here's her chance." Frankie said sarcastically
and laughed.

Kansas laughed just as hard. "Hey, I saw your girl
when I got off the elevator. What she have to say?"

"Nothing worth talkin' about," Frankie answered.

Frankie's doctor entered the room and interrupted their visit. "I'm sorry to barge in on you, Miss Graham." He eyed Kansas from the top of her blond braids to the top of her run-over wedge heeled sandals.

"No problem, Doc." Frankie cleared her throat.

"How are you feeling today? I've been concerned about your lingering low-grade fever. I can't discharge you until we get it under control." He approached her bedside and began checking her heart rate and pulse. "If you don't mind, I'd like to talk to you in private," he said, his eyes shifting in Kansas's direction.

"I'm going downstairs for a smoke. I'll be back a little later," Kansas told her.

"Okay, I'll see you in a minute." Frankie nodded slowly.

As the door closed behind her, the doctor didn't waste any time. "Now tell me, how are you really feeling? And be truthful," he asked.

"I'm tired and I ache all over."

"That's understandable. You were involved in a serious accident. One that could have very well been fatal."

"Yeah, I'm lucky, huh?"

"Some would call it that. Others would say that you're blessed."

A withdrawn, terrified look enveloped Frankie's face. She watched her doctor as he continued his examination. "You . . . have . . ." his voice faded out with every word that trailed out of his mouth.

"No, it's a mistake," Frankie screamed. A nurse appeared from out of nowhere with a syringe in her hand. "I don't want a shot." The doctor didn't seem to hear a word she said. His lips kept moving as she drifted off into a heavy, sedated sleep.

20

*"No matter how badly your heart is broken, the world does not
stop for your grief."*
—*Unknown*

With the fight gone out of her, Frankie relented and
moved in with her parents after being discharged
from the hospital. She had no place else to go even if she
wanted to. Unable to rid her mind of what the doctor had
told her, she sunk into a deep depression. She didn't
want to be bothered with anyone. If only she could be
left alone, but with the casts still on her legs and her arm
in a sling, she could barely do anything for herself. She
was at the mercy of others, something she despised.

Audrey did her best to take care of Frankie. She
wanted to bring in a certified nurse assistant, but Rena
volunteered to help instead since she hadn't started her
new job.

It was difficult for Rena to watch Frankie lie helplessly
in bed day after day. Rena did everything she could to try
to cheer her up, but it seemed the harder she tried to
make her laugh, the deeper Frankie withdrew.

"Frankie, you have to pull yourself out of this funk
you're in. You're not behaving like the Frankie I know.
I'd rather see you screaming at me instead of lying here

in this bed like you have nothing to live for," Rena told her one day.

"I don't have anything to live for. My life is over."

"Come on, Frankie. Why are you talking like this? You know as well as I do that it's going to take some time for you to completely recover. That car accident was no joke. You were seriously injured."

Rena sat on the edge of Frankie's bed, preparing her medications for the day. She studied each of the bottles, something she hadn't taken the time to do before. "I know what some of these pills are for, and the other ones I don't have a clue as to what they're supposed to be helping," Rena commented. "Looks like a mini pharmacy in here." Rena eyed the bottles sitting on Frankie's nightstand.

"Look, why don't you leave. I really don't feel like your snooping around." Frankie managed to turn over in the bed with her back facing Rena.

"Come on, take your medicine. After I get you cleaned up, I'll leave you alone to rest. How's that?"

Frankie managed to look over her shoulder and glare at Rena with burning hostility. "I don't need you coming around here pretending like you're so concerned about me. Don't you think you should be getting ready for your wedding Saturday?"

"I want to be here for you, Frankie." Rena attempted to touch Frankie's hand but decided against it. "As for the wedding, everything is ready. Oh, and Pastor said he would make sure to have someone help to get you into the church."

"Don't bother, I'm not going. I've told you that more than once. You and Momma are getting on my nerves, trying to force me to come to that stupid, fake wedding."

"Frankie, don't do this. I want you there. It's bad enough

that you aren't going to be my maid of honor, but for you not to be at the wedding at all. I mean, what will . . ."

"I know what you're about to say, Audrey number two. What will people think? Well, I don't give a darn what they think. If you want to act like you're head over heels in love, go 'head. But I'm not going to be a part of your charade. And another thing, have you bothered to tell him about me and you yet?" Frankie looked over her shoulder again, this time to see the expression on Rena's face.

"No, no I haven't." Her body stiffened in shock, "And I don't plan on telling him. There's no need. Stiles knows that we've always been best friends. There's no need to elaborate on anything else that happened in the past between us. You know for yourself that it would destroy a lot of people's lives if they knew about us."

"Now you want to get all sensitive on me. Girl, puh-leeze. Get on outta here. I need time to think about when I should tell my brother about his little bride. Before or after the wedding," Frankie snarled and then coughed so hard she began to sweat.

Rena circled around the bed to face Frankie. She reached over and touched her. "Frankie, I know you aren't going to do that. You'll ruin my life. Please, I'll do whatever you want me to do. But promise me that you won't tell Stiles, or anyone else, about us." Rena cried and fell down to her knees on the side of the bed, tugging at Frankie's side.

Without so much as an ounce of emotion in her voice, Frankie answered, "Your tears don't mean a thing to me. Why should they? Nobody has ever cared about me. Not even my own mother. It's always been Stiles this, and Stiles that. She thinks the sun rises and sets on him. But me, she despises me, and you know it, Rena. I used to think that you were the only one who cared about me, but you're just like her and all the rest. You're a phony, a hypocrite just like she is. Now get out of my room before I start screaming," Frankie yelled between coughs. "And you don't want me to start screaming because if I do I'm going to spill my guts, and you and no one else will be able to stop me," Frankie said angrily.

Rena, wiping the tears from her eyes with the back of her hands, got up off her knees and practically ran out of Frankie's room, closing the door behind her. Her heart was beating so fast she thought she would collapse. *What am I going to do? Oh God, help me through this. Please don't let Frankie tell it. Please.*

"Rena, sweetheart," she heard Audrey calling her.

Rena rushed inside the hall bathroom before Audrey saw her. Closing the door behind her, she answered, "I'm in the bathroom, Audrey. I'll be out in just a minute."

"Take your time," Audrey answered back.

Several minutes later, Rena opened the door when she no longer heard Audrey's voice. The door to Frankie's room remained closed. She prayed that her face wouldn't expose the fear she felt as she walked up the hallway. Entering the kitchen, Rena saw Audrey on the porch talking to one of the neighbors from across the street. As usual, Audrey's arms were flailing and she appeared to be dominating the conversation. Rena sat down on the stool at the kitchen island and rested her head in the palms of her hands. *How could Frankie be so wicked? It has to be jealousy. Why else would she threaten me?*

Audrey finally came inside. "Honey, are you all right? You were in the bathroom a mighty long time."

"Yes, I'm fine, Audrey. Just a little upset stomach, that's all."

"You have wedding jitters. But it'll all be over in a couple of days. Then you and my baby can live happily ever after." A satisfied smile came over Audrey's thin lips. She leaned over and squeezed Rena's shoulders before pecking her on the cheek. "What do you say we go over some last minute details for the wedding?" Audrey picked up the paper and pen off the table and looked over the list of items. "I want to make sure we haven't left anything off. Did you tell Francesca that we've made arrangements to get her to the wedding?" Audrey's eyes were hopeful.

"Yes, I told her. But she's not going to come. I guess that's understandable. She's been through a lot these past few months." Rena found it hard to maintain her composure, but she had to if she didn't want Audrey to suspect that anything was wrong.

"I guess you're right. That's one of the reasons I love you so much."

"What are you talking about?" Confused, Rena crinkled her face and slightly tilted her head.

"Your compassionate and forgiving spirit." Audrey smiled at Rena. "Anyway, enough of that. Come on," she patted the chair next to her, "let's go over this list again. When Meryl returns tomorrow, we're going to be busy putting the final touches in place."

Later that evening, after Rena, Audrey, and Meryl made their final plans for the wedding, Meryl accepted Audrey's invitation to spend the night at Emerald Estates. After preparing for bed, she paused as she reached Francesca's door, and tapped. "Francesca, honey it's Meryl. May I come in?"

Frankie refused to answer. She didn't want to see anyone, definitely not Rena's mother. Meryl knocked several more times before turning the knob and peaking inside the room. Frankie closed her eyes and it appeared as if she was sleeping peacefully. Not wanting to disturb her, Meryl closed the door and left.

Frankie opened her eyes when she was certain Meryl had left. She reached for the phone and called Kansas.

Over the next two days, Rena, Meryl and Audrey had little time to devote to Frankie, so Audrey relented and called in a certified nursing assistant to assist with Frankie's care.

The morning before the wedding, Rena turned the knob and walked inside Frankie's bedroom, without knocking.

"You didn't hear me tell you to come in," Frankie said.

"Okay, so you've made your point." Rena didn't feel like any of Frankie's dramatic antics. "I stopped by to check on you. I know I haven't been around much these past couple of days, but this wedding has kept me going. How do you feel this morning?"

"Besides the fact that I'm stuck here in this bed, in this house, with you people, I guess you can say that I'm just fine." Frankie answered cuttingly.

Rena stood next to Frankie's bed with an awkward, uncomfortable look on her face.

"Shouldn't you be getting ready for your wedding?" Frankie remarked sarcastically.

"I will not entertain your insults and curt remarks today, Frankie. I hoped that you would be happy for me, and that your attitude about this whole thing somehow might have softened up a bit."

"No, you couldn't have expected that. Anyway, go on. I hope you and Stiles have the kinda life you two deserve." Frankie turned her face away from Rena and stared at the wall instead.

"Have it your way. I don't know what else to say or do

to make things right. I thought our friendship meant much more to you than this." Rena sighed heavily and walked away. By the time she reached the door and turned the handle, the words spewed like venom from Frankie's mouth and made Rena's knees go weak and her head swim.

"I thought you might want to know that I have genital herpes."

21

"Loneliness and the feeling of being unwanted is the most terrible."
—*Mother Teresa*

Rena began to hyperventilate as she stumbled out of Frankie's room. Holding onto the sides of the patterned wallpaper walls, trying to catch her breath, she made it to the hall bathroom. Her head spun like she had been on a drinking binge all night. This should have been the best day of her life but now, thanks to Frankie, her hideous past life was about to be brought from the dark into the light. Rena anticipated the most traumatic turn of events, she just didn't know when, where or what time.

"Herpes? No, she has to be lying. She'll do anything to make me miserable before my wedding. Yes, that's it. That's exactly what she's trying to do," Rena continued talking to the flushed red, tear-streaked face staring back at her in the mirror. "It's not going to work." She managed to release a fake snicker. "Frankie always was a drama queen. And to think, I was about to fall for her bull." Rena kept trying to convince herself that everything was a hoax. Oh how she prayed it was.

Rena's heart continued to beat thunderously against

her chest. She ran cold water and dapped her face with it. Inhaling, she dried her hands on the thick, swanky hand towels and waltzed back toward Frankie's room. *For once and for all, I am not going to let you ruin my wedding day.* Pastor appeared and thwarted her plans.

"How's my daughter-in-law-to-be?" he asked with outstretched arms as she came near him.

"A little nervous," she admitted shakily as she allowed him to embrace her.

"The first lady should be returning from the church in just a few minutes. You know that woman, she has to make sure every *I* is dotted and every *T* is crossed. I ran into Meryl too. She wanted me to tell you that we need to be at church in a couple of hours for the rehearsal dinner. She's going to the hotel to make sure everyone else is ready on time."

"Thanks for telling me. She called me earlier and told me too. Pastor," Rena paused. She had no idea what was about to come out of her mouth.

"Yes, sweetheart?" Pastor focused his full attention on Rena.

"I, well, what if I'm not doing the right thing? I want to be a good wife. But I don't feel like, well like I'm good enough."

"Come with me for a minute," Pastor urged and led her by the hand into his study. Have a seat." He pointed to the brown leather sofa. "Now you listen to me, young lady. You are a wonderful person. You're kind, you're intelligent, you love my son, but even more important than that, you love God. One day you're going to make a fine first lady. You've been part of this family since you were a teenager. And you and Frankie are the best of friends. The first lady adores you, and both us know that if First Lady loves you, then you must be something special." Pastor chuckled and continued. "As for Stiles, the two of you are perfect for each other. You're nervous, and that's normal. But remember that God's Word says, 'He who findeth a wife, findeth a good thing,' and you are a good thing, Rena. Don't let the enemy poison your mind with negative thoughts. This wedding is something Audrey has wanted for Stiles for a long time. And I don't think he could have chosen a more perfect bride than you."

"Thank you, Pastor." Rena felt like the phony Frankie told her she was, sitting in front of Pastor knowing full well that her life was far from what everyone believed it to be.

Pastor's words began to disconnect with Rena's spirit. All she could hear were Frankie's words ringing in her ear, *I have genital herpes. I have genital herpes* Over and over, the words kept growing louder and louder in her mind.

"Are you sure you're going to be okay, my dear?" Pastor asked, massaging her hand gently.

"Yes, I'll be fine. I'm going to push these negative thoughts aside."

Suddenly, they heard Audrey bursting through the door, calling out Rena's name.

"I'm in the study," Rena responded.

Audrey walked toward Pastor and kissed him briefly on the top of his gray balding head. "Rena, come on, it's time for you to start getting your things together. We don't want to rush and forget anything. We have to be back at the church by six o'clock." Audrey glanced at her shining diamond-encrusted watch that Pastor had given her last Christmas.

Rena stood and looked at Pastor with admiration. She paused before leaving. "Thank you, Pastor."

Audrey stared first at Pastor then at Rena. "What's going on? Thanks for what?"

"Oh nothing, honey. Rena and I just had a little pre-father-in-law/daughter-in-law talk. That's all." This time it was Pastor's turn to stand. "While you ladies are getting things together, I'm going to go and sit with my Frankie and see how she's doing. I know she's terribly disappointed that she won't be able to be at the wedding tomorrow."

"Honey, not to worry. We're having it placed on DVD. Now come along, Rena." Audrey motioned her long thin hands.

Despite the wave of nausea that washed over her, Rena managed to go through the motions of getting ready for the wedding, smiling for the photographers and pretending like she didn't have a care in the world. When it was time to line up for the wedding, she heard Frankie's words. "*I have genital herpes.*" She thought she was about to faint. She turned to her mother.

"Honey, what's wrong? Nervous bride?" her mother asked after noticing the pale look on her daughter's face.

"Momma, I don't know if I can go through with this."

"Honey, you're going to be just fine. It happens to the best of us. You should have seen me on my wedding day. When I married your father I thought I had come down with the flu. I was sweating, feverish, sick to my stomach, the whole nine yards. But as soon as we exchanged vows, all I felt was peace and calm. You'll see for yourself. You look so beautiful, Rena," her mother complimented.

"Thank you, Momma."

Meryl embraced her daughter. "Now, come on, we have a wedding to attend."

Rena followed her mother out to the atrium. Rena's eyes were bright and her palms were sweaty. The organist played, "Here Comes the Bride." Rena's father stood proudly next to his daughter. Then he led his daughter down the aisle to present her to her mate. .

Rena looked gorgeous in her white satin and chiffon dress. She moved cautiously until she stood next to the man of her dreams.

Gazing into one another's eyes, they pledged their love to one another.

Stiles began his promises. "I, Stiles, take you, Rena, to be my partner, loving what I know of you, and trusting what I do not yet know."

Rena was frozen in limbo, and her mind reeled out of control as she listened to the promises that Stiles spoke.

"I promise I will trust you and respect you, laugh with you and cry with you," he said with tears glistening in his eyes. "Loving you faithfully through good times and bad, regardless of the obstacles we may face together."

"I, Rena, take you, Stiles, to be my husband, to have and to hold from this day forward, for better or for worse, for richer, for poorer, in sickness and in health, to love and to cherish; from this day forward until death do us part. I eagerly anticipate the chance to grow together, getting to know the man you will become, and falling in love a little more every day."

Stiles looked at Rena with eyes that seemed to penetrate her soul. He ended his vows by saying, "Rena, I give you my hand, my heart, and my love, from this day forward for as long as we both shall live. Love and cherish you through whatever life may bring us."

On the outside, Rena glowed with beauty, and her mouth was upturned in a smile shaped in love. On the inside, she felt deceitful and dirty as Pastor pronounced them husband and wife.

* * *

Stiles had dreamed about his wedding night for a long time. But he was sitting on the side of the bed at a five-star hotel in St. Simons Island. The breathtaking view of the Atlantic Ocean, with the waves pounding against the beach outside of their hotel suite, meant nothing to him because all he heard was his bride in the hotel bathroom throwing up. He couldn't, for the life of him, understand what was going on. All he knew was that it started at the wedding reception. She told him she wasn't feeling well, but he didn't know that she was actually sick for real. He'd tried several times to hold her and caress her, hoping that would make her feel at ease just in case it was a bad bout of nerves.

Their flight had been just as horrible. Rena's complexion was pale, and looking at her no one could tell this was her wedding day. When they arrived in St. Simons, the hour-long drive to their hotel was filled with a dull silence.

"I don't know what's wrong with me. I'm sorry, but I feel awful." She held her stomach, wretched, and raced to the bathroom, closing the door behind her.

"Rena, honey, let me come in," he pleaded with her from the other side of the locked bathroom door.

"I don't want you to see me like this on our wedding night. I'll try to be out in a minute. I think the nausea is passing."

Rena sat on the ice cold tile floor of the luxurious bathroom thinking about what she was going to do, or not do. *There's no way I can be intimate with Stiles. Not until I find a way to get tested or at least get to a computer to find out more about herpes. I can't take the chance. Even if what Frankie said turns out to be a lie, she's managed to ruin the most important night of my life. Some way to spend my wedding night.* She curled up in a knot on the floor and wept with Stiles on the outside pleading with her to come out or let him come in.

After almost two hours, she finally unlocked the door and tip-toed out of the bathroom. A shirtless Stiles was laying on the king-sized bed, snoring lightly and curled in a fetal position. She ambled over to the bed, lightly pulled back the satin sheets and climbed between them.

Stiles turned over and pulled her body next to his. She tried to resist his butterfly kisses as they landed delicately upon her neck and along her shoulder. His need for her was evident. Before she could muster up a protest, he turned her face toward his and covered her mouth with his. Rena was no match for his sexual fervor, and she gasped with desire of her own. There was no turning back. She whispered a prayer within her spirit that what she was about to let happen would not be the beginning of their end. Then she gave in to her husband's physical needs and her own.

Five days later, Rena and Stiles returned from their honeymoon. She was sick with worry. What kind of person was she? She had chosen to deceive her husband rather than reveal the truth to him about her past, and the possibility that she might have an STD. What a way to start a marriage. After arriving at their new home, Rena tried to rush past Stiles as he carried in their luggage. They had shopped for the house three weeks before settling on the three-bedroom, three-bath brick home on Berry Hill Drive.

"Hey, hold up. What's your hurry, Mrs. Graham?" he asked her.

"Oh, nothing. I'm just anxious to see our new home; the place we're going to spend the rest of our lives," she told him with a broad, fake smile embracing her cherub face.

Stiles set the luggage down in the foyer and reached for his wife. Pulling her toward him by her narrow waist, he scooped her up in his arms and passionately kissed her.

"Welcome home, Mrs. Graham," he remarked and proceeded to carry her across the threshold of their modest home and into the master bedroom.

Standing in the master bedroom, inches from their provocatively enticing king bed, Stiles yearned for his wife. "Hey," he said and nibbled on her ear. "It's time we christen 689 Berry Hill Drive." He used his husbandly rights to become familiar with her waist, thighs, and buttocks. Tilting her head backward he tasted the saltiness of her breath.

"Stiles," Rena giggled but escaped from his arms. "Baby, we have time for that. We've been gone a week. You know you should go to check on Frankie and your parents, and . . ." She held her breath for a moment, "I need to check on some things too, like my mail, and I plan to run by and see Frankie." Rena walked up on him and rubbed her hands along the contours of his chest. She smiled and patted his cheek

Stiles wasn't falling for it. "Listen, I don't want a confrontation but, baby, we've barely been married a week, and starting off arguing is something neither of us should want. I can understand your being nervous and apprehensive on our wedding night. For God's sake, you were a virgin and terrified at that. But, baby, look at me. He shifted his eyes downward at his manhood. Rena's eyes followed against her will.

In a tender baby silk voice, Rena worked things to her advantage. "Look, I promise I won't be gone long. If you go check on Frankie and your parents then I'll go to the post office, grab our mail, and stop at the neighborhood market to get us something to eat. We're going to need our energy," she said teasingly, biting his bottom lip.

Stiles relented easily. "Okay, but I want to be with you,
Mrs. Graham, and only you." He kissed her upper back.
Rubbing her butt, he took a half step back. "Promise me
you'll be back soon. I'm only going to run by Emerald Estates and make sure everyone's fine. Then I'm headed
back here to spend the rest of the evening and night with
the most beautiful wife in the world."

Rena flippantly threw her hand, grabbed her purse
and keys and threw him a kiss. "I love you, Stiles," she
said and scooted past the box of items in the foyer.

Rena couldn't chance waiting another minute. If she
ever hoped to have a satisfying marriage with Stiles, she
had to know if she had contracted an STD. She drove
downtown to the Shelby County Health Department.
The drive was one of the most frightening times in all of
her twenty-four years of life. She dashed inside the clinic
and searched for the STD department. With her head
bowed, shielding her embarrassment and humiliation from
the others in the waiting room, Rena grabbed a number
from the counter like the receptionist told her. She waited
several hours in the waiting area before a slender, young
Asian woman called her number. She didn't care that the
brochure on the table next to her said that for every 1,000
people tested, one would test positive for an STD; she
didn't want to be that one.

"What are you going to do?" Rena asked the pleasant,
black-haired nurse as she led her back to a tiny room and
motioned her to sit.

The phlebotomist appeared close to Rena's age. She
pulled up a chair and sat in front of her "Tell me why
you're here, and be truthful. Nothing goes outside of this
room." The woman's tone calmed her.

In that case I guess I'm ashamed of the life I've lived. I'm
nasty and disgusting and I've been sleeping with another
woman for ten years. How's that for telling the truth?. Oh, did

I mention that I feel ugly, filthy and most of all, ashamed for letting God down? Her clamored thoughts gave way to her stammering voice. Nervously, she rubbed her hands together hoping somehow to ignore the pulsing knot that formed in her stomach. "I believe I've contracted an STD," Rena answered without going into detail. "I just married a wonderful man. I didn't know I might be infected until recently. And before you ask, there's no chance I contracted it from him. I can't tell him, I just can't," Rena repeated with her head hung low. "If I'm infected it would destroy everything." She covered her glistening eyes with her hands.

"Before you jump to conclusions, let's find out once and for sure. I don't think you can grasp the stories I've heard from people just like yourself. Sometimes things just happen, so don't be so hard on yourself. I want you to relax as much as you can." She broke into an open, friendly smile.

Rena exhaled slowly. "Thank you. I feel a little better."

"Good. Now, the first test I'm going to give you is a rapid HIV test. It detects antibodies to HIV-1 that are found in blood specimens. It requires a tiny finger-stick." The phlebotomist reached for Rena's trembling hand.

Rena pulled her hand back. An alarm went off in her head. "Why do I need an HIV test? I know I don't have that," she insisted.

"I don't think you want to take any chances. You're here because you think you've contracted an STD. If it turns out that you have, you need to know what it is. That means I need to check for them all. Okay?"

"Okay," answered Rena wondering what she would do if Stiles suddenly burst through the door. She shook her head slightly to dispel the thought.

The nurse reached for Rena's hand a second time, and this time Rena didn't object. "This will take barely a nanosecond," she said and pricked Rena's finger before she had time to react. She placed a cotton ball on the tip of Rena's finger and held it in place until the blood clotted. "I'll know the results in about twenty minutes. If it comes back non-reactive, that means your final result will be negative. But if it reacts, I'll have to do a confirmatory test."

"What's that?"

"It involves doing an actual blood test. It takes about one week for the results to come back. There's also a possibility that you could react on the first step and not be infected. The final test result is not HIV positive unless both steps are reactive."

"Oh, my God. What have I done?"

"Look at it like this; everyone needs to take the same battery of tests every couple of years. What you're doing makes sense if you want to do what's best for yourself and your husband. More people should do this before they suspect they have an STD." The nurse stood. "Let me take this to the lab. While we're waiting on the results of your HIV test, I'll start the next series."

Rena stood and paced around the cramped space. Her head felt like a spinning top. "God, help me. You said if I confess my sins, you would be faithful to forgive me and cleanse me. Do it, Lord. Forgive me and cleanse me of any diseases." The nagging thoughts in the back of her mind refused to be still. Startled, her body jerked, and she covered her heart with her hand.

"Sorry, I frightened you," the nurse apologized when she witnessed Rena's uneasiness. "Are you ready to get the rest of the tests done and over with?"

Rena shook her head and sat down. Awkwardly she cleared her throat. "What will the next tests be for?" asked Rena, her pretty face clouded with uneasiness.

"They can detect chlamydia, herpes, syphilis, and a

few others. May I ask you something a little more personal?

"What do you want to ask?" Rena responded with apprehension.

"Do you believe?"

"I beg your pardon?" The waxed eyebrows gathered on Rena's face.

"I asked you if you believed. You know, believe in God?" The nurse looked up toward the ceiling as she said the words, believe in God.

"Yes. Yes, of course I do. My husband is a minister." Rena responded slowly.

"Then no matter what happened to bring you to this place, God is big enough to handle it. Don't go around condemning yourself. Everyone has a past. Everyone," the nurse emphasized.

"Thank you for sharing that. I just feel so ashamed. And I don't know how to tell my husband, or if I can tell him." Rena couldn't hold back the tears that had gathered in the corners of her eyes and trickled down her face. 'I'll destroy his life, our marriage and the lives of his parents and mine." Rena leaned her head down and continued sobbing. *Oh God, Frankie What have you done?*

"Your spouse still has a right to know. You have a moral obligation to tell him. And if your tests come back negative, you still aren't out of the woods, especially when it comes to HIV and genital herpes." The nurse reached over to her left side and grabbed the box of tissue on the desk.

"What do you mean?"

Passing the box to Rena, she said, "Take HIV for example. The tests could come back negative but it could be too soon for the antibodies to show up. You should be retested every six months for at least two years. As for genital herpes, up to ninety-percent of those with the virus don't know they're infected. They may have had symptoms but didn't recognize it or either confused it with something else. The herpes virus, similar to HIV, can lie dormant in a person's body for years; and having genital herpes increases the risk of contracting HIV."

Teary-eyed, Rena stared ahead.

"I'm all done," the nurse said, after taking several vials of blood from Rena's upper arm. "It will be two, maybe two and a half hours before I have the results. At that time I'll tell you the results of your rapid HIV test too. You can go to the reception area and wait or, if you want to, you can leave and come back. But make sure you inform the receptionist up front if you do decide to leave. The nurse gathered the vials and placed them in a container. "I'm praying for you, sweetie. But you need to pray for yourself too."

The nurse closed the door behind her, leaving Rena alone in the testing room. Rena sobbed and prayed. Wiping her red eyes again, she opened the door and walked to the reception area. *How could I have been so naïve?* Finding a seat next to a magazine rack, she picked up a pamphlet that discussed, of all subjects, STDs and lesbians. She became transfixed on what she read. '. . . Oral herpes can be transmitted to the genitals, and vice versa. Symptoms are similar . . . Lesbian women are at risk for many of the same STDs as heterosexual women . . . Lesbians can transmit HIV through genital skin-to-skin contact . . . Lesbians can transmit genital herpes through intimate contact with someone with a lesion or by touching infected skin, even when an outbreak is not visible.'

The nurse had definitely not exaggerated. Rena drifted off into a light sleep. Her eyes lazily opened when after three hours of waiting, she heard her name called.

"Well, God does answer prayer," the kind nurse said as soon as they entered the lab.

A grin as wide as the Mississippi River spread over Rena's face. She listened to the nurse go over each test result. A giant sense of relief consumed her when the nurse told her that her test results were negative.

"Thank you, God," Rena screamed and threw her hands in the air.

"Let me explain,' the nurse continued. "You're not totally out of the woods yet. Remember that I told you that you should have an HIV test every six months for the next two years?"

Rena shook her head hurriedly up and down. "Yes, yes, I know that. But God has heard my prayers. He's answered me. I don't have any STD." Rena cried and raised her hands up in total praise to God. Rena barely heard the words coming forth from the nurse. At this moment, she was far too happy, but she tried to listen. "Nurse, what did you say? I'm just so filled right now, I can hardly contain myself."

"I know that, and I'm happy for you. But you know I have to do my job here too," the nurse said and chuckled. "Okay, now where was I? I hope you follow through on the series of HIV tests. The next test I want to touch on is the one we did for herpes, which was your main concern when you came here."

"But didn't you say all of my tests were negative? So why do we need to keep beating a dead horse?" Rena asked, with a critical voice.

"You're right but let me remind you that herpes is hard to detect, especially when there is no sign of an outbreak. Like I said, it can be tricky. I know your test results are negative but I strongly advise you to see your internist or gynecologist if you detect a sore, lesion, redness, burning, or irritation in your genital area. "Promise me that you'll do that," the nurse emphasized. "It would be even better if you and your husband used a condom during sex. At least until we're one hundred percent sure that your HIV and herpes tests are 100 percent negative."

"A condom?" Rena's cheerfulness gave way to a look of confusion. "I hear what you're saying. But it's not that easy," Rena eagerly replied. "If I could convince my husband to use protection when we made love, just until I finished the series of HIV tests, then you're right, I would feel so much better, but I already know that he wouldn't agree to anything like that, unless I told him the reason. Imagine me going home tonight, the very day we returned from our honeymoon and telling him he needs to wear a condom. I'm his wife, for God's sake. A red flag larger than the Statue of Liberty would start flying. So to be honest with you," Rena commented with gritted teeth and annoyance in her eyes, "There's no reason to tell him anything. You said it yourself, my tests are negative. This nightmare is over."

"I understand, but listen to me . . ."

"No, you listen. My husband and I want to have children right away. Now, I'll take the series of HIV tests, which I don't think I need to do, but I will. But as for anything else, and certainly suggesting that we use a condom, it's out of the question. I want a child just as much as he does. Don't you think I would take your advice if I believed for one second that I would endanger him or a baby? You asked me if I believed in God. I told you I did. I prayed and asked Him to forgive me and to let every test be negative. He did just what I asked. Now you're standing here like you don't believe he is the author and finisher of our faith. I'm telling you one last time—I'm healed. I thank God because it was you who reminded me of his awesome power. I've been cleansed. Thank God, I've been forgiven." Opening the door, Rena gulped hard and hot tears slipped down her cheeks.

* * *

Stiles arrived at Emerald Estates.

"Stiles, why are you here alone?" Audrey asked after she opened the door and didn't see her daughter-in-law. "I know you haven't left your beautiful bride alone already."

"It's more like she left me alone," answered Stiles smiling. "She had some things she said she couldn't put off." He looked around the room for some sign of her. "She was supposed to stop by and visit Frankie while she was out."

"Maybe she did, but Pastor and I just pulled up before you did. We had an exquisite lunch at Madidi. You know Morgan Freeman's restaurant in Clarksdale, Mississippi," Audrey gushed with pleasure. "I barely had a moment to kick off my shoes before you rang the doorbell, so I haven't had a chance to check with Frankie to see if anyone stopped by while we were gone. Pastor is in his study on the phone."

"Well, I'll be back after I check on Frankie. I want to here all about Madidi's." Walking away, Stiles stopped midway by the family room and teased, "I might have to start keeping tabs on you two lovebirds.

"Boy, go on now, and check on your sister. Tell her that I'll be in there later." Joy bubbled in Audrey's laugh and shone in her eyes.

Stiles turned and walked away. He tapped on Frankie's door.

"Come in."

"Hey, there."

Frankie was sitting in her gingham covered recliner with the remote in one hand and a Jolie Du Pré novel in the other.

"Hey, yourself," she answered, looking up at her handsome brother. "So you're back from your honeymoon, huh?"

"Yep."

"Did you have a good time?" She looked and listened for any sign that Rena had told him, but it was obvious she hadn't after hearing how happy he was.

"Yeah, as a matter of fact, we had a wonderful time. But Rena probably told you already."

"I haven't heard from Rena."

"Oh, I see."

"Was I supposed to?"

"Not really. She said she was going to come by to check on you while she was out, that's all. But I'm here, and that's what matters." He leaned over and kissed Frankie on her forehead."

"Don't tell me you're suspicious of yo bride already?" asked Frankie as she watched him with smug delight.

"Who, me? Now you, of all people, know me better than that. I'm not the jealous type."

"Every man is the jealous type," Frankie rebuffed.

Stiles changed the subject. "When are you going to come out of those casts?"

"I have to go to the doctor tomorrow. They're sposed to cut'em off. I'll wear somethin' called a boot walker for nine weeks and do some physical therapy. Doc says I'm likely gonna have a limp for the rest of my life. As for my arm, it actually feels pretty good. The swelling has almost gone away completely."

"Everything's going to be fine. I've been keeping you in my prayers. The sister I know is not going to let a little thing like being banged up from a car accident stop her, I know," he joked.

"Naw, it's gonna take somethin' worse than that to keep this girl down."

"I heard that. Well, I'll let you get back to reading your novel and watching TV. How you do both at the same time, I have no idea." His head tilted back when he chuckled.

"It's called multi-taskin'," Frankie laughed.

Stiles bent down and kissed her on the back of her hand and then on her forehead.

"Take it easy, sis. Audrey said she'll be in here later to check on you."

"Dang, you just had to find a way to ruin my day, didn't cha?"

Grinning, Stiles said, "Call and let me know if they cut off those things tomorrow." He pointed at her casts while walking to the door.

"Sure thang."

Stiles talked to his parents about their lunch at Madidi's. After close to an hour of non-stop chatter from Audrey about their day's adventure, not allowing Pastor to barely get a word in, Stiles told them he was going to leave.

He turned the engine on and eyed his rearview mirror. His cell phone rang with the lyrics, "Every time you hold me, Hold me like this is the last time." He smiled as he listened to Alicia Keyes, knowing it was Rena on the other end.

"Hi, sweetheart. I'm on my way home. Where are you?" she asked him.

"Just pulling off from your in-laws. They wanted to know where my beautiful bride had run off to."

"Did you tell them that I had some errands to run?"

"Sure. But as you know, Audrey had to behave like the diva she is. She and Daddy went to Morgan Freeman's restaurant in Clarksdale today. They said they had an unbelievable time."

"Oooh, that sounds so romantic. Just think about it, baby, we have our entire lives to do things like that. And

Frankie? How was she? I had every intention of getting over there, but time went by so fast."

"No need to worry. They're all fine. Frankie might get her casts off tomorrow."

"That's great news. I know she'll be glad. Baby, I was thinking about ordering some take-out from Applebee's, unless you have other plans."

"Take-out sounds fine. And the plans I have include being alone with my wife. Monday morning will be here before we know it, which means I want to spend this weekend with the woman of my dreams," Stiles flirted.

Rena's heart fluttered as she imagined lying inside the curve of his muscular arms. "You will, baby. I promise you that," she returned in her own sexy voice. "I'll see you soon."

"Bye, love."

Rena pulled into Applebee's, went inside, and ordered food for her and Stiles. When she returned outside twenty minutes later, the wind had picked up and the sudden drop of the temperature chilled her to the bones. She hurried and climbed inside her mild gray Acura. Once inside, she dialed her in-laws. The person she wanted to talk to answered the phone.

"What is it?" Frankie asked without saying hello.

"My tests results were all negative. You were probably lying all along. You're so evil, Francesca," Rena snarled, knowing how Frankie hated the name, Francesca. The sound of Rena's voice revealed her apparent anger.

"If you wanna believe I lied, so be it. But it is what is."

"Don't start again, Frankie. Because of your lies, I have to be tested for HIV every six months for the next two years.

"I don't know why you gotta do that. I didn't say nothing about havin' no HIV. You're the one that's full of crap."

"If you knew anything about anything, then you would know that when you go to the health department, they test for all STDs. You should try it sometime," Rena barked. "I don't understand you. As good as I've been to you. Why would you put me through something like this?"

"Do what to you? You are so full of it, you know that, Frankie exclaimed. "Have you for one minute thought about what I have to deal with? I'm sitting here in this room, barely able to do anything for myself, and then I have to sit here and live with the fact that I have herpes and I'm going to be crippled the rest of my life. And you have the nerve to accuse me of being a liar. My God, if Audrey and Pastor find me out, I'll never hear the end of Audrey's mouth about how embarrassed she is, and what a terrible, twisted daughter she and Pastor produced. I'm tired, Rena. I'm sick, and I'm tired. But nobody seems to give a doggone about me."

"You're right. Frankie, I'm so sorry. How could I be so selfish? You must be going through changes too. That's what you expect me to say? Well, I don't feel sorry for you anymore. You did this to yourself, but you won't do it to me ever again. I'm married to Stiles. He loves me and I love him. You will never be able to change that."

The shock of Rena's words caused Frankie's words to lodge in her throat. Her fury toward Rena mounted. "Yeah, whatever," Frankie responded. "But remember this one thang, sweetie, time will tell. It always does." Frankie hung up the phone abruptly.

Surprised at the way she talked up to Frankie, Rena drove the rest of the way home as if her car had a mind of its own. *Suppose Frankie is telling the truth? Suppose she does have herpes? Then what? What if she really does tell Stiles? I've really pissed her off.* Before Rena realized it, she had made the right on Berry Hill Drive. Pushing the remote, she eased inside of the garage and parked next to Stiles. For the next several minutes, she sat in the car, hoping to regain some composure.

Reaching for the bag of food, Rena stepped out of her car. With each step, her legs seemed to grow heavier as the weight of her bevy of lies and deceit grew deeper, but for now she couldn't afford to worry. She had enough worries to last two lifetimes. As for tomorrow, it would have to take care of itself.

"Stiles, baby . . . I'm home."

22

"There is love of course. And then there's life, its enemy."
—Jean Anouilh

Rena was tested again during the seven months she'd been married. Thank God, the HIV test came back negative again, yet, she couldn't dispel her 'what about the next time' thoughts. From what she read in the brochure at the Health Department, contracting HIV through lesbian sex was rare, but it increased if one, or both, partners had herpes. Determined to believe that Frankie had lied about having the STD as a way to ruin things between her and Stiles, Rena continued to think "what if."

Nearing the one year mark of her marriage, Rena made up her mind to let go and let God, without understanding exactly what the words meant. She stayed away from Frankie as much as possible to avoid confrontations. When it came to Stiles, Rena couldn't bring herself to become overly anxious to indulge in sex with him. She tried to be the wife Stiles deserved, and she hated herself for freezing up when he reached out to make love to her.

* * *

All too soon, reality knocked and Rena was reminded about the uncertainty of life. The morning of their one year wedding anniversary, she was awakened by a tingling, burning sensation between her legs. It was the beginning of the worse time of her life. She looked at Stiles sleeping on his back with a peaceful look on his face. She stared with longing at him, taken off guard by the sudden lurch of excitement mounting within her.

Easing out of the king-sized bed, Rena tipped into the master bath. Opening the vanity cabinet, she reached for her magnifying make-up mirror then took a seat on the toilet. Spreading her legs, she viewed her private areas and almost fainted when she saw a cluster of red ulcer like sores spread on her genital area. *Oh, no. No, God. Please not this!* Unable to remove the mirror, she kept staring, hoping she would wake up and find that she had a nightmare. The tingling sensation intensified, accompanied by a slight throbbing. Hot tears poured down her face as she bent over. When the mirror fell from her hand, crashing on to the cold, ceramic tile, Rena was startled.

"Rena, Rena," she heard Stiles's voice calling her from the other side of the bathroom door. "Are you all right in there?"

"Yes, I'm . . . I'm fine, honey. I dropped my make-up mirror. I guess I'm silly Suzy this morning," she pretended to joke.

"Be careful, sweetheart."

"I will. I'll be out in a minute."

"You know what they say about breaking a mirror," he joked.

Rena stood and moved in front of the wall mirror. Her eyes had begun swelling from her tears. She dashed cold water on her eyes several times hoping to reduce some of the puffiness. Going to work today was out of the question. She had to see a doctor right away. After spending time praying and sulking, Rena finally came out.

Stiles reached both hands out toward her while he sat up in bed. "You're up mighty early. What do you say we use the extra time practicing on making our baby?" His gaze fell to the creamy expanse of her neck. "I want to start our anniversary off right. Just because we both have to go to work today, doesn't mean we can't do a little early morning celebrating," he crooned sexily.

Ignoring his need for her, Rena walked to their huge walk-in closet.

"Honey, you know I need to be at work early," she told him as she fumbled for an outfit.

Stiles's chest deflated when Rena didn't acknowledge his need for affection.

"What is up with you, Rena?" He could no longer hide his irritation.

"Nothing's up with me," Rena retorted. "I can't help it if I have to be at work. This isn't like my job in Marion, Stiles. I don't know how many times we've discussed this."

"That's the problem. We're always discussing this, as you put it, because when I want to make love to my wife, there seems to be one excuse after another."

Rena detected the hurt in his voice and bit her lips in dismay. She stopped shuffling through the closet and turned to face him. "Stiles, I'm sorry. I really am. But I still don't think you're being exactly fair either. You act like we never make love. My God, we've been married one year today. I didn't know we were supposed to be counting how many times we've made love," she shot back.

Stiles clenched his teeth; he was furious. It was becoming more and more difficult for him to contain his emotions. "I don't know what to say or do anymore, Rena. One minute you treat me like I'm the best thing since sliced bread, and the next minute you're cold as ice toward me. Sometimes I feel like a stranger to you rather than your husband." Stiles frowned and threw back the bed covers. "My prayers for strength keep me going, but my physical desire for you is hard to hold back. What man in his right mind wouldn't want to make love to a beautiful woman like you, Rena?

Stiles climbed out of their California king-sized bed, and walked over to the closet where Rena stood. He positioned his half-naked body behind her. Grabbing and pulling her next to him, he nibbled on her neck and shoulders. "It's our anniversary," he sung sweetly in her ear.

Rena eased out of his gentle, bear-like hug. "Honey, I can't. I just told you that I have to leave early this morning." She pulled her tomato-red jersey knit dress off the hanger and eased past him, pretending that his touch meant nothing to her.

"It's not about you having to leave early and you know it. It's about me and you, Rena. You act like I have some contagious disease or something. Do I disgust you that much?"

Rena jumped and a big lump formed in her throat. *It's not you who's contagious. It's me. Oh God, it's me.*

Laying her dress across the chair, Rena turned but barely faced him. "Look, I don't want to argue with you this morning. And I wish you would stop being so paranoid. I love you, and I think our marriage is just fine. And I'm ecstatic that today is our anniversary," she said nervously and pecked him on the cheek, but stepped back. "I know there are times when I'm not as interested in sex as much as you'd like me to be, but I can't help it. But you have to believe me when I say that it's not you.

It's me, Stiles. Just give me a little more time. Please, sweetheart," she pleaded while maintaining her distance.

Stiles released a heavy sigh before he spoke. "Things are fine between us, well almost. And believe me; I know that sex isn't everything. Our marriage shouldn't be based solely on sexual intimacy. But I'm married to a gorgeous, hot woman. I love you, and it's hard not to want you twenty-four seven."

"Just give me a little more time to get accustomed to our life together. I promise soon you'll be begging me to let you rest," Rena winked at him. There was no doubt in her mind he loved her, and she loved him just as much, if not more. If only she could show him she desired him just as much as he yearned for her. Every time she looked at him, her body called for his, but there was no way she could submit to her urges, definitely not now. "Look, Stiles, I really need to shower and get dressed. We'll talk later, okay?" Before he had time to answer, Rena dashed inside the bathroom again. Leaning against the closed door, she closed her eyes and heaved as her heart beat rapidly against her chest wall.

Driving down Elvis Presley Boulevard, Rena called her supervisor to inform him that she would be late reporting in to work. Next she called the doctor's office and listened to the answering service relay the office hours. Glancing at the clock in the car for the first time, she saw that it was only 8:00. Dr. Mitchell's office opened at 9:30. She pulled up to the drive thru of Danver's Restaurant and ordered a cup of decaf and a bacon and egg biscuit. After paying for her order, Rena drove to Dr. Mitchell's office despite the earliness. She took two bites of the sandwich and a sip of her coffee before she lost her appetite.

The burning sensation below her waist produced a flurry of thoughts. *What if I do have an STD? That means I could have passed it on to Stiles. What will happen to me and Stiles? Will he leave me? What will my parents and the Grahams think of me?* The sound of a blaring horn brought her back to her senses. She looked across at the driver next to her just in time to witness a red-haired woman flip her the birdie.

After fighting her way through the maddening early morning expressway traffic, Rena turned into the parking lot of Dr. Mitchell's office at a quarter after nine. She didn't have an appointment, and she didn't care. If she had to sit all day in order to see him, she was prepared to do so. There was no way she was going to leave until he told her what was wrong.

She called her supervisor again after sitting in Dr. Mitchell's waiting room for almost two hours. Rena told him now that it was unlikely that she would be coming in at all.

"Mrs. Graham, you can come back, please," Dr. Mitchell's nurse said as she stood in the opened door of the waiting room.

Rena followed the nurse down the hall to the lab.

She instructed her to get on the scales. "One hundred and twenty-two pounds," the nurse commented. "That's good, now let's get your blood pressure. You can have a seat if you'd like," the nurse gestured at the chair in the corner. "Your pressure's fine too. Why are you here today, Mrs. Graham?" the nurse eyed her curiously.

"Uh, well, I have some female problems that I'd like to talk to Dr. Mitchell about."

"What kind of female problems?"

"I'd rather talk to the doctor about it, if you don't mind."

"Of course, come this way, please." The nurse scribbled in Rena's chart while she led Rena down the hall to patient room five. The nurse opened the table drawer and pulled out a disposable gown and passed it to Rena. "Remove all of your clothes and put this on. It opens in the front."

Seeing the name on the nurse's button, Rena replied, "Thank you, Clarice."

"You're welcome. The doctor will be in shortly," she responded with a smile and closed the door as she exited the room.

Rena did as she was told and removed all of her clothes and put on the gown. Climbing on the examination table, she fidgeted nervously, trying to concentrate on anything but why she was at Dr. Mitchell's office.

When he came in, Rena felt a sense of shame. Dr. Mitchell was a fine, sophisticated, and strikingly debonair black man. She stared at him, and instead of seeing his face, she saw Stiles. Her mouth refused to address the reason she was there.

"Mrs. Graham," he said, pulling her out of her daydream. "What is it I can do for you this morning?" he asked for the second time.

"I . . . I really don't know how to say this."

"There's no need to be nervous. Just tell me what's going on with you today." He reassured her with a pat on her hand and a friendly smile.

"I woke up this morning with a burning sensation in my," Rena hung her head down, and her shoulders slumped over. "In my vaginal area. I have a rash down there too."

"I see. I want you to put both feet in the stirrups, scoot as close to the end of the table and lay back." His voice was gentle, and he didn't sound the least bit judgmental. He stood at the end of the table. "A little more," he instructed.

"Doctor, there's something else I need to tell you," Rena added. "There's a chance I might have herpes."

"Before we go any further, would you be more comfortable if I have my nurse to come in during the exam?" he kindly offered.

"No, I'm fine."

"Let's see if we can find what's going on," he remarked. He put on a pair of latex gloves and pulled an exam light next to her. "What makes you think what you have could be herpes?" he asked while he examined her. "Have you had an outbreak before?" he asked.

"I was sexually active with someone who told me they have it. I hoped the person was lying," she stuttered. Feeling deftly uncomfortable with his probing examination and invasive questions, Rena fought to maintain control of her emotions.

"So this is the first time you've had an outbreak of this kind?"

"I think so. It's the first time I ever had a rash and burning down there. For the past couple of days I've been feeling weak and achy. I thought I was coming down with the flu or a cold."

"Herpes can display flu-like symptoms," he told her. "Relax a little. What you're feeling now is me swabbing your vaginal area. I'm going to run a culture on you. My nurse will be in to draw some blood. You can get dressed now." He patted Rena on the shoulder again as she sat up. "I'm going to send everything to our lab upstairs. It'll take forty-five minutes to an hour for them to run it through, depending on how many are ahead of you," Dr. Mitchell patiently explained. "In the meantime, I suggest you make yourself comfortable. I'll be back as soon as they let me know the results are in.

"Thank you, Dr. Mitchell."

Dr. Mitchell left Rena in the room alone. The hour and

a half Rena waited was the longest wait in her life. She flipped through the out-of-date magazines in the room, read all of the wall charts what seemed like a thousand times, and she prayed just as much.

The light tap on the door made Rena jump, as the doctor turned the knob and stepped inside. "Mrs. Graham." The doctor sat on the round stool. "Your results," he said in a somber like voice, "unfortunately were positive for genital herpes. Your outbreak is pretty severe, but I can prescribe something to ease your discomfort. I don't know how much you know about the disease," he spoke calmly as if he'd recited the same speech a thousand and one times before. "Though it's incurable, it is treatable. It usually doesn't cause serious health problems. It causes more emotional effects because of the stigma that the disease carries. However, it may play a role in the spread of HIV by making people more susceptible to HIV infection."

Rena sat huddled in the chair, listening like a frightened child being scolded by a parent. Tears rested in the corners of each eye, waiting patiently until just the right time to cascade along her cheeks and onto her dress.

"Are you married?" he asked while he studied her chart.

"Yes." Her head dropped a second time.

"Is there a chance you're pregnant?"

"No, I haven't missed a period, if that's what you're asking." Rena answered with a slight tremor in her voice.

"Is your husband infected?"

"No, I . . . I don't know," Rena shamefully responded.

"I'm going to do a pregnancy test before you leave. We need to be certain. I don't want to alarm you unnecessarily," Dr. Mitchell spoke as empathetic yet candidly as possible. "but genital herpes can be life threatening for an unborn child. If it turns out that you aren't pregnant but you and your husband plan on having children, let me give you a word of caution. There is a chance that you can pass it to your baby."

"What will happen to my baby?"

"A baby that is born, and let me reiterate, I said born with herpes, could die or have serious brain, skin, or eye problems."

"Oh, my God, no," Rena screamed.

"Mrs. Graham, please, just listen," Dr. Mitchell said in an even gentler voice. He stepped closer to Rena and held her hand. "If you are pregnant, or become pregnant, we will work through this together. I will refer you to a good obstetrician and you, your husband and the doctor can make a plan that can reduce the baby's risk of getting infected. Babies born with herpes do better if the disease is recognized and treated early. There have been many cases where infants are born without the disease. But as for now, I don't want you to worry about that. I want to get you to feeling better."

Rena's hands shielded her reddened face and caught the tears that fell.

"There is one more precaution you must take."

Rena's head jerked upwards as if from an allergic reaction. The jerk of her head caused tears to splatter from her eyes.

Dr. Mitchell turned to the right and grabbed the box of tissue from the supply table and passed the box to Rena. "Until I give you the okay, you're not to engage in sex or have any genital contact whatsoever with your husband, or anyone, not even with a condom."

Rena gasped. *What does he mean, with anyone else? He probably thinks I'm a slut, or one of those wives who sleep around on their husbands.*

"Let me suggest counseling, proper counseling that is, for you and your spouse. It can help you to learn how to cope with this disease. For instance, you'll learn condoms can decrease the transmission of the disease, but transmission can occur even if condoms are used correctly because they may not cover all infected areas. Let me assure you that with proper education, you and your husband can enjoy a satisfying sex life.

Dr. Mitchell reached inside of his white doctor's coat and pulled out a prescription pad and wrote out a prescription before telling her that he wanted to see her back in his office in one week. He emphasized again the importance of not being sexually intimate for at least two to three weeks, depending on the length of her outbreak.

Rena arrived home late that night. She couldn't face seeing Stiles after what the doctor told her. Today should have been a time of celebration for them, but her past wouldn't leave her alone. She didn't feel right giving him the anniversary gift she'd bought. Rena opened the garage, and exhaled slightly when she saw Stiles car was not there.

Rena awoke and saw Stiles sitting on the side of the bed. "What time is it?" she asked groggily.

"It's late. I didn't mean to wake you." Stiles brushed a lock of her hair away from her face with his hand.

Rena sat up and leaned against the headboard. "Stiles."

He placed a finger against her lips. "Shhh," he said before he kissed her tenderly. "Happy anniversary, Rena." Stiles eyes were dark and his face was somber.

"Happy anniversary to you, Stiles," she responded sadly.

"Here, this is for you." He passed her a black rectangular box.

"Oh, Stiles." She opened the black box. Inside was a white gold necklace with a single diamond dangling from it. Rena gasped and threw her hand against her lips in total surprise. "It's gorgeous." She continued to stare at the exquisite piece of jewelry, and guilt filled her heart. "I . . . I have something for you too," she said and climbed out of the bed and walked to the chest of drawers. She pulled the bottom drawer open and lifted the gift bag out. "This is for you," she said as she returned and sat next to him.

Stiles looked inside the bag. He pulled out a bottle of his favorite cologne, and a navy leather journal. His eyes brightened, and he turned kiss her on the cheek. "Thank you. I love it."

"I thought you might like to keep your sermon notes in it," Rena said as she ran her hand over the kid-soft leather.

"I will." Stiles placed the gifts on the night table while Rena picked up the black box and studied the contents again before she did the same thing.

Stiles stood and undressed down to his underwear. Rena's heart fluttered at the thought of having to tell him, no, again. Surprisingly, Stiles walked to the other side of the bed. He knelt beside the bed and prayed. When he finished praying, he climbed in the bed and pulled the cover up to his waist. "Goodnight, Rena," he said in a wounded voice.

Over the next several weeks, Rena was forced to come up with one weak excuse after another to keep Stiles from touching her. Tension mounted in the house at Berry Hill Drive. Would her marriage survive? With each passing day, Rena had her doubts. What she didn't know was Stiles had begun to have his doubts too.

23

*"The saddest thing in the world is loving someone who used
to love you."*
—*Anonymous*

"Pastor, do you have a minute?" Stiles asked one
day after noon Bible study.

"Always for you, Son. Sit down," he ordered. and
pointed to the oversized leather chair in his church study.

Following his father's instructions, Stiles sat down.
His face looked worn. He ran his hand through his hair
and held his head down slightly.

Pastor observed the troubled look on his son's face.

"What is it, Son?"

Not really knowing if his feelings were justified, Stiles
hesitated before sharing his troubles.

"I don't know how to say this but to say it. But my
marriage to Rena has been less than perfect. What I
hoped and prayed for in a wife is not who Rena is." Stiles
clasped his hands together and rested his elbows on the
chair arms.

"Tell me what you mean by less than perfect."

"It's like with each passing day, my will is being
tested. I feel like my ministry is suffering because I'm
suffering emotionally and I'm ashamed to tell you, but

physically too. Pastor, my wife is a beautiful, desirable woman, yet there's a gaping hole that's keeping us from being husband and wife." Stiles hurriedly wiped away a tear.

Pastor sat quietly and listened. His years in the ministry had granted him years of experience in counseling, and there was probably nothing anyone could say that would surprise him. But seeing the deep hurt etched on his son's face shook him to the core.

"Dad, you know I love Rena. I love her with all of my heart." Stiles placed his hand over his heart. His shoulders drooped. "But, I'm telling you, this moat separating us is draining the life out of what should be a blossoming marriage." Stiles rubbed his forehead with the palm of his hand and let out a heavy sigh.

"Son, marriage takes work—hard work. No one said it would be easy."

"I know that. I've seen you and Mom work through a lot of things. I didn't expect it to be easy, but I didn't know that it would hit me head-on like this. I mean, we've been married a year now."

"Stiles, I'm talking to you as father to son right now. I understand all too well your frustration. Here you are, a vibrant, virile young man with a beautiful wife, and she's not interested in sex. Have you and Rena sat down and openly discussed the issues and problems in your marriage? If you haven't, you need to do it and you need to do it right away."

"We haven't exactly sat down and talked about it. It's either one extreme or the other."

"What do you mean by that?"

"What I mean is either we're arguing about it or we're going about our day to day lives like it's something we dare not admit. Like some hush-hush thing between the two of us."

"Communication, open communication I should say, is one of the main ingredients you're going to need if your marriage is going to survive," Pastor advised.

"She tells me that I'm paranoid, but I know that I'm not. Shoot, I got more attention from her before we recited our vows than I do now that she's my wife."

"Son, listen to me. Go home to your wife. Sit her down, and the two of you talk. You're not going to solve anything by keeping your feelings bottled up inside. Rena needs to know how this is affecting you, and you need to know what's going on with her too."

"I'll try to talk to her again, but I already know it's not going to be easy. It's not going to be easy at all."

Pastor moved from behind his desk, walked over to his son, and placed a hand on Stiles' shoulder. He said, "Let's pray, Son."

Rena went to Emerald Estates and spent some time talking to Audrey. When the phone rang, Audrey excused herself and Rena grabbed the opportunity to go talk to Frankie. She knocked on Frankie's bedroom door. Silence answered her knock. Just as she turned to walk away, she heard Frankie's voice behind her.

"What do you want?" Frankie snapped, as she stepped out of the bathroom and into the hallway.

Rena met Frankie's unwavering stare with one of her own. "I thought I'd stop by to see how you were doing. But it looks like you're doing pretty well. I'm glad to see you up and about."

"Humph." Frankie moved past her, went in her bedroom and sat on the edge of the bed.

"Is that all you have to say?" Rena's lips puckered in annoyance.

"Look, I don't have time for your 'holier than thou'

mess this afternoon. I'm getting out of this place. It's driving me crazy."

"Where could you be going? You know you can't drive, and you can barely walk, so get used to it."

"I'm not going to get used to anything," Frankie shouted. "I'm sick and tired of being cramped up in this house. Kansas is coming to get me out of here."

"You're so stupid," Rena lashed out.

Frankie's limp allowed her to move at a snail's pace. Coupled with the fact that she had limited use of her right arm, Frankie was barely ambulatory.

"You must really be sick in the head. How can you call yourself going somewhere when you can barely walk from the bedroom to the bathroom?"

In an angry and perturbed tone, Frankie shot back through gritted teeth, "It ain't your business."

Rena swooshed around, flippantly throwing her right hand up in the air at Frankie as she proceeded down the hallway away from her former friend. "You know something, Frankie. You're not the one that's stupid. I am. I don't believe you ever loved me. I've come to realize that now, especially after what you've done to me. You're so doggone miserable and hateful. I made a mistake a long time ago, and I'm paying for it now. I thought I had a second chance when me and Stiles fell in love, but you won't let me have that bit of happiness either. Here I am, standing here arguing with the same low-down, evil person who ruined my life, and I have the nerve to still care about what happens to you. Never again, I'm out of here and I'm done with you," Rena huffed before she turned and stormed out of Frankie's room and the Graham house.

Frankie slowly made her way to the front door minutes after Rena's abrupt departure. The wound that Rena had left in her heart hurt more than her physical wounds.

She thought about the things Rena had said. So what if she gave Rena herpes? It was no big deal. But when it came to her life, God acted like He was her personal tormentor rather than the personal savior she had grown up being told He was. Why was the hand that God dealt her full of pain and betrayal? Frankie wrestled with trying for years to understand the reasons she was subjected to such a tormented life.

Memories of Fonda's molestation plagued her mind and brought tears to her eyes. Then there was Minister Travis. She thought of him as a demon sent to pick up where Fonda left off—to destroy her and turn her into the person she was today. Now there was no turning back for Frankie, no future, no one to understand, no one, not even Rena.

Frankie opened the front door and ambled outside to wait for Kansas. Frankie unleashed a wave of sobs that had been bottled up for years. Thank God, Audrey was in her room on the phone talking to somebody about somebody else's business. Frankie managed to steady herself with her quad cane and used her weak arm to brush away the tears. No way would she let Kansas see her crying.

Through the years, she managed to maintain a pretty tough exterior since those dreadful times in her life. Everything she'd been raised to believe about God disappeared back then. Each time Cousin Fonda came to visit, another callous formed over Frankie's heart. Minister Travis was a knife to her abdomen. How could God, who was supposed to be good, who was supposed to love her so much, allow her to be molested over and over again? Why did he turn a deaf ear and a blind eye to her torment and her hurt? She was a young girl who loved God with all of her heart, soul, spirit, and mind. Now the very thought of church and religion, forgiveness and reconciliation, meant nothing to Francesca Graham. The life she lived was tarnished, and Frankie believed it would never sparkle again. That's why, as a teenager, she refused to obey Pastor and Audrey when they tried to force her to go to church. She preferred to face the wrath of the rod than sit on another church pew. The whippings were far better tolerated than listening to Pastor's messages about God's promises and power of protection. Where was God's protection when she had needed Him the most?

KaPow! The loud sound cracked her ears. Frankie looked up to see Kansas turn the corner in her wrecked front-end 1989 Grand Prix with a trail of smoke so thick, she could barely see the houses across the street. Frankie quickly brushed the last bucket of tears away from her lightly scarred face just as Kansas managed to steer the car into the driveway. Turning off the ignition, the vehicle sputtered and spat like it had a mind of its own, while Kansas shuffled up the walkway to aid Frankie.

Pecking her on the cheek, she asked, "Whuzzup? Who helped you get out here?"

Still frazzled over the thoughts that had saturated her mind, her speech reflected her displeasure.

"I didn't need no help," she snapped.

Kansas responded by displaying both palms in a show of defense. "You ready to vamp?"

"If only you could imagine just how ready I am." Frankie wobbled alongside Kansas until they made it to the now quiet-as-a-whistle automobile. She allowed Kansas to open the passenger door for her to climb inside. After Frankie settled inside the car, Kansas turned the ignition on. The car sputtered and shook, and a white cloud of smoke filled the air again.

Frankie laid her head back against the worn headrest and sighed heavily. "Dang, you don't know how good it feels to get away from that dungeon. I gotta do something, Kansas. I need a place of my own again. I'm telling you, I can't take it."

"Man, it's like that up in there? I guess having a preacher for a daddy has to be rough, huh?"

"Rough ain't the word. Anyway, my daddy ain't the one. It's Audrey who gives me the blues. I swear; I can't stay in that house with that woman any longer. She drives me insane. She makes my skin crawl." Frankie scratched her arm like she had fleas.

"It's that bad?"

"Yeaaa, it's that bad. If I told you the real deal about her, you might start choosin' up on men," Frankie laughed harshly.

"Aww, Lawd." Kansas laughed. "Puhleeze, don't tell me a thang about your momma if it's gonna make me do somethin' crazy like that, girl." Kansas lit a cigarette, passed it over to Frankie and proceeded to drive in the direction of Interstate 240.

Stiles paced back and forth over the area rug in the den. His mind was made up. He was going to follow Pastor's advice and talk to Rena. This time, he wouldn't let her weasel her way out of it either. He sat on the couch and picked up a *Jet* magazine when he heard the garage door going down and Rena's key jingle in the kitchen door.

"Stiles, are you here?"

"In the den," he answered.

Rena followed the sound of her husband's voice, placed her purse on the sofa before going in the den. She planted a light kiss on his lips. She asked, "How was your day?"

"I guess you can say it was business as usual."

Rena picked up on the eerie calmness of his voice. Had he discovered her dreadful secret? Did Frankie call and tell him? The harder she tried to ignore the truth the more the thought persisted.

"What about you?"

"What do you mean?" Rena's paranoia set in. She fumbled with the buttons on her shirt,

"I mean, how was work today? You look a little tired."

Rena relaxed. "I am. The library was packed today. We had busload after busload of school children. It's Read Across America Month, and busy isn't the word for what's been happening around that place the past couple of days. What if I prepare one of those thirty minute meals for us?"

Stiles was determined to bring everything to a head tonight. "Don't bother on my account. I'm not hungry. I ate earlier," Stiles told her.

"Oh, well, that's fine. I'm going to take a shower, and then I'm going to fix me a sandwich. I think I'm going to call it an early evening. I'm beat."

"Rena, we need to talk, and we need to talk tonight."

"Talk? Talk about what?" Rena hoped the knot forming in her throat wasn't noticeable. She swallowed hard.

"About us. And don't tell me there's nothing wrong, because you and I both know there's plenty wrong in this marriage. The only way we're going to work through this is by communicating. Come on, sit down." Stiles patted the cushion next to him.

Rena cautiously sat down.

"Rena, I love you. Do you know that?"

"What kind of question is that? Of course, I know you love me. I love you too. What's this all about?"

"Us. You and me." She noticed that he was watching her intently. "I believe our marriage is in trouble. I mean, you barely say anything to me anymore. You don't want me to touch you. You're always avoiding me, and basically I don't feel like you're giving 100 percent to this marriage."

Rena's ears began to burn. Stiles was right, to a certain point, but not for the reasons he thought.

"Stiles, I don't know what you expect from me." She looked at him then quickly looked away. With her head held down, she tried to think of what to say next. Glancing back up at his sad countenance, she told him, "I love you. I love you so much. I know that I haven't been affectionate or wanting intimacy lately. But all I can tell you is that I need time." A quick and disturbing thought came to her, then she said, "Sex, well I . . . all I can say is that I don't seem to enjoy it as much as you. I don't know why, but the thought of being intimate frightens me, Stiles. Maybe I should see a doctor." *God, more lies.* But it was all she could think to say at the time.

"I think that's a good idea. I don't want to come off like something must be wrong with you, but maybe there's some underlying reason for your lack of interest. I mean all I do is think about you, about touching you and making love to you. I want you to have my children, Rena. When I see you, I want to reach out and grab hold of you and never let you go." Stiles's face lit up like Christmas lights. He took hold of Rena's hands and kneaded them inside of his own.

"Rena, if it's me, please, please tell me, sweetheart. I don't ever want to hurt you. I want to satisfy you. I don't want to force you to do anything that you don't want to do. I want you to want me. Tell me, is there someone else? Are you sorry that you married me? Just tell me what it is, so we can work it out."

"Stiles, no," she gasped. "You have it all wrong. There could never be anyone but you. You're everything to me. And not for one moment have I ever regretted marrying you."

"Well, talk to me, then. Tell me what's going on? Is there some, some problem I don't know about? Is there something about me that turns you off? Something you're afraid to tell me? Whatever it is, you have to believe that, with God, we can get through it."

"Baby, it's nothing like that." Rena could barely stand to hear him blame himself for the strain in their marriage. She was the blame for everything. Everything was her fault. When they got married, she had visions of being a mother, the perfect wife.

"And children? We agreed we wanted to have children right away. So much is going through my head." Stiles stood and paced in front of Rena. "I don't know what to do. I don't know how to fix this, Rena. All I know is that I can't do it by myself." His voice sounded raised, and Rena detected the yearning for answers in his voice.

"I want the same thing, baby. Look, why don't I make an appointment with a gynecologist and make sure that there isn't anything physically wrong with me. Until then, try to be a little more patient with me. Just a while longer, Stiles," Rena pleaded, and tried to erase the guilty thoughts creeping through her mind.

"Let me know when you make the appointment. I want to go with you," Stiles told her.

Rena hadn't expected him to say he wanted to go with her. She tripped over her own words as alarm stole away in her heart and mind. "That won't be necessary, honey," she managed to say and added a fake smile.

"Are you sure?" he asked firmly.

"I'm sure. If it turns up that something is wrong, then I'll ask you to go with me."

"Just so you know, we're in this thing together. Now come on, I'll start the shower for you," he said and leaned down to kiss her full on her lips.

His lips pressed against hers felt heavenly. Her heart pounded with desire and her body slightly trembled.

Stiles eased one hand and then the other along the length of her arms. Slowly he pulled her up from the sofa and allowed his eyes to seduce her as they boldly raked over her. His warm, full lips met hers in a slow, drugging kiss.

"Rena, baby, I need you so badly," he groaned with yearning desire as his need for her pressed between her thighs. "I need you, baby. Please, let me love you. If you'll trust me, you know I won't hurt you. You know I would never do that," he said hungrily.

"Stiles, I told you," she said apologetically. A single tear sparkled like a diamond in the crest of her left eye. "How I wish I could, but I can't." Pushing away from him, Rena rushed out of the den and went back to their bedroom. She hurried into the master bathroom, and closed the door behind her.

Stiles stood as if time had came to a halt. Feeling dejected and confused, he rubbed his head with the palm of his hand and sat back down on the couch . . . alone.

Later on that night, Rena tossed and turned while Stiles slept. She reached over and with the tips of her fingers she traced light feathery strokes along his chest.

You look so peaceful. God, I love you, but I've ruined your life. How do I tell you? How?

Ring, ring.

Rena jumped at the sound of the ringing phone. "Who in the world is calling at this time of night?" She glanced at Stiles who continued to sleep undisturbed.

The caller ID read "blocked call," and at first thought Rena started not to answer. With her curiosity mounted, she picked up the phone.

"Hello."

"Yeah, skip the small talk."

"Why are you calling here at this time of night?" Rena asked as soon as she recognized Frankie's voice.

"We need to talk." Frankie's voice hardened.

"Are you crazy? It's after midnight. What do we need to talk about anyway?" Rena whispered and glanced over her shoulder to make sure Stiles was still asleep.

"We need to talk about when you're going to tell my brother, and your husband, the truth." With each slurred word that escaped Frankie's mouth, Rena could tell that Frankie was high. She always could.

Rena heard talking and loud music in the background. "Where are you?"

"Don't worry about that. You just concentrate on where you are," Frankie responded with her off-the-wall answer. "I so sick of you tryin' to live like you so good, and you so perfect. You ain't doing nothin' but making a fool of my brother."

Rena eased out of the bed and tip-toed into the hallway. "Look, I don't have time for this tonight. You need to sleep off that high you're on, then call me," Rena answered sharply.

"Don't you dare tell me what to do," she screamed in a stern and threatening voice. "Now you listen to me, you lil' sneaky, conniving trick. If you don't tell Stiles by tomorrow night, I'm gonna tell 'em for you." Frankie slammed down the phone so hard that Rena's ears rang.

Rena paced the hall; she frantically tried several numbers, hoping she could reach Frankie. After several failed attempts, Rena turned off the ringer just in case Frankie tried to call back. Just as quietly as she left, she returned to the bedroom and lay back in the bed. Praying within, she begged God for His mercy. Her marriage was sure to be over if Stiles found out the truth. The past was about to catch up with her. Looking at Stiles again, Rena turned on her side with her back to him. *God, help me. Please, help me.* Part of a passage of scripture she learned as a little girl came to Rena's mind—" for I will forgive their iniquity, and I will remember their sin no more." God, I know I have to suffer the consequences of my sin, even if you have forgiven me. But does Stiles have to suffer because of me and Frankie's mistakes?

Suddenly, Rena's head began to pound. Tears spilled from her eyes and on to the sheets. The skeletons inside of her closet were beating against the door . . . hard. They'd been hidden away far too long and were ready to come out.

24

"Nothing ends nicely, that's why it ends."
—Tom Cruise

Rena woke up late the next morning with swollen eyes, with her hair matted down where tears had settled during the night. Stiles's side of the bed was empty. Looking at the desk clock, Rena saw that it was almost ten o'clock. Normally, on Saturday mornings, she was awake no later than eight-thirty. After recalling what the previous night, Rena rubbed her face with her hands. She picked up the cordless phone and scrolled through the caller ID to see if Frankie had called back. There was another blocked call.

Rena jumped up from the bed. A faint feeling came over her at the thought that Frankie may have already told Stiles everything. She went to see if Stiles was in the house. An uncanny stillness came over her at the emptiness that filled the house on Berry Hill. Too frightened to call his name, Rena moved quietly from room to room until she realized that Stiles wasn't there. She ran to the door that led to the garage. His car was gone.

"Where is he? He usually wakes me up to tell me that he's leaving. Oh, God, this isn't good. This isn't good at

all." Spying the cordless phone on the kitchen countertop, Rena headed for it. Immediately she dialed the Graham resident, only for Audrey to tell her that Frankie left
sometime the day before and hadn't come back or called.

The phone rang just after Rena hung up from talking
to Audrey. Rena snatched the phone off the counter.
"Hello."

"You told your husband yet?"

"Frankie, where are you? I am not about to play games
with you," Rena yelled into the receiver.

"Who's talkin' about games?" Frankie snarled. "I told
you, you tell Stiles today, or I will."

"Where are you?" asked Rena, desperation pleading in
her voice.

"What does it matter?" The coldness in Frankie's voice
was enough to chill an entire room.

Rena's anger transformed to slush. "Because we need
to talk. If I'm going to tell Stiles, I want to talk to you
first."

"Be at Pastor and Audrey's house at one o'clock. I'll be
there by then," Frankie ordered and hung up the phone.

Rena loathed the control Frankie still had over her.
Rena tried to call Stiles on his cell phone but it went
straight to voicemail. "Lord, this might be a set up. Stiles
could be there waiting on me too. But I don't have a
choice. I have to go because if he isn't there, then Frankie
is sure to tell him. If he isn't then maybe I can find a way
to talk her out of telling him. She can't hate me that
much. We've been through too much together," Rena
tried to convince herself.

At 12:25, Rena retrieved her cell phone and clutch
purse. She grabbed the keys from the kitchen key holder,
she entered the codes on the security keypad and
slammed the kitchen door.

In less than twenty minutes, fifteen and a half to be

exact, Rena pulled into her in-laws' driveway. She jumped out, ran to the door, and rang the doorbell.

It was almost three minutes before Frankie opened it and nodded for Rena to come in.

The first thing Rena noticed was how bad Frankie looked. Her hair was packed down on her head, deep circles cradled her eyes and her pimpled skin was dry as a bone. Rena stepped inside and looked around to see if there was any sign of Pastor and Audrey.

"There's no one here, if that's whatcha tryin' to see." Frankie said, closing the door.

The two of them went into the family room. Frankie slowly maneuvered herself so she could sit down in the recliner facing Rena, but Rena continued to stand. Her folded arms and hands resting under her armpits revealed her uneasiness.

"Rena, I'm going to get straight to the point. It's time for you to come clean."

"Did you just say come clean?" remarked Rena, with an expression like that of a marble statue plastered across her face. "How can telling Stiles that I had a sexual relationship with another woman possibly be called coming clean? And then it was with you, his sister?" Rena lashed out.

"Whaddaya mean, it was with me? You sound like the fool that you are. But baa-by, you ain't Miss Innocent, so girl, puhleeze. Marrying my brother don't make you a saint." Frankie screamed.

Rena stomped across the floor. "You've always been selfish, Frankie. Always. Just because you've managed to screw up your life, you want to screw up mine too. Isn't it bad enough that you gave me an incurable STD? Haven't you done enough? How can I tell my husband about that? And how can we ever have children? Don't you have an ounce of goodness left in you?" Rena's fair skin turned a glowing red as she unleashed the fury inside her.

Frankie leaned forward slightly, in the chair as if she was about to get up. "Obviously, I don't 'cause what you sayin' sounds like a personal problem to me. Maybe you shoulda thought about that before you married him, considering the lifestyle we were leading, you know. I have no pity for you. If I'm gay, then so are you. You're just a fool trying to hide behind religion to shield what you really are. You're stupid, Rena—a stupid, lesbian wench." Frankie laughed out loud at the sickened look that came on Rena's face.

Rena balled her fists and went toward Frankie to strike her, but an invisible force kept her from doing so.

"Go on, hit me. That's the real you, Rena. Let it come out."

They were arguing so loudly, neither of the women heard the front door open and then close. Pastor followed the voices he recognized as Francesca's and Rena's. He stood in the kitchen by the refrigerator, hidden from their view, and listened to the blaze of accusations spewing from their mouths. *My God, Lord I know what I'm hearing can't be true.* Pastor walked toward the family room to stop the vicious words between Frankie and Rena. He ignored the sudden lightheadedness and his unsteady gait.

Oblivious to Pastor's presence on the other side of the family room, Frankie and Rena continued their tirade until, without warning, a thunderous thud severed the heated quarrel.

Rena looked up and gasped when she saw Pastor lying in the floor. His body twitched before it became deftly still. She dashed over to his still figure.

"Pastor," Rena screamed. She knelt down beside him, and her hand flew up to her mouth when she saw how badly his mouth was twisted. He struggled to speak, but his words came out garbled and unintelligible, followed by an unresponsive look of unspoken pain.

Frankie struggled to get up from the chair. As fast as her lame legs would take her, she made her way over to where Pastor lay and looked down at him. Hot tears spilled from her bloodshot eyes. "Daddy, Daddy?" she screamed. With eyes that narrowed like slits, she glared at Rena. "This is your fault. It's all your fault. Call 911," ordered Frankie.

Rena jumped up from her frozen state like she had been prodded with a cattle prod. She ran to get the phone and called 911 like she was told. With the phone against her ear, Rena ran back to Pastor. "Operator, I have an emergency at 3290 Pepper Oaks in Emerald Estates. Please send an ambulance."

The 9-1-1 operator remained calm. "Tell me what's going on." the man instructed.

"It's my father-in-law. He . . . he just collapsed on the floor. I think he must have hit his head."

"Is he conscious?"

"Yes. No. I mean no. He's not conscious. He's bleeding from the back of his head. Please, send someone now," Rena tearfully pleaded while Frankie called Pastor's name in the background.

"Did you say that he's conscious or unconscious, ma'am?"

"He's not saying anything, but his eyes are open. Oh, my God, don't let him die. Please don't let him die." Rena leaned closer to Pastor's body. Thank God, he was breathing.

"Forget all the questions. Tell them to send help," Frankie screamed. "My father needs help now," she bellowed loudly in the background.

The 911 operator assured Rena that help was on the

way. Though it seemed to take ages, an ambulance arrived within minutes. Rena rushed to the door to let the paramedics in. The paramedics immediately began working on pastor.

Audrey, returning from the beauty shop, rushed inside when she saw the ambulance parked in the driveway and the front door wide open. *What has happened? What has that child of mine done now?*

"Pastor, Pastor what's going on?" Audrey asked and ran to the family room where she heard the commotion. At the sight of Pastor being placed on a stretcher, Audrey became uncontrollable. "What . . . what happened to my husband? Oh, my God," Audrey sobbed as her trembling hands reached out for Pastor, at the same time the paramedics were wheeling him outside to the waiting ambulance.

Frankie managed to make it outside and planted herself next to her mother. "Audrey, we don't know what happened. Me and Rena were . . ."

"We were talking," Rena interrupted. "There was no one here but the two of us. The next thing we knew, there was a loud noise. We looked up, and Pastor was lying on the floor. We didn't even know he had come home."

"Yeah, and that's when I told Rena to call 911," a distraught Frankie further explained.

"Ma'am," the paramedic said, looking in Audrey's direction. "Are you going to ride in the ambulance?"

"Yes, certainly," Audrey answered and allowed the paramedic to help her inside the back of the ambulance next to her husband. Between sobs, she looked at both Frankie and Rena. "Something happened to cause this. It's always something when you come around," she accused Frankie. "You rest assured, I'm going to find out," she warned.

* * *

The ride to the hospital with Rena ignited Frankie's temper even more.

"If Pastor heard what we were talking 'bout, I'll never forgive you." She shouted so loud, Rena thought the car windows would crack.

"Forgive me? You must still be doing drugs," Rena rebuffed. "You're the one to blame for all of this. If you weren't so bent on ruining my life, none of this would have happened. Anyway, who's to say anyway that Pastor heard us?"

"Never in a million years would I have thought you would turn out to be my worst enemy instead of my best friend."

Rena was too mad to reply. Instead, she pushed harder on the accelerator. Simultaneously she reached for her cell phone to call Stiles.

His phone went straight to voicemail—again. *Where can he be? Somewhere still pouting,* Rena concluded.

Frankie jerked her head around to glare at Rena. "What are you trying to do, kill us?"

Rena didn't bother to answer. She pulled into a parking space, shut off the engine, and jumped from the car, leaving Frankie to fend for herself. The compassion Rena normally felt for others was nowhere to be found; she'd had more than her share of Frankie Graham.

Rena rushed through the double doors and up the hospital corridor until she arrived at the information desk. Her heavy breathing and rushed talking signaled to the desk clerk that something major had happened.

"Settle down, miss," the nurse told her politely. "Take a deep breath, and tell me what's wrong."

"My, my father-in-law was just brought in here minutes ago." Rena tried to slow her speech but found it hard to do. "The ambulance brought him."

Frankie arrived at the nurse's station and quickly exerted her authority. "My father," Frankie emphasized and gave Rena a wicked look, "Pastor Chauncey Graham, was brought in here. Can you tell me where he is?"

"Are the two of you together?" the nurse asked.

"Certainly not by choice, but yes, we are," Frankie answered.

"Just a minute, let me see what I can find out."

Rena paced the milky white corridor while Frankie leaned against the nurse's station counter. The nurse hastily returned and gave Rena and Frankie directions to the trauma unit waiting room.

"How is my father?" Frankie demanded to know before she left the nurse's station.

"I really can't tell you anything, ma'am. All I can say is that he's being examined. The trauma team will tell you as soon as they know something."

They walked to the trauma unit in silence. Rena glanced at Frankie as she hobbled down the hall like she was propelling her weak body to move as fast as she could. Rena thought of her husband and his whereabouts. Concerned for Pastor, Rena ignored the 'No Cell Phone Use' sign and dialed Stiles' number again—voicemail.

A gentleman stepped ahead of Frankie and opened the door when she reached the trauma unit. Stiles and Audrey were already there. Rena couldn't imagine how Stiles made it to the hospital before her, and he hadn't bothered to return her calls. Her anger was quickly forgotten and she bypassed Frankie, running into his arms. Rena released a fresh bucket of tears that spilled on to Stiles's crisp white dress shirt. He held onto her and rested his head on top of hers.

Frankie stood alone at the entrance, watching. Audrey, with red eyes, sat with one hand supporting her bowed head.

Rena eased back and looked up at her husband. "How is he?"

"I don't know. I just arrived before the two of you," he answered as his eyes shifted toward Frankie. "Mother said the doctors are still working on him. They haven't told her a thing since they brought him here, only that he's still unconscious." The worry was evident in Stiles' speech. He shifted his weight from side to side and rubbed his hair with the palm of his hand. "What happened? Mother says that you and Frankie were there when Pastor collapsed."

Frankie had made her way to where Stiles and Rena stood and heard his question.

"Rena and I were in the family room talkin', so we don't know when Pastor came in. All I can tell you is that we heard a loud noise, looked up, and saw him lying in the floor. He must have fallen and hit his head on the end table."

Rena fidgeted with each word Frankie spoke.

"What exactly were you two talking about that was so important that you didn't hear him come inside?" questioned Stiles.

Frankie tried to speak up, but not before Rena said, "Now is not the time to discuss that. We're here to see about Pastor."

"I agree," Audrey butted in.

"Anyway, I'm sure your wife will tell you everything very soon. Won't you, Rena?" Frankie coyly remarked, with an upraised eyebrow and a sneer on her hardened face.

Rena sashayed off in Audrey's direction without saying a word. She wrapped her arm around Audrey's shoulders and hugged her.

"Everything is going to be fine, you'll see."

Audrey rocked back and forth, and hot tears streamed

down her face. Stiles consoled Frankie until Audrey called for him to come to her. He took hold of his sister's arm and guided her along with him.

After making sure Frankie was seated comfortably, Stiles sat down next to Audrey. Rena was still seated on the other side of her mother-in-law. Audrey looked up when she saw the doctor walking toward them.

"Mrs. Graham?" he asked, looking at each woman.

"I'm Mrs. Graham," Audrey answered. "How is my husband? Is he conscious?"

The dark-haired doctor sat in the chair across from the Graham family. "Your husband has suffered an ischemic stroke. He probably hit his head after falling when he had the stroke. Unfortunately the fall made his condition worse. He has regained consciousness and right now we have him stable, but he's still not out of the woods just yet."

Audrey cried, and Stiles pulled her against him for support. Frankie's eyes filled with tears too while Rena sat across from the doctor in distress.

"May I see him?"

"Ma'am, not right now, I'm afraid; maybe in a couple of hours. We want to run a few more tests to make sure he didn't sustain any brain injury. Like I said, he's stable, but he's still in serious condition."

"Doctor, can you tell if the stroke did any permanent damage?" asked Stiles.

"I can't say if there will be permanent damage, but he is experiencing some paralysis on the right side. He is quite disoriented and has difficulty speaking. We're working to get his blood pressure under control. There is a chance that his long term care can be improved since he arrived in the emergency room fairly soon after having the stroke which gave us the chance to treat him right away."

"Thank you, doctor," Stiles told him. "We appreciate you."

The doctor stood, and so did Stiles. Stiles extended his hand in gratitude, and the two men shook hands. He then turned to Audrey. "Mrs. Graham, we're doing everything we can. You have my word, as soon as it's okay for you to see him, the nurse will be in to let you know."

"Thank you," Audrey whispered solemnly.

Rena and Frankie remained quiet, hanging onto every word.

Rena's mind flooded with a bevy of questions. *How much, if anything, did Pastor hear? Were she and Frankie responsible for his stroke? What will he say when he begins to talk?*

Frankie pulled herself up from her chair. She watched Rena's facial expression as she managed a small, tentative smile when Stiles sat down and embraced her. *You're going to pay for all the trouble you've caused. There's no way I'm gonna walk around crippled, while you come off like the Virgin Mary. If it's the last thing I do, Stiles will know everything about you, Miss Rena. Believe that.*

25

*"Lucky is the man who is the first love of a woman, but luckier is
the woman who is the last love of a man."*
—Unknown

Pastor's doctor made his daily rounds. Like always,
Audrey was by her husband's bedside.

"Hello, Pastor Graham. Are you about ready to go
home?" the short doctor asked Pastor with a broad grin
on his face.

One corner of Pastor's mouth pulled into a slight smile
and he could hardly lift his voice beyond a whisper.
"Yes," he strained.

"Doctor, may God bless you for everything you've
done to help my husband." Audrey's face split into a
wide grin too. "This has been the most dreadful two
weeks I've experienced."

"I want to go over your condition," the doctor said
and glanced from Pastor to Audrey. "The stroke left you
with right-sided weakness which is the reason you're unable to do much, if any ambulating right now. I believe
with physical therapy, you might be able to eventually
walk with the use of a walker or quad cane. You'll continue to have problems with your cognitive thinking, at-

tention span, and short-term memory, which may or may not improve over time; it's hard to say." His voice remained calm and he continued to shift.

"And his speech? You know he is a preacher. It's his whole life." Audrey's voice was shakier than she wanted it to be.

"It's hard to give you a definitive answer. However, I believe with speech therapy, it will improve. I wish I could tell you that you'll fully recover your speech, Pastor Graham, but again, only time will tell. I've written in your discharge papers that you're to attend physical therapy three times a week and speech therapy two times a week over the next few months. I want to see you back in the office in one month." The doctor reached down and grabbed Pastor's hand and shook it lightly. "Do you have any other questions?" he asked patiently.

Audrey nodded her head, and Pastor remained silent.

Holy Rock faced the repercussions of Pastor's illness just as much as the Graham family. Gone, for now, were the days of Pastor's prolific preaching and soul-stirring sermons. The deacons and trustees nominated Stiles to step up as interim pastor. The nomination was presented to the congregation that Stiles should have the position.

Stiles sat on the bed in his pajama pants and ran his fingers through his short hair. His eyes darkened with emotion while he peered at the notes he held in his other hand. "I dreamed of one day following in my father's footsteps, and being the pastor of Holy Rock. I wanted his legacy to live on. I wanted to fill his shoes, Rena, but not like this." Stiles put the sermon that he'd prepared for Sunday worship service on the nightstand.

"Baby, this is what Pastor wants." Rena lovingly stroked his back. Their home life was still strained, but aside from their bedroom issues, Stiles could count on

Rena being a good wife. She stepped up to the plate and supported him fully. "He can't preach any more, so you know he wants you to keep sending forth the word of God."

Stiles relaxed and laid his head on Rena's shoulder.

"There's no time to dwell on the way you hoped things would be. The future is here, and you're the shepherd of Holy Rock now. Lead your sheep, sweetheart. Don't worry about a thing because God is on your side, and so am I."

"O Lord, my God, your people called out to you for help, and you healed the man of God. Some of you might say that Pastor isn't healed because he can't speak like he used to. But I'm here to tell you this morning, that Pastor is healed because he is alive. The devil may have stilled his tongue, and his body may be frail, but God will not be stopped," Stiles's voice rang with vigor and faith. The congregation seemed on fire. Hands went up in the air, the organist played mightily and shouts of praises resonated throughout the packed sanctuary.

"He'll make the rocks cry out in praise if He has to. Not only is He a healer, but He's Jehovah-Jireh, the Lord who provides. Stiles jumped up and down in the pulpit. "I feel my help coming. Yes, yes, yes. I said I feel my help coming, y'all!" Stiles preached with certainty. "God is Jehovah Nissi, God our Banner, Jehovah-Shalom, the Lord of Peace, Jehovah Tsidneku, The Lord of Righteousness, Jehovah-Rohi, the Lord Our Shepherd. I can keep telling you who God is, but you need to know Him for yourself."

"Tell it, Pastor. Preach the word." Rena sat on the second row, her heart about to burst with praise for the work God was doing in Stiles' life and the healing in hers. God had given her a second chance. When the choir broke out singing, Marvin Sapp's, "never would have made it, never could have made it without you," Rena couldn't sit any longer. She stood, reared her head back, and began clapping her hands and praising God.

Monday morning, Rena waltzed into Dr. Mitchell's office with calm assurance. Her outbreaks had ceased since she started her prescribed medication. It was difficult but she had managed to abstain from sex, even though at times it seemed like it would destroy her marriage. Her check-up with Dr. Mitchell left her feeling refreshed, revived, and renewed when he gave her clearance to engage in sex, except during the times she felt the signs of an outbreak. Rena could be the wife Stiles deserved, totally and completely. If she became pregnant, she believed God would work that out as well. She thought back to what Dr. Mitchell had told her. *There are people walking around every day leading successful lives, with fulfilled happy marriages and healthy children, who have the same STD.* "If you worked it out for them, being no respecter of persons, Lord I know you'll take care of me too," she said and climbed in her car.

After leaving Dr. Mitchell's office, Rena went to work. The day moved quickly. Her supervisor, Mr. Bolden, commented and chuckled, "Rena, I don't know what it is, but it seems like you have an extra stride in your step today. I know you haven't been feeling the best these past few months but it seems like the old Rena is slowly coming back." He patted her on her shoulder, glad to see the fresh smile on her face.

"Thank you, Mr. Bolden. I do feel better, much better." When he walked away, Rena turned and focused on the computer screen. She hummed the song from yesterday's service while she worked.

On her way home from work, Rena stopped at the

store and picked up several of Stiles' favorite foods. She was going all out for her husband tonight. Tonight would be the end of worrying about anything, including Frankie. She'd experienced enough outbreaks to know the signs of an oncoming one, and Dr. Mitchell told her that he believed she would be just fine. The longer she took her medication, the fewer her outbreaks would be, he told her. And she had to keep her stress levels down. What better way to reduce her stress than by making love to her husband?

Stiles opened the door and the aroma of a home-cooked meal slipped underneath his nose. He sniffed lightly and "oohed" as the aroma drew him inside the house like a magnet.

"Rena," he called. No answer. Stiles walked slowly through the kitchen but halted momentarily to inhale the tantalizing aroma of food again. "Rena." No answer. He went to the living room and was in awe when he saw the table set for two with some of the never-before-used china they had received as wedding gifts. Candles lit the otherwise dim room and Stiles saw a spread of food fit for a king.

He dropped his coat where he stood, unloosened his tie, and walked slowly past the table, drooling over the array of delicious dishes.

"How do you like it?" Rena asked, stepping from behind the wall that divided the living room from the entrance into the hallway.

His mouth dropped open when he saw her posed seductively, each hand strategically placed on her hips. The sexy red cocktail dress clung to every inch of her curvaceous frame like glue. Stiles couldn't help it—he rubbed his eyes to make sure he wasn't dreaming. He rubbed them again, harder this time, just to be sure.

Rena inched a smidgen closer to him, and the scent of Chanel excited him. He was ravenous, but not for food.

"Hi," she finally greeted him. "I know you must be hungry after such a long day." Her voice was melodious, soft, and eager to please.

He managed to speak. "What? What's . . ."

She silenced him by placing her hands against his lips. With his tie already loosened, Rena unbuttoned the first couple of buttons on his shirt and teasingly rubbed his chest. She took hold of his hand, and led him to the table.

"Baby, everything is, well, I can't explain it," he stuttered aimlessly.

"I wanted to do something special for you, sweetheart. I love you so much, and I know you've been dealing with a lot lately. It's time for you to relax a little."

The two of them talked like they hadn't done in a long time. Stiles not only savored every bite of food, but he looked at his wife like he was photographing her with his eyes. When they finished eating, Rena rose from the chair slowly, slightly bending over so he could get the perfect view of her cleavage.

"Where are you going?" he asked, as if afraid he would wake up and discover he had been dreaming all along.

"You'll see. Follow me," she ordered, and grabbed his neck tie and led him behind her like a dog on a short leash. He didn't protest but watched her behind as she moved slowly up the hallway like a stealth cat. His excitement and desire grew with each step he took. Once they were in the bedroom, Rena stopped, turned and kissed him passionately. His hands lightly traced a path over her skin while she explored his body like she'd longed to do for so long. He smothered her lips with demanding mastery.

Backing away from him, Stiles froze, expecting to here the dreaded words, "I'm sorry, I just can't." He dropped his hands, but she grabbed hold of them before they landed by his side.

Leading him further inside the bedroom, she whispered enticingly in his ear, "Time for dessert."

26

*"The enthusiasm of a woman's love is even beyond
the biographer's."*
—Jane Austin

Audrey sat in the chair next to Pastor's bed and read the Bible out loud to him. Today she read the twenty-ninth chapter of Psalms, one of his favorite chapters. Afterward, she gingerly placed his hands inside of hers and prayed. "Do you want to get in your chair, honey?" she asked tenderly.

He nodded yes.

Rena helped him to the chair. "The remote is right here by your left hand. I'm going to fix myself a cup of coffee, and I'll be back in a minute." Audrey kissed him on his forehead.

Ring. Ring. Ring.

Rena was about to hang up when Audrey picked up the phone. Out of breath, she answered, "Hello."

"Good morning, Audrey. Why are you breathing so heavy?"

"I was trying to find the phone. Pastor and I just finished our morning devotion when I heard it. It was in the family room. How are you this morning?"

"Fine. I just thought I'd call before Stiles and I left for

church. We'll be praying for you and Pastor. When church is over, we'll stop by Piccadilly's and bring you both some dinner."

"You're such an angel, Rena. My son is blessed to have you." Audrey's animosity she directed toward Rena for Pastor's stroke had basically disappeared. Audrey reasoned if anyone was to blame, it was Frankie. Frankie's lifestyle, the car accident, drugs, and her refusal to turn her life over to God wore heavily on Pastor's mind and heart constantly. His bouts of depression and emotional outbursts since his stroke were truly taking a toll on Audrey, but she was determined to stand by her man. Pastor rescued her and Stiles from a life of mediocrity and opened her heart to love again. She was devoted to him completely, and if she had to, for the rest of her life, she would take care of Pastor.

"Audrey, you and Pastor are my family. I love you. Oh, hold on a minute. Stiles wants to say something." Rena passed the phone to Stiles.

"Good morning, Mother. How's my favorite girl?" he asked, winking at Rena while talking into the receiver.

"Don't you let your wife hear you say that," Audrey laughed.

"Don't worry, she isn't listening." Stiles chuckled while Rena stood smiling next to him with her hands positioned on her waist. Changing to a serious tone, Stiles inquired, "How's Pastor?"

"He had a pretty rough night. Sometimes he has quite a bit of pain on his weak side, and it makes it hard for him to sleep well. He ate a good breakfast. Bacon, eggs, and French toast."

"Good. I'm glad his appetite is still strong. Is he awake? I want to have a word or two with him."

"Sure, sweetheart. Hold on a minute." Audrey walked

down the hallway and into the bedroom where Pastor sat in his chair at the window. He watched the birds like he did every morning, even before he had the stroke. Something about the birds soothed his spirit.

"Stiles is on the phone."

A faint smile formed on his twisted face. Audrey placed the receiver up to his left ear and Pastor managed to hold the phone in place between his head and shoulder.

"Uhh," Pastor grunted into the receiver.

"Morning, Pastor," Stiles said happily. "I'm on my way to church. And just like you taught me, I'm going to be there early rather than late."

Pastor grunted his approval into the phone again.

"This morning I'm preaching from the New International Version. I know you prefer King James, but I want to make sure every one understands where I'm coming from. My text comes from Psalms 101 verse 7."

Pastor slowly mumbled, struggling to speak, he finally mouthed the words, "Good choice."

"I know you know the verse. I don't think there's a passage in the Bible that you don't know. Anyway, here goes. 'No one who practices deceit will dwell in my house; no one who speaks falsely will stand in my presence.'"

Rena jumped away like an arrow was headed for her heart. Deceit? She didn't know if she could listen to the message. She felt like she was more than deceitful. She felt like a hypocrite.

"I'll bring my typed sermon notes over with me when I come over there after church. How is that?" Stiles asked Pastor.

Pastor grunted his approval.

Stiles prayed with him. Afterward, Audrey gently removed the phone from his ear. "Stiles, you and Rena have a good time at church. Tell everyone that Pastor sends his love, and we thank everyone for their prayers, gifts, visits, cards, and telephone calls."

"I'll tell them, Mother. We'll see you this afternoon." Stiles hung up the phone, turned around. He didn't see Rena. "Honey, where are you?

"In the kitchen," Rena answered.

Stiles grabbed his Bible and suit jacket from off the bed and walked out of the bedroom.

One look at her and Stiles asked, "What's wrong? Are you all right?"

"Yes, of course. My stomach is a little queasy. It's nothing, just a bout of gas."

"Gas? Ooh, wee. Let it all out now, First Lady. I don't want Holy Rock to know that the first lady is a pootie lady," Stiles teased and squeezed his nose with his thumb and forefinger.

Rena laughed along and jokingly hit Stiles on the shoulder with her handbag before they walked out to the garage.

Listening to Stiles' sermon, Rena was captivated by his powerful message. At that moment, he sounded so much like Pastor. His words were dynamic, and Rena felt like the hand of God was guiding her husband's life.

"There are times in life when we face moments of weakness. David faced a moment of weakness, yet he was a man after God's own heart. He broke God's law. He intentionally set out to steal Bathsheba, the wife of Uriah. He went so far as to have Uriah killed in order to get the woman he lusted after and keep himself clear from the adultery he had committed with her."

"Preach, Pastor, preach," someone in the congregation shouted.

"Deceit is dangerous, my people. Deceit is a deadly

game that the devil loves to play. But the only way the devil wins is if we let him. Remember, there is no condemnation in Christ Jesus. Whatever sin you have committed, God is faithful and just to forgive you and to cleanse you from all unrighteousness. Not some unrighteousness, but all unrighteousness," Stiles stressed. "But, my people, you have to ask and seek His forgiveness. If you're living a life of shame, deceit, or fear, God wants you to know that there is no problem, no situation, and no sinful act that is too hard for Him to turn around. Nothing you've done is so terrible that He won't forgive you. The devil wants to mislead you. He wants you to believe that you're unworthy. He wants you to believe that the sin you've committed is too bad to ever seek God's mercy."

Rena hung her head down when she saw Stiles look in her direction.

"If we stand at God's door and knock, He promises to hear us and answer us. He'll open wide the door of forgiveness. He'll extend a hand of mercy and His grace never runs out."

Stiles' words convicted Rena's spirit. As he opened the doors of the church, she wanted to stand up and walk down to the front of the sanctuary and submit her life back over to Jesus. She wanted to so badly, but her feet felt like they were glued to the floor of the sanctuary. The weight of her past sins held her back. Before she realized it, the new members' ministry had taken those who had come down the aisle to the counseling area. She remained on the pew and slowly wiped the tears from her red cheeks.

27

*"Friend deceives friend, and no one speaks the truth. They
have taught their tongues to lie; they weary themselves
with sinning."*
—Jer. 9:5 NIV

"I'm glad they had Pastor's favorite, cornbread and
dressing, today," Stiles remarked.

"Yeah, they used to have it every day, but they've
stopped. I'm not sure why," commented Rena.

"How did you enjoy today's sermon?" Stiles asked,
seeking his wife's approval. He couldn't explain how
great he felt since the night Rena showed him how much
she wanted their marriage to work. He felt like he'd been
given a new lease on life. He thanked God every day for
healing his broken marriage.

Rena inhaled, and then exhaled slightly, to keep herself from bursting into tears. "It was powerful, Stiles. I
don't know how to explain it, but I could see the favor of
God on your life when you were in that pulpit. No matter what, please don't let the devil distinguish that fire in
you."

Stiles took his eyes off the road for a second and
looked at his wife. "Honey, thank you for that. I love
you."

"I love you too. And I want you to know that I would never do anything, and I mean anything to hurt you."

"Whoa, what do you mean by that?"

"Your message hit home in so many ways. It made me realize how important it is to forgive and to seek God in all that we do in life. That's all, baby."

"Praise God, praise God," Stiles said. The couple parked the car, retrieved the Piccadilly bags and went up the walkway.

As soon as they walked inside the house, Rena almost dropped the bag of food when she heard Audrey and Frankie exchanging powerfully heated words.

"You're no daughter of mine," Audrey yelled.

Stiles placed his bag on the table in the foyer before he sprinted toward the sound of the voices emitting from Pastor's study.

"Hey, hey, what's going on in here?" Stiles asked with Rena now standing behind him.

"I want your sister out of here. I want her out of this house for good. I mean it. Get her out of here," Audrey yelled, pointing at the doorway.

"Come on, you two. What's this all about?" asked Stiles.

"I'll tell you what it's all about," Frankie yelled. Her piercing brown eyes locked with Rena's. "Better yet, why don't you tell him, Rena?"

Stiles' eyes quickly darted from Rena and then back to his sister. "What has Rena got to do with any of this? Honey, do you know what Frankie is talking about?"

Stuttering, Rena set the drinks down on the desk so she wouldn't drop them. "No, I don't know what any of this is about," she replied nervously.

"So, it's like that, huh? You want to keep on lying, huh?" Frankie screamed again.

Audrey jerked her head around and looked at Rena

too. "What on earth could she possibly have to do with any of this?"

"Frankie, don't do this. Now is not the time." Rena pleaded.

"Not the time for what? Will somebody please tell me what's going on?" demanded Stiles.

"Yes, I want to know too," Audrey yelled. "But if I know Frankie, she has another far-fetched lie up her sleeve. You come in my house high, letting one sleazy, nasty woman after another up in this house. You don't do a darn thing to help with Pastor. The man that's been good to you all of your life, who loves you even though you don't care about him, or anyone else, but yourself," Audrey accused as she moved closer to Frankie.

"Don't try to turn this around and put the blame on me. It's your fault that I'm the way I am," Frankie lashed out. For the first time in a long time, Frankie cried. "I'm sick of you and your fakeness, Audrey. You want everybody to think that you're so good. Well, you're not. You're nothing but a phony and I hate you." The venomous words spewed from her mouth like a geyser.

"Don't you talk to Mother like that. What's wrong with you?" Stiles' jaws flexed and he pointed angrily at Frankie

Pastor slowly rolled up in his scooter to the entrance of his study and grunted. Everyone turned around.

"Now look what you've done. You've gotten Pastor all upset," Audrey accused Frankie and pointed her finger inches away from her face.

Rena wanted to disappear, to get away from the madness and what she knew was about to happen.

"Pastor doesn't know the half of it." Frankie looked at Pastor.

Pastor slowly forced words to come forward. "I . . ." he struggled to form the words with his mouth. "I."

Audrey went to her husband and kneeled down beside him. "Don't try to talk, Pastor. Everything is all right. We just had a minor disagreement."

Pastor continued with his struggle. "I . . . know." he paused and tried to regain the wind that had gone out of him. "I . . . heard."

Rena grabbed her chest when she realized what he said. As if on automatic cruise control her head diverted in the direction of Frankie.

"You know? You heard?" Audrey asked. "Honey, I know you heard us arguing, but believe me, sweetheart, everything is fine."

Pastor appeared agitated. His grunts escalated. Stiles moved closer to his father like a realm of protection.

"Pastor, Mother is right. Everything is fine. Right everybody?" he asked looking at Frankie, Audrey, and Rena.

They each answered, "Yes."

Pastor slowly raised his left arm. "I heard," he said again, "Fran, Rena."

Audrey turned her head and looked over her shoulder at Rena. "What on earth is he talking about?"

Frankie stepped up in front of Pastor then glared over her shoulder at Rena. "Are you ready to tell my brotha the truth?"

"The truth? The truth about what?" Stiles focused his eyes on his wife.

Frankie spoke out again, and looked vehemently at Rena, "That you were involved with someone else before you married him? Someone that you were in love with?"

Stiles' jaw tightened, and he gnashed his teeth. He looked at his sister for the first time with disdain. He turned his fuming, questioning gaze toward Rena. "What is she talking about?"

Rena walked up and took hold of her husband's arm.

"Stiles, now is not the time. We'll talk when we get home."

He jerked away from her and Rena quickly moved back. "No, I want to know what Frankie is talking about. And I want to know now." Stiles shot her a cold look and yelled. His voice echoed throughout the house.

"Stiles, I was young and naïve." Rena looked at Frankie and at that moment she hated her.

"Why do you keep looking at her, Rena? Tell me," he replied with contempt that forbade any further argument. He moved in closer to Rena.

He was frightening her. She'd never seen Stiles behave in such a manner.

"We were best friends, Stiles. Two young kids who didn't know what we were doing. One thing led to another and, and, it kept on happening over and over again."

"Yeah, Stiles, over and over again up until you moved back to Memphis," Frankie added.

"Who was it, Rena? Who were you in love with?" Audrey paused in thought and suddenly put two and two together. "Oh, my, Lord, no. How could you?" Audrey snapped. "You, of all people, I trusted," Audrey told Rena. "I thought you loved my son."

"I did. I mean, I do love him," Rena cried while Frankie enjoyed the scene. Pastor trembled slightly in his scooter.

"Mother, be quiet. I want to hear what Rena has to say," ordered Stiles.

Audrey crouched like a scared child and positioned herself behind Pastor's scooter.

"I said, who was it that you were in love with?"

Again, Rena's eyes fell on Frankie. This time Stiles noticed the lingering look in Rena's eyes, and the knowing look in Frankie's.

"Nooo," Stiles yelled, the words moved in slow motion. "My sister? You were having an affair with Francesca?"

Audrey was stunned. A tear streamed down Pastor's face. Rena held her head down.

"Tell me this isn't happening," Stiles cried.

Walking hastily to where Rena stood, Audrey screamed, "How could you? How could you do this? You're, you're no better than, than her," Audrey hollered, while pointing at Frankie.

Rena almost fell to the floor as Audrey's hand went hard across her face. Warm liquid oozed down the side of her mouth, and Rena tasted her own blood.

"You deceitful little tramp," Audrey yelled and went for her again. Stiles grabbed Audrey's hand before she could land another blow.

"You . . . "Stiles cried out. Then he focused on Frankie. "And you, my own sister. How could you do something like this? Wasn't it enough for you to live your sick life around Mother and Pastor? Wasn't it enough that your homosexual acts were a mockery to everything that our father taught us without you having to bring Rena into your twisted, maniacal world?"

"Don't you stand there and try to make me out to be the bad one. I'm tired of it all," Frankie yelled even louder. Stomping her feet and moving toward Audrey, she continued yelling at the top of her voice. "This is your fault. Your fault," screamed Frankie as particles of spit sprayed over Audrey's face. Next she lifted a nail stubbed finger, and pointed it at Audrey like it was jagged edged knife.

"Get out of my face, you lying little wench," Audrey commanded. "Stiles, you better get your sister before I do something drastic to her."

"Noooo," Pastor managed to say and tried desperately to raise his weakened hand in protest.

"Ohhh, yes, Daddy, I'm afraid it's time you know everything." Frankie retorted. "Let me tell you about your sweet Audrey because you don't know half the story. You see, Pastor," Frankie released everything that she had kept bottled up inside of her since she was a child. "First Lady Audrey here knew; she knew all along. Didn't you, Mommie Dearest?" Frankie asked sarcastically, her voice flamed and belligerent.

"What did she know? What is she talking about, Mother?" asked Stiles. His brows were furrowed in a show of confusion.

"I'm talking about Fonda, that's who, Stiles. Cousin Fonda. When I was just a girl, she molested me."

"Shut up! You shut up right now," Audrey cried out.

"Are you satisfied? Are you?" Frankie screamed.

"You're a liar," Audrey yelled. "And you know it. Get her out of here." Audrey flailed her hands and head back and forth and from side to side, like she was having convulsions.

Rena wiped another trickle of blood from her lip with the back of her hand, but what she heard hurt more than any slap ever could.

"That's what you want people to think. You want everybody to believe that I'm a bad seed. Maybe I am, but at least I don't pretend to be anybody but who I am. But you," Frankie pointed an outstretched arm and finger at her mother. "You're the real liar; the real deceiver in all of this," she accused. "You knew all along what Fonda did, and you did nothing about it. When I told you how she hurt me, you did nothing, nothing to stop her. You blamed me instead. You said I was fast and hot in the pants. All these years I carried this guilt around inside of me alone. I never said a word to you," Frankie screamed at Audrey, and tears trickled down her face. "But I wasn't fast or hot, mother. I didn't want Fonda to do those things to me. I was a child. I was only a child," Frankie repeated, her face turned red and loud sobs pelted from her belly. The stream of hot tears ran down her face-mixing with snot.

By this time, Rena was sobbing too and Pastor's hands shook uncontrollably. Stiles' eyes had gotten large and his frame was as still as a department store mannequin.

"It wasn't enough that Fonda did what she did to me, but you had to go and make me feel dirty and nasty, Audrey. Then years later, it happened again when Minister Travis came to Holy Rock. Some youth minister he was," mocked Frankie. "Why do you think he's in prison for the next thirty years? It sho ain't for preachin' the word! He's a daggone freakin' pedophile!" screamed Frankie. An uncontrollable rage filled her spirit and at that moment she hated every one of them. "Yea, the great youth minister raped me! Did you know that too, mother? I wouldn't be surprised if you paid him to go away."

Pastor swayed in the scooter like he was about to fall out of it.

"Raped you?" barked Stiles. "My God, why didn't you tell somebody? Anybody?" he asked with questioning eyes.

"Why you ungrateful, disgusting little tramp. Don't you see everybody, she's lying." Audrey looked at everyone in the room, searching for someone to stand with her against Frankie's vicious attack, but no one said a word. "She always has wanted somebody to feel sorry for her. You're going to burn in hell for this, Francesca Graham. Mark my words."

"Oh, shut up. Your words don't mean a thing to me, Mother. If I go to hell, you'll be right there beside me," Frankie shot back.

"Stop it!" Stiles hollered and walked over to his sister.

He tried to hold her and comfort her, but she moved away from the grasp of his arms.

Rena rested against the arm of the sofa chair, trying to keep from passing out. Too much was happening. "Oh, my God. Frankie, I didn't know. Why didn't you tell me?" Rena asked with pleading grief-stricken eyes.

Frankie looked at Pastor, but ignored Rena. "I used to believe that you were the one who I could count on to be there for me, Pastor. The one that I hoped really loved me. But you believed everything Audrey said. Did she tell you about Fonda, Pastor? Did she?" Frankie continued to sob and tremble.

Pastor moved his head from side to side like he was trying hard to process what was going on around him. But Frankie could imagine what her father was thinking. His perfect family was falling apart right before his tear-stained eyes, and there was literally nothing he could do or say about it. Her eyes shifted from Pastor and settled on Stiles.

"And you, dear brother. You were always wrapped up in yoself. You didn't have time to see what was going on inside this so-called Christian home," Frankie continued. "You couldn't see what was goin' on right in front of your own eyes. Why do ya think Rena was takin' care of me every time I was locked up? Huh? Why do you think we wuz always together and that no matter what, she was the one that had to tell y'all where I was? Duh?" Frankie chuckled wickedly and pointed her finger on the side of her head.

Stiles remained motionless. Frankie knew her brother. His mind, like a computer, more than likely was trying to gather everything she'd just said about Fonda, Minister Travis, and his precious Rena.

Limping slowly, and with what resembled a mask of

hatred on her face, Frankie made her way to Rena. "And you," she said vilely, standing face to face with Rena. "I used to believe you were my friend, but you turned out to be no betta than her." Frankie pointed to Audrey with her eyes. "Wantin' folks to think you so much. You deceived my brotha. You tricked him into believing that you were so pure, so holy, when all the time you just as nasty as me."

Stiles couldn't take any more. He couldn't stay inside the house one minute longer. He turned and rushed out of the room. Stiles spotted Clarence, one of his friends from back in the day, driving down Pepper Oaks just as he had bolted out of the house. The timing couldn't have been more perfect. Clarence slowed down to say hello to Stiles, whom he hadn't seen in close to a year. As soon as Stiles made it to Clarence's car, he asked Clarence to give him a ride home. Clarence looked over his shoulder and saw Stiles' car sitting in the Graham's driveway.

"Everything all right, man?" questioned Clarence.

"Naw, everything is jacked up. But I can't talk about it right now. You know. I just need to get to the crib. I'll give you some gas money." Stiles reached inside his pants pocket and retrieved his wallet.

Shoving his hand in Stiles' direction, Clarence answered, "I'm not worried about gas money. I'm worried about you. But I won't press the issue. If you need a ride home, a ride home is what you'll get. No problem." Clarence made a U-turn in the street and sped off.

"Stiles, wait," Rena bellowed. She was no match for his athletic swiftness. All she heard was the sound of the front door closing so hard it could have popped off of its hinges.

She turned around and started searching nervously for

her purse. Frankie and Audrey became enthralled in another yelling match.

"Stop . . . it," Pastor stammered.

"Get out of here." Audrey angrily demanded of Rena.

Rena ignored Audrey and walked over to Frankie. "You talk about me not being a friend to you. Well you're the lowest of the lowest. How could you hurt your family like this? How could you be so cruel and evil? You could have told me about your cousin and about Minister Travis. I was your friend, and I would have tried to help you. But you never gave me a chance. You used me, Frankie. You were the one who pretended to care about me. You're the one who pretended like you were my friend and that you loved me. But you're just as big a phony as me. I admit what I did was wrong. It was down right terrible, and I'm ashamed of myself. I'm ashamed of me and you. But you, I feel sorry for you, Frankie." Rena turned and walked out, and left Frankie, Audrey, and Pastor to face the demons that had taken up residence at 3290 Pepper Oaks.

Outside, in the driveway, Rena fumbled through her purse in search of her keys to Stiles' car. After she found them, she drove up and down through the streets of Emerald Estates in search of Stiles. *How could he have disappeared so quickly when his car is still here? Lord, why? Why is all this happening? And how can I tell Stiles that not only have I been involved with another woman, but I have a disease too?* Rena drove through the neighborhood for twenty minutes before she gave up and headed home.

Thanks to Clarence, Stiles was at home. His mind was going in circles. He went into the kitchen, and then in a daze, started back to the bedroom. "God, what just happened back there? How could my life take such a deadly turn in a matter of seconds?" Stiles raised both hands toward the bedroom ceiling. "What do you want from me? What am I supposed to do now?" Stiles cried out loud to God. Hitting the bed with his fists, he grabbed the pillows off of the perfectly made king-sized bed and threw them against the wall. A soft thud followed. Next, he yanked the spread off of the bed. Like a madman, Stiles swiped his hands across the dresser and in one swoop everything crashed to the floor. Falling on his knees, he placed his head in his hands and pleaded for God's mercy.

Rena walked inside of the house and suddenly encountered coldness like she'd never experienced before. Stiles was here; she could feel him. Hair stood up on the back of her neck, and she shivered. Slowly, and cautiously she walked toward the bedroom and met up with the glare of his bloodshot eyes. Her eyes scanned the trashed room and a knot formed in the base of her throat. For a moment, she said nothing, and then she reached her hand out toward him. Stiles jerked away from her grasp.

"Don't you even think of touching me. You make me sick to my stomach. It's all clear to me now. Everything about you, and then you have the audacity to judge my sister? Now I know why you couldn't stand for me to make love to you. All the time making up one excuse after another one."

"Stiles, please. Listen to me. It wasn't like that. I wanted to tell you. I wanted to tell you so badly, but I didn't know how. What happened between me and Frankie was a long time ago. It's you I love. You have to believe me."

"Believe you? Why would I believe anything you have to say? You proved that you're just as much a liar as Frankie, and Audrey too, for that matter. Did you know that Francesca had been molested? Did you?" he demanded as he drew in closer to her face.

Tilting her head back in fear, Rena answered, "No, I didn't know anything about that. Frankie never told me."

"I can't believe this crap. I can't. And Pastor heard you and Frankie talking about this? That's why he had the stroke, isn't it? Because of you two sick . . ." Stiles threw his hands up and folded his lips before the words he wanted so badly to call her burst forth.

Rena's eyes grew as large as baseballs. She didn't know what to say because as bad as she hated to face it, Stiles was telling the truth. It was her and Frankie's fault. Pastor had heard them and it was too much for him to take.

"Didn't you hear me?" Stiles continued hollering. "It's your fault that my father almost died! Yours and Frankie's. I have to get away from you. I can't stand the sight of you."

Stiles abruptly turned, pounced into their closet, and began pulling clothes off the hangers. He reached above his head on the top shelf of the closet and grabbed a piece of his luggage. Throwing his clothes into it, he shoved past Rena and stepped over the mess he'd made, before he stopped in front of the chest of drawers. He yanked out underwear and socks.

"Stiles, don't do this. We need to talk. Please, I need to tell you everything."

Without missing a beat, Stiles continued stuffing the suitcase. "There's nothing else you can tell me, Rena. You've already managed to destroy my life. What else could you possibly have to say?" He didn't turn to look at her.

"I haven't been exactly truthful about the reason I wouldn't let you well, you know, make love to me."

This time Stiles did stop and turn around. With a white T-shirt in hand, he looked at her. Her hair was crumpled. Her cheeks were red, and her eyes were puffy.

"Why would you want to explain the reason for something that I already know? I just said it, or didn't you hear me? Maybe you were too busy trying to make me feel sorry for what you did to me." He huffed and hit his chest. "But come on, give it a shot. Let's hear what else you have to say, Rena."

"Stiles, it's important that you know I never meant to hurt you. I love you. I love you with all of my heart and soul. You deserve to know all of the truth, not part of it." Shaking, she moved to the bed and sat down. There was no way she could remain standing for what she was about confess.

Stiles stood in the same place, next to the chest of drawers, in total silence.

"I didn't . . . I couldn't let you make love to me." Again, Rena's head dropped in shame. "I couldn't because," she paused as a knot formed in her throat. "Because I contracted an STD from Frankie." Hot, fresh tears spouted.

With one step, Stiles was standing over her. "What did you just say?

Rena repeated herself with fear in her eyes and in her spirit.

"An STD?" He flipped his hands up in the air and twirled around, his head tilted back until his body had made a 360 degree turn. Looking at Rena again, with balled fists, he tried to hold back the fury that demanded to be set free. "What kind of STD?" he asked between clenched teeth.

Slowly, as if in slow motion, Rena raised her head. "Genital herpes."

Stiles' head began to swim. The pulse in his temples pounded like a heart beating against his chest. Sweat popped out on his forehead, and his tightened fists tightened even more. Without warning, a sickening, growling type of laugh emanated from his throat.

Rena leaned back, afraid of what Stiles was about to do. Crawling across the bed, she tried to escape from his reach, but his long arms grabbed her by her ankles and pulled her back toward him. He violently jerked her and she flipped on her back to face his wrath. Tears pounded her face. His tears, not hers. Rena braced herself when she saw the rage in his eyes and the perfectly formed fist coming toward her.

Stiles towered on top of her with an anger he'd never experienced before in his life. An inch from her face, his hand was stilled by a power greater than his own, and he jumped up off of his wife.

Rena hopped off the bed, rushed inside of the bathroom, and locked the door behind her. Shaking, she slid down the cold ceramic tiled wall and cried.

Stiles stepped over the partially packed suitcase and stormed out of the bedroom without it. He grabbed his keys off of the kitchen countertop, bolted outside, and climbed into his car. His rage had frightened even him. He drove along Berry Hill Drive until he was out of their neighborhood. Blinded by confusion, anger, and hurt, Stiles drove and didn't stop until he reached the church.

When he pulled into Pastor's personal parking space, Stiles was greeted by the building engineer.

"Pastor Stiles, what are you doing back here so late? Did you forget something?"

"No, I need to spend some time with just me and the Lord, so don't bother about me. I'm going to be here a while."

"Sure. I'm about to lock up then. How is Pastor's recuperation coming along?"

"He's faring better. God is able, you know," Stiles told him with little enthusiasm in his normally confident voice.

"That's good. Tell him I asked about him, if you will, and that I'm keeping him in my prayers."

"Sure, I'll let him know."

"Thank you, Pastor Stiles. Well, I'm going to get out of your way. I'll see you tomorrow, if it's the Lord's will." The engineer tilted his baseball cap at Stiles and walked off in the direction of his Dodge Ram.

Once inside his study, Stiles sat in his father's chair. He saw the open Bible on the side bar of his father's desk and picked it up. It was open to the third chapter of James, a chapter Pastor had preached from many times. Not understanding why, Stiles read it to himself.

"Not many of you should presume to be teachers, my brothers, because you know that we who teach will be judged more strictly. We all stumble in many ways. If anyone is never at fault in what he says, he is a perfect man, able to keep his whole body in check. When we put bits into the mouths of horses to make them obey us, we can turn the whole animal . . . Who is wise and understanding among you? Let him show it by his good life, by deeds done in the humility that comes from wisdom. But if you harbor bitter envy and selfish ambition in your hearts, do not boast about it or deny the truth. Such wisdom does not come down from heaven but is earthly, unspiritual, of the devil. Or where you have envy and selfish ambition, there you find disorder and every evil practice. But the wisdom that comes from heaven is first of all pure; then peace-loving, considerate, submissive, full of mercy and good fruit, impartial and sincere. Peacemakers who sow in peace raise a harvest of righteousness."

Clasping his hands together, Stiles looked up. "Father, what are you trying to tell me? That I should forget about everything that my sister and my wife have done and said? You want me to forgive them and pretend like it never happened? I don't understand, Lord. I'm your servant, but this time, Lord, I need some time. I'm not strong enough. I'm not like Pastor. My wife and sister just confessed that they've been having a homosexual love affair. I can't just let that go."

This wasn't how his life was supposed to be. He had given his all to do the work of God. He'd gone to school, studied religion, knew the Bible like the back of his hand, prayed every day several times a day, married who he thought was the perfect girl, but where had it all gotten him? More tears came. The sound of his sobbing echoed off the hollow walls. When the flow of tears stopped, Stiles leaned back, still trying to make sense of everything that had happened, but his mind and spirit were too tired. He folded his arms together on the cherry oak desk and used them as a pillow. Sleep replaced his scattered thoughts and messed up life.

28

*"There's no place like home, there's no place like home, there's
no place like home."*
—*Wizard of Oz*

Rena eased out of the bathroom with a measure of caution. She searched around the cluttered room until she found the cordless phone. With shaky fingers, Rena dialed the only number that could give her comfort.

"Hello," the mild-mannered voice on the other end said.

Rena didn't say anything.

"Hello," the voice repeated. "Rena, is that you?"

With careful words, Rena responded. "Yes, it's me, Mother. I need you."

"Honey, what is it? What's going on?"

"I can't tell you over the phone. I just need to come home. But I don't want you to tell Poppa anything."

"You're frightening me, child. Where's Stiles?"

"He's not here. Mother, so much has happened. I've ruined my life, and I've ruined Stiles' life."

"Honey, now you listen to me. You do what you have to do, but I want you to get here as soon as you can. You hear me?"

"Yes. I'm going to see if I can get on the next flight to Andover."

"You do that, baby. You do that right now."

"One more thing, Mother." Rena rubbed the back of her neck and twisted her head to relieve the mounting tension.

"What is it, honey?"

"I don't want to come to the house. I'm going to book a hotel, and I want you to come to where I am."

"Rena, I can't lie to your father. Anyway, what could be so bad that you can't come home, I mean to the house?"

"Trust me, Mother. Please, if you never trust me again, I need you to trust me now and do this for me."

"Honey, if this is what you want, then I'll do it." Meryl Jackson soon agreed. "But, I tell you this, Rena, whatever's going on, your father is going to have to be told, sooner or later."

"It'll have to be later, Ma. Much later," responded Rena in a drawl. "I'll call and let you know my flight. Bye."

Meryl hung up the phone and began to pray immediately. "Lord, whatever is going on sounds serious. So serious, father, that my child feels the need to come home. Lord, whatever it is, fix it. Work it out. Bring her here safely, Father, and help me not to be anxious and worried."

Back at the Graham household, Audrey placed Pastor in his bed. The afternoon's events had proven too much for him. His agitation showed with each word that he tried to force from his lips. Dribbles of drool, not words, burst forth.

Audrey gave him a Xanax to calm him down. She

stood beside his bed, and watched as he struggled to swallow the pill, Audrey wished she could take one of the pills herself; anything to help drown out everything that had transpired. Instead, she sat down in the chair next to the window, rested her head against the back of it, and stared blankly. It didn't take long for Pastor to drift off to sleep. She stood quietly, so as not to awaken him, left the bedroom, and closed the door behind her. She couldn't wait to march straight to Frankie's room. Audrey didn't bother to knock; she barged inside.

Frankie was propped up by several pillows on the bed, with the remote in her hand.

"How could I give birth to a child so wicked?" asked Audrey, with eyes that blazed like fire.

Frankie, lying back on her bed, eased upright and used the head post for support.

"Spare me your antics, Mother. And you call me wicked? Have you ever thought that you gave birth to someone just like you?" Frankie yelled.

"Why, you good-for-nothing," Audrey reached out to hit Frankie, but the reflex in Frankie's good arm reacted in time before the palm of Audrey's hand reached its intended target.

"Don't you dare try to make this my fault." She continued holding Audrey's arm with as much strength as she could muster. "All of my adult life, I've kept quiet about what Fonda did to me. I didn't say a word about you and the way you flippantly dismissed what happened. Don't you realize how much that hurt? Not just physically, but you helped to mess me up emotionally. It saddens me to know that my mother cares more about what other people might say or think than about her own daughter." Frankie's voice this time was not harsh. Rather, she sounded almost like a little girl in pain. She slowly released her tight grip on Audrey's arm.

Throwing her hand again toward Frankie, Audrey exhaled, not moved by Frankie's words. "You've always been an exaggerator. Where you get your wild thoughts from, I don't know. But I do know that what I saw that night when I walked in on you and Fonda was not molestation. You weren't crying or trying to get away from her. You were the one on top of her when I walked in that room."

"You walked in the room? You saw what she did to me?"

Audrey was stunned. Raising her hands to her mouth, she tried to think of what she'd just blurted out.

"Fonda told me that you knew, and she said that you wouldn't do anything about it. Oh, my God. She was right. How could you not do anything? How could you let her hurt me?" Frankie became hysterical. "I hate you!" she screamed.

"Because, it was your fault, Francesca. That's why. Fonda told me all about it. You were the one who did all of those things you accused her of doing. If anyone should be scarred, it should be Fonda." Audrey pointed with anger dripping from her lips.

"I was a little girl, Mother! What part of that don't you understand? Fonda made me do those things. I hated her. I prayed to God every night for her to die. I just wanted the pain to stop." This time Frankie's voice raised a notch. "How many times do I have to tell you that? Fonda threatened to kill me if I told anyone. She said that she would make you and Pastor believe that I was bad and that I was a child of the devil. What else was I to do?" This time, Frankie began to cry.

"You should have come to me. That's what you should have done." Audrey folded her arms and stood defiantly.

"I did come to you, but you never told me that you saw what happened. You never told me that Fonda had already blamed me. I was a scared child. I didn't want Fonda to kill you or Pastor."

"Don't be ridiculous. Fonda would do no such thing. You've been on drugs far too long. They've definitely burned your brain cells."

"I'm not going to let you get away this time, Mother. Say what you want to say, but you know I'm telling you the truth." Frankie's tightened jaw line flexed with each word. "After Fonda kept molesting me, I knew I had to tell you. Pastor was at church the night I came to you. I remember I cried so hard that night, and I prayed that Fonda wouldn't do anything to you, Pastor, or Stiles. But when I told you what she did to me, you slapped me so hard that I fell on the floor and bruised my leg, and your handprint stayed on my face for hours. You said that I was nothing but a fast little girl, and that I was lying on Fonda. You told me never to mention anything like that to you again."

Audrey's eyes bored into Frankie, but she said nothing.

"After that night, you made me stay in my room after school every day for a month. I couldn't get off punishment until I admitted that I was lying. That's what you told me, and that's how it happened. You know it, and I know it. Tell me something. How could you believe Fonda over me? And when Pastor Travis did the same thing to me, I had no one to turn to, Momma. He raped me. I was a virgin, Momma!" Frankie sobbed.

"Oh, please. I don't want to hear any more of this, Francesca." Audrey waved her hand at Frankie and began to turn around to leave.

"Don't you dare leave out of here, or I'll go and tell Poppa so fast, it'll make the weave on your head spin," Frankie threatened. "Do you hear me? That so-called man of God raped me. He's in jail right this minute for doing to someone else what he did to me."

"If he's in jail, why haven't we heard about it, Francesca?" Audrey folded her arms and tapped her foot nervously.

"Don't play with me, you do know. You sure didn't act surprised when I told y'all earlier. But I don't have to prove anything to you anymore, Audrey. You and no one else can change what happened. I couldn't tell Pastor, and you already warned me never to come to you again. I didn't want Pastor to look at me and be disgraced. I didn't want the church to look at him differently because of me. So I didn't say a word to anyone about Minister Travis. There was no one there for me, Mother. No one." Frankie wiped her face with the back of her hand. She refused to cry any longer.

Audrey shuffled from one foot to the other. "Child, you missed your calling. Do you know that? You should be on somebody's movie screen. How dare you accuse Minister Travis of such a disgusting act? You don't know when to stop, Francesca. You always have to make a mountain out of a mole hill." Pointing her manicured finger at her daughter, Audrey continued her slanderous attack. "God don't like ugly. Minister Travis was a kind soul. The young people loved him, including you, as I recall. What happened? He wouldn't fall for your advances so you thought you'd fabricate some tall tale about him too? Thank God you had the sense not to spread that lie."

Frankie listened at the words that spewed from Audrey's mouth. The more Audrey talked, the harder Frankie's heart grew. With each word, Frankie became numb until there was no feeling in her spirit whatsoever.

"You need to be on your knees begging God to forgive you, girl. If you don't, you're going straight to hell for sure." Audrey stared at Frankie for a few moments without saying anything, then she swiftly turned around and walked out of Frankie's room. Before Frankie could release a sigh, Audrey returned.

"I want you out of here." Audrey spoke with an eerie calmness. "I want you out of this house now." She disappeared down the hallway. Fluffing her hair, Audrey added, "And let me remind you, I haven't worn weave in months," Audrey chided and slammed Frankie's door.

Frankie wiped away her tears. She picked up her cell phone and dialed. "You got a ride?"

"I can get one."

"Well, get one. I need to get out of here, and I need to get out now. When you get here, knock on the door because I need you to come in and help me get my stuff together."

"You moving out?"

"Yeah, you better believe it. Now hurry up."

Frankie slammed the phone back on its base after speaking with Kansas. She searched for her duffle bag. As quickly as her mangled body would move, she gathered her small array of personal items and stuffed them inside. *No more tears. Don't you dare shed another tear. When you leave this time, don't look back, and don't ever come back. 3290 Pepper Oaks and everything it was supposed to stand for is a thing of the past.* Patiently waiting for Kansas, Frankie sat on the bed, looking around the room. If only for a short time it had held pleasant memories, but it was now filled with nothing but skeletal remains.

29

"Love does not begin and end the way we seem to think it does."
—*James Baldwin*

"Mom, I found a flight, but it doesn't leave until tomorrow morning at six."

"All right. But I wish you would tell me what's going on. I've been worried sick every since you called this evening," Meryl told her.

"Mother, all I can tell you is that I've done something shameful. I don't even know how I'm going to tell you . . . or Poppa, for that matter. But I will tell you this much, my marriage is probably over, and I don't want you to be mad at Stiles. I'm to blame and no one else."

"We'll talk when you get here. But I won't accept what you're saying. There's more to whatever is going on and I intend to find out about it all. Do you understand, Rena?"

"Yes, I understand, Mother." *I just hope you will.* "I'll call you when I get there. I'll be checking into the Holiday Inn off I-93. You know the one on the Andover South Shore."

"I'll find it. I'll see you tomorrow, sweetheart."

"Mom, please, remember what I told you."

"I know. I won't say a thing to your father." Meryl promised again. "Now you get your things packed and then try to get you some sleep, okay?"

"Okay, Momma."

"And, sweetheart?"

"Yes, Momma?"

"No matter what it is, I want you to know that I love you. You hold on to that. I love you, and God loves you even more. You hear me?"

"Yes. I hear you." Rena slowly hung up the phone. *If only I could believe that God really does love me after the mess I've made of my life.*

The sun had set when Stiles returned home to find Rena curled up in a knot asleep with her clothes still on. Standing at the entrance of their bedroom, he watched her sleeping. How could a woman so beautiful, so perfect, be so wrong for him? Stiles lingered for a few more minutes then walked away to the guest bedroom.

He stripped down to his Joe boxers, not bothering to shower. Not only was his body exhausted, but his mind and spirit were heavy, and he felt absolutely drained. On bended knees, he prayed. He felt the tug of the Holy Spirit saying, *Trust in the Lord with all of your heart, Stiles. Lean not unto your own understanding. In all your ways acknowledge me, and I will direct your path.* After confessing his fears and weaknesses to God again, he pulled back the Tiffany Jacquard comforter, slipped between the sheets and quickly succumbed to the call of sleep.

Rena awoke to find her husband's side of the bed empty. Lying on her back, Rena rubbed her eyes and thought of how much had happened to her marriage. How things had quickly changed. It was true—up one minute, down the next. The noise startled her from her thoughts. Lying as still as she possibly could, she listened. When she heard the familiar snore, she realized that Stiles was home.

Rena climbed out of bed and eased down the hallway. The door to the guest bedroom was ajar, and she could see her husband sleeping soundly. He didn't snore often, but whenever he did, it was usually because he was exhausted both mentally and physically. No doubt, today had been one such day.

Rena returned to her room. How was she going to leave Stiles? What would she say to him? Maybe he would be glad to see her go away. He had said she made him sick and he didn't want her in his sight. And to see Stiles become so angry to the point of almost physically abusing her, sent a wave of chills down Rena's spine. Pulling the covers up around her neck, she stared again at the ceiling. She wondered if Frankie was satisfied now that everyone knew their dirty little family secrets. *One day you're going to see the error of your ways, Francesca Graham. And when you do, you'll be sorry. Oh, so sorry.*

"Is this everything?" asked Kansas as she lifted the stuffed duffle bag onto her shoulder.

"Yeah, all that I care to take. Now, let's get out of here."

As they walked out of Frankie's room, she instructed Kansas to go outside to the car. At first, Kansas hesitated, but then did as she was told.

Frankie stood still, holding herself steady until she made up her mind about what she was getting ready to do. Looking back down the hallway, she slowly turned, limping in the direction of Pastor and Audrey's room. As she neared the door, she reached for the handle but stopped just as she heard Audrey's voice.

"Lord, you know the evil that's been lurking around this house for a long time. Father, I'm praying that right now, you remove every ungodly presence from 3290

Pepper Oaks. God, you are not a God of confusion. And as much as I would like for things to be different around here, they're not. Not as long as my daughter is being ruled by the devil. So Father in heaven, please . . ."

Frankie refused to listen to Audrey's prayers anymore. She would have to say good bye to Pastor some other time. But as for now, it was time to leave and never look back.

Early the next morning, Stiles confronted Rena when he saw her carrying her suitcase into the kitchen. He had been up since three o'clock, unable to sleep. Sipping a cup of decaf, he cocked his head to the side as she walked in like a frightened kitten.

"You leaving?" he asked her without much expression.

"For a few days. I think it's the best thing to do right now."

"The best thing for whom? You?"

"No, Stiles. The best thing for the both of us. I've admitted that I was wrong." Rena said apologetically.

"Wrong? You are more than wrong, Rena. It's not that simple. You can't wipe away what you've done by leaving for a few days," Stiles said, snapping his finger. "Life isn't like that."

"For goodness sakes, you're a man of God, Stiles. What do you have to say about forgiveness?"

"Don't you turn the scriptures back on me. I know all about forgiveness. I believe in forgiveness. And I also believe that the just shall live by faith. I had faith in not only God, but in you, Rena. I had faith enough that I was willing to wait until you were more comfortable for me to make love to you, not knowing it wasn't me you wanted—it was my sister. I forgave you time and time again when you pushed me away. Then when you did reach out to me, I believed once more that you really loved me. Now you want to put what you've done all on me by throwing God up in my face, when you put my very life in danger and deceived me?" Stiles grew angrier as he talked.

"I am not throwing God up in your face. That's not what I'm doing at all. I'm asking you to forgive me, Stiles. And I always wanted to make love with you. But I couldn't because of the love I have for you."

"Sooo, that's supposed to make me feel better. It doesn't, Rena, because it doesn't change what you are and who you are."

"If you would just listen to everything I have to say, then maybe you could at least think about forgiving me."

"You want me to forgive you and act as if nothing has happened? I'm a man of God, that much is true. But that's all I am—a man. A man who has been called by God to preach His word. But I'm frail, and I'm weak, and I'm made up of flesh just like you, in case you forgot. That's why I have to pray a little harder and a little longer for the strength to forgive you, and my sister. That's about as honest as I can be."

Rena forced the tears to stay back. She sucked in a deep breath. "I'm going to Andover for a few days."

"Why, so you can make your folks believe that I'm the bad guy in all of this?" snarled Stiles.

"No, I'm going to get away; to give us some space. My father has no idea that I'm even coming home. I told my mother, and I'm going to be staying at a hotel while I'm there."

"What do you want me to say?"

"I don't want you to say anything. Not a thing." Rena repositioned the luggage in her hand and walked toward the garage. "I'm parking my car at the airport."

"Do whatever you have to do. And you're right; we don't need to be in the same house together. If you

weren't leaving, I sure as heck would be out of here myself. So as for now, I don't see how we can remain together as husband and wife. You've not only engaged in
a sinful, homosexual lifestyle with my sister, but you've
acquired an STD that you may have passed on to me.
This is a little too much to ingest, don't you think, Rena?"

"It is. But now you see why I couldn't let you make
love to me."

"Oh, I beg to differ, because you did let me make love
to you. Whether it was one time or three, it doesn't matter. You willingly kept your disease and your relationship a secret. Now you want me to believe that you love
me?" Shooing her away, he threw up his hands in her direction. "Yeah, you need to go. Hurry up and leave."

Rena walked into the garage and closed the door behind her. Stiles stood at the kitchen island. A lone tear caressed his high cheekbone.

Rena listened as the boarding agent called her flight
number. Walking down the airport boarding area, she realized the magnitude of being untruthful, and it hurt her
to the core of her heart. With each step that took her far-
ther away from Stiles, her feet felt heavier. There was no
future for her in Memphis anymore, or so it seemed. She
hadn't bothered to call Mr. Bolden to tell him she wouldn't
be in for the next few days. At the moment, she didn't
care. Let him fire her. It didn't matter anymore; nothing
did.

30

*"Only those who will risk going too far can possibly find out
how far one can go."*
—*T. S. Elliott.*

Pastor wrestled with the bevy of thoughts that flooded
his mind since everything had exploded last Sunday.
Audrey, his sweet Audrey. Were the things Francesca accused Audrey of really true, or were they another way of
hurting her mother? What he had heard the day of his
stroke was more than he could stand. Francesca and his
daughter-in-law engaged in a secret homosexual affair?
The very thought of everything that happened wounded
him deeply.

*God I thought I raised God-fearing children who understood
the deadly consequences of sin. Francesca has lost her way,
Lord, and I feel like I'm to blame. Your servant, called by you to
send forth your Word and I couldn't even keep my own household from crumbling. Now my tongue is bound, and I can't say
what I'm thinking. Is this a form of chastisement, Father?*

With unsteady hands, he reached over to the bedside
desk where his Bible lay. Fumbling through one of the
many passages he'd come to love, he turned to the first
chapter of Romans. The people the Apostle Paul wrote
about in Romans had turned away from God. They knew

God but yet refused to thank him and acknowledge him. Pastor read word for word, until his eyes rested on verse twenty-six. The tears that he'd held back now overflowed. He read verse twenty-six for a second time before completing the rest of the chapter. *Lord, heal this family. Heal my child, Father God. Heal us all.*

Stiles considered asking Rena for a divorce when she returned. On one hand he wanted out of the marriage, but what would the people of Holy Rock think of him? They wouldn't know the details of what had happened between him and Rena, so they would form their own opinions. He was contemplating whether to stay in the marriage for the church's sake or get out of it, for his own sake. Stiles understood all too well the ramifications he would face if he divorced Rena. He needed to talk to Pastor. There had to be a way for Pastor to tell him how he felt about the situation.

Stiles informed the church secretary that he would be away for a couple of hours. He didn't waste any time driving to Emerald Estates. He jogged up the walkway. After ringing the doorbell, no answer, he used his own key to the house. When he walked in, the house was unusually quiet. Stiles didn't see or hear Audrey anywhere as he perused the house like a skilled detective. He stood in front of their bedroom and tapped lightly. No answer. He reached for the brass doorknob, slowly opened the door, and stole a peak inside. Pastor was asleep with his Bible on top of his sunken chest. Approaching his bed, Stiles reached down and touched his father's wrinkled, cool hand, and Pastor opened his eyes. He smiled when he saw Stiles.

"Hello, Pastor. How are you feeling this afternoon?" Stiles walked around the other side of the bed and cracked the wooden blinds.

Pastor mouthed the word, "Son."

"Pastor, I need to talk to you. Do you feel up to it?"

Pastor nodded.

Moving the Bible from his chest, Stiles placed it on the table next to Pastor where it would still be within his reach; then he helped him sit upright in the bed. It had been a long time since they had one of their father-son talks. The stroke had stripped away so much from Pastor, but when he sat in the chair next to him, the rush of memories about those times hit Stiles head on, and he smiled.

It didn't bother Stiles that he had to do most of the talking, while Pastor responded whenever he could with short answers or nodded according to whether he agreed or disagreed.

Pastor knew what he wanted to tell his son but his aggravation over not being able to do so was etched in the deep frowns that traveled along his withered face. *God, maybe you want my tongue stilled. That way Stiles and the rest of the family can't run to me for my Godly advice. They have to go directly to the source, which is you, heavenly Father. And as for me, you're the only one who I can talk to without saying a word. Thank you, Lord.* The very thought of God's awesome power overjoyed Pastor. His hands twitched and tears streamed down his aging face.

Stiles misread his father's reaction, and quickly apologized. "I'm sorry. I didn't mean to upset you." Stiles paused like he was in deep thought. "My spirit tells me that I need to pray and listen for God's direction in all of this."

Relieved that Stiles' spirit had connected with God's, Pastor formed his mouth to speak. He managed, after some time, to say, "That is right."

"You've been here for me whenever I've needed you. You raised me like I was your own flesh and blood, and

I'm so grateful to God for having a stepfather like you. I wish there was some way I could repay you for all you've done." He took hold of his father's hand and massaged it between his strong ones.

"Daddy, I love you." He and Pastor both could count on one hand the times Stiles had referred to him as "Daddy." It felt awkward calling him "Daddy" like he was disrespecting Pastor in some small way, but at the same time, it seemed so right. Stiles hugged his father, and the tears of the two men meshed.

"Pastor, I'm going to leave now. You've helped me more than you can imagine. I'm going back to church. I don't want you to worry, everything is fine. I promise to come by Sunday and take you to church."

Pastor nodded his approval.

Stiles suddenly remembered to ask about Audrey. "Where is Mother? I know she can't be far," Stiles chuckled. "That woman doesn't want to leave you for a second."

Pastor's eyes shifted toward the table where his Bible lay. "Store."

Stiles saw the blue sticky note on the table and picked it up. "Says here that she went to Walgreen's to pick up your prescription. She'll be back in thirty minutes." Stiles looked at his watch. "In that case, she should be here in a minute or two. I'll hang around until she gets back."

Turning onto Pepper Oaks, Audrey spotted Stiles' car in their driveway. No way could she avoid him today. It was time for her to face the music. She still found it hard to believe that Francesca accused her of being a terrible mother. She would never allow her daughter or Stiles to be abused or molested and not do anything about it.

Turning off the ignition, Audrey sat in the car for a while. *Sometimes I think that girl should have been an actress for real. She always wants people to believe the worst things about me every since I saw through her lies that night. My God, that was such a long time ago. I can't believe she's trying to use that against me. All I told her was the truth when she came to me with all that mess. Little girl, my tail. Lord you know she's always been more than a handful. I still can't believe she blames me for her irresponsible behavior. I've always tried to be a good mother. She's just full of anger because I saw through her even back then.* Audrey shook her head back and forth. *And Minister Travis, that is such a debauchery; accusing that poor man of molestation. Why would he want to do anything to her when he had a gorgeous wife at home?* She popped out of her daydream, gathered Pastor's medication, and went inside.

"Pastor, I'm back," Audrey said in a loud voice. Placing the items on the kitchen counter, she walked back to the bedroom. Stiles met her at the bedroom door.

With a stiff countenance about her, she spoke. "Hello, Son."

"Hi, Mother."

Walking past him, she went directly to Pastor's bedside, bent over, and kissed him on his lips. "Honey, are you all right?"

"Yes." answered Pastor.

"Mother, he's fine. We had a nice visit," Stiles stated.

"That's good," Audrey replied without enthusiasm.

"Since you're back, I guess I'll head back to the church."

Audrey jerked her head around. "Don't leave on my account." Her voice rang with coldness.

"I didn't mean it like that, Mother. I told Pastor that I would stay here until you came back. We had a good visit, but now that you're back, I really do need to leave. I have a couple of meetings later this afternoon. I told Pastor that I would pick him up Sunday for church."

"We'll see. It depends on how he's feeling. I don't want him to tire himself out. Anyway, I can get him to church if that's what he wants." Audrey shifted her attention back in the direction of Pastor. "Pastor, you know whatever you want to do, I'll help you to do it. You don't have to worry, Stiles," she said to him lovingly and gently stroked the side of his wrinkled face.

Stiles watched the tenderness his mother bestowed on Pastor. How could someone who could act so cold and callous toward her own daughter be so loving, kind, and compassionate toward her husband?

"I'm going to walk Stiles to the door, sweetheart. While I'm up front, I'll fix us some vanilla wafers and bologna. It's almost time for *Judge Mathis*, you know." Audrey patted him on his leg. The couple watched *Judge Mathis* five days a week. Every day, right before it was time for his show, Audrey prepared a snack for the both of them before she crawled in their king-sized bed and snuggled next to him.

In the kitchen, she asked Stiles about Rena. "Where's your wife?"

"Andover. She went to visit her parents."

"Have you decided what you're going to do? You know that what she's done is unforgivable. The girl deceived you. My own daughter-in-law, how disgusting," Audrey blasted.

"I don't know what I'm going to do."

Audrey changed from evasive and cool to calm and compassionate. She walked over to her son and gathered his face between her cottony soft hands.

"Listen to me, son. Believe me when I tell you that your sister is nothing but a liar. Everything she said about me, about Fonda and Minister Travis—all of it is fabricated in her sin-sick mind. And Rena. Well, Rena has proven to be just as bad as Francesca, because she flat out deceived all of us. I would expect something like this from Francesca, but never Rena. I think she married you so she could hide behind you and your spotless reputation." Removing her hands from his face, Audrey reached for his right hand, lifted it up to her lips and gently kissed it. "Stiles, honey, I love you, and I don't want anything or anyone to ever hurt you like that girl has done. Do you hear me?"

"Yes, I hear you, and I love you too." Stiles returned his mother's affection by embracing her in a tight squeeze and kissing her on top of her coiffed hair.

"Now, look, I have to get back to church. I'll call and check on you and Pastor later."

"You do that. You're such a wonderful man. With God's help we're going to get past this."

Closing the door behind him, Audrey went about preparing the cookies and bologna. The clock on the microwave indicated that she had less than ten minutes before *Judge Mathis.* She hurried about her business, humming and singing a song by Hezekiah Walker that Pastor loved . . . *Grateful, grateful, grateful, grateful . . . gratefulness.*

31

"Oh what a tangled web we weave, when first we
practice to deceive!"
—Sir W. Scott

"Rena, you will have been here a week tomorrow. It's time you went home to face your problems."

"Momma, I don't think I can. Stiles hasn't tried to call me, and when I call him, if he answers, he tells me he doesn't want to talk, so it's obvious that he doesn't want me there."

"You have to clear up a lot of things, Rena, and you can't do it by hiding away in a hotel room here in Andover. What you confessed to me, I must say that I am quite upset by it all. But I'm your mother, Rena. Nothing can ever change that. I love you, and no matter what you've done, and regardless of all the mistakes you've made, I will always love you. Nothing can ever change that."

Rena moved from the sofa in the hotel suite and walked over to where her mother sat on the side of the double bed. She sat down beside Meryl and laid her head against her mother's shoulder.

"Thank you for being the best mother in the world.

Not once have you judged me harshly. You haven't made me feel ashamed or anything."

"Listen to what you're saying, child. Think about it. If I can love you no matter what you've done, who you are, or where you've been, can't you see that God can and does too? I've always told you that God loves you more than you can ever begin to imagine. He loves you unconditionally. Not like Audrey, or Stiles, or even Francesca. That kind of love is based on what you do and who you are and how you make this person feel or that person feel. But God, yes, but God," Meryl said with a joyful spirit. "God loves you, and me, and the Grahams, no matter what. Even in the midst of your act of homosexuality. It sounds terrible I know, but it's nothing that God won't forgive you for. He wants you to give it all to Him, sweetheart." Rubbing her daughter's hair, Meryl hugged her and then kissed her on the forehead.

Rena lifted her head from her mother's shoulder. Only silence separated them.

"It's time? What are you talking about, Momma?"

"It's time you go home and face your problems."

Rena collected her bags from baggage claim and struck out for her car. It took almost ten minutes for her to get to the short-term parking area. Part of her was anxious and excited about returning home, but she didn't know what to expect from Stiles.

Rena was overcome with emotion the moment she walked inside. So much had changed in so little time. How could she forget the past and the things that lay behind like the Bible said when the past had resurrected itself back into her life? Shuffling through the house, Rena carried her bags to the bedroom and began to unpack. Once she completed that task, she watered her plants that were droopy from lack of nourishment. She performed several other small tasks in the house that Stiles had neglected and then ran herself a warm bath. The plane ride had been exhausting. She decided to take a nap; it felt good to be home and in her own bed.

Stiles was surprised when he opened the garage and saw Rena's car. "I didn't know you were coming home today. But then again, why would I?" He asked out loud.

He walked through the house and discovered Rena curled up in the bed. She was asleep.

The jolt against the bed as he passed by woke her and she saw Stiles going into their walk-in closet. Clearing the sleep from her eyes, she watched his lean physique. She lay quietly while he searched for an outfit. Their eyes connected when he walked out of the closet.

"So, you decided to come back, huh?"

"Yeah, I did."

"Okay, so what now?"

"That's what I hoped we could talk about, Stiles. I know one thing; we can't go on like this."

"While you were gone, I thought the best thing would be to see a lawyer about a divorce."

Rena's pulse beat rapidly.

"But I thought about it some more and I recognized that I have a responsibility to more than myself." He pointed a finger at his chest. "I have a moral responsibility to God. As bad as I may want to call it quits, I don't believe it's God's will, at least not now." He stood at the foot of the bed, arms folded.

Rena sat up. "Stiles, don't stay with me because you don't want to look bad before the church."

"Like I said, I have a responsibility, and I'm going to do what God has called me to do. My suggestion is for us to remain married. I'll move my things in the guest room.

You won't have to be bothered with me. All I ask is that you refrain from disgracing me and yourself further."

Rena's voice was sharp. "What's that supposed to mean?"

"It means," he quickly spoke up, "that you're not to run to my sister's bed anymore, Rena. As long as I'm in that pulpit, I'm demanding for you to act like the woman God expects you to be. Outside of these doors, I expect you to carry yourself in a morally correct way. Stand by my side as my wife," he said in a harsh raw voice. "Inside these doors, I don't expect you to do anything for me, and you surely don't have to worry your pretty little head about me asking you for sex."

Rena sat on the bed surrounded by sheer terror at the thought of her future. "As much as I dislike your demands on my life, I agree that we should stay married. I'll walk the walk, talk the talk, and play the role, if that's what God wants me to do. The last thing I want to do is embarrass you, your family, and the church." She took a deep breath punctuated with several even gasps. "So, I'm willing to live with your decision. But I promise you this, somehow, I'm going to prove to you, Stiles, that I've changed and that I'm worthy of being Mrs. Graham, in every way."

Rena returned to work, thankful to Mr. Bolden for standing up on her behalf.

Mr. Bolden hugged her when she walked in. "How are you, Rena?"

Rena returned his hug. "Things are better." Without going into details she explained that she had to deal with some serious family issues.

He listened to Rena, without reservation. Since she was one of his best librarians, he was eager to have her back. "I'm glad you're back, Rena. This place has been a mad house. In one week alone, we've had forty-one tours. Can you believe that?"

"My goodness, that's phenomenal. Seems like I'll be too busy to think about my problems."

"I couldn't agree more. Plus, you know I'm here for you. Any time you need a shoulder, I've got one for you."

"Mr. Bolden, thank you for everything."

"Sure. Now come on," he jokingly snapped his fingers at Rena and chuckled. "No more messing off. It's time to get some work done around this place."

Sunday morning arrived way too soon for Rena. Standing in front of the full-length mirror in the master bath, she surveyed her less than perfect body. It was almost show time and she had to put on her game face. Her choice of a flutter-sleeved charcoal dress with an empire bottom made her look sweet and sophisticated. Accented with the perfect pair of earrings and shoes, Rena dabbed perfume behind each ear, the base of her throat and on her wrists.

From the sound coming from the front of the house rather than the guest room, Rena gathered that Stiles was more than likely up and dressed already. Sucking in a deep breath, she nervously walked out of the room and up the hall.

"Good morning," she greeted as she entered the kitchen.

Sipping on decaf from his favorite mug, he barely acknowledged her presence. "Are you ready?"

"Yes."

He finally looked at her. "I think we should keep our same routine. You drive your car, and I'll drive mine. I won't be home right after church. I want to visit some of our sick and shut-in."

"Sure." Rena eased past him. With her purse and keys

in hand, she opened the garage door and walked to her car.

Stiles followed suit, pausing long enough for her to maneuver out of the two-car garage before doing the same.

Rena drove along East Shelby Drive with her radio tuned to Hallelujah FM 95.7, listening to her favorite radio personality, Christie Taylor, play one gospel hit after another. One of her favorite songs by the Clark Sisters was interrupted by her cell phone. The ring tone let her know it was Stiles calling. *What does he want?*

"Hello."

"I forgot to let you know that I'm going to swing by Emerald Estates and pick up Pastor."

"Oh, that's good. I didn't know he was strong enough to get out."

"God is able, Rena. Pastor is a man of faith. He expects to be healed."

"I'll see you at church." Rena abruptly ended the call, barely able to contain her irritation. He acted like she was a stranger who didn't know anything about Pastor. She turned the corner and accelerated, going at least ten miles above speed limit.

Hands went up and shouts of praise filled the sanctuary when Stiles wheeled Pastor up the aisle of the sanctuary. A broad smile enveloped Pastor's face and the first lady beamed with pride as she walked next to her husband and Stiles.

Rena turned and watched as the three of them made their way down front. Two of the deacons and close friends of Pastor and Audrey helped him to the pulpit. The church roared even louder with praise and thanksgiving.

Audrey went directly to the section reserved for the pastor's family. Judging from the glow on Audrey's face and the kiss and hug she gave Rena when she sat next to her, there was probably no one who imagined that Audrey despised her son's wife.

Rena played her part well too, by smiling and greeting her mother-in-law. The order of service followed. The choir sang Pastor's favorite song, "Grateful," and he almost bopped out of the pulpit chair. Tears streamed down his face, his hands flew up in total praise, and from his crooked mouth came, "Hallelujah, I'm grateful. I'm so grateful, Lord, God."

Stiles walked to the podium with an air of confidence. "The power of the Most High God is definitely in this place today." Stiles repeated himself in a stronger tone. "I said, the power of the Most High God is definitely in this place today." His lofty frame was supported by his size twelve's as he rose up on his toes. Like Pastor, his hands stretched out and upward, and his head reared back in reverence to God. "This is a day that the Lord God has made. We will rejoice and be glad in it. Aren't you glad this morning, church?"

"Amen, Praise God, and Hallelujah" reverberated off the walls of the church building.

Stiles turned sideways and looked at his father. "Don't tell me what God can't do," he shouted. "Don't tell me that my God is not a healer. Don't tell me that there's anything too hard for my God."

Audrey bounced up from her seat. "Thank you, Lord. Thank, you, Lord," she shouted, with hands tucked behind her back and her head jerking back and forth so hard that her First Lady's designer hat almost popped off.

Rena clapped her hands but inside her heart she felt totally different. *Hypocrites*, she thought when she looked at Audrey and Stiles. *Praising God, while all the time treating me like I'm the daughter of Judas Iscariot.*

At the close of service, Rena dashed out so she could

avoid being detained by any of the members. She didn't feel like faking the funk. Leaving church, she wasn't ready to face an empty, gloomy house, not just yet. She drove in the direction of Cordova. *I think I'll do a little window shopping, maybe even treat myself to a new dress.* She went to Wolfchase Galleria and parked on the end near Macy's. For the next hour, she window shopped, and just like she hoped, being away from dissension soothed her.

Rena walked in the direction of one of the mall restaurants, when she heard her stomach growl. Just two stores from the restaurant, she was pulled by the sight of a sailor-blue square neck knit dress in the window at New York and Company, and stopped to look.

"Excuse me," a woman who was standing next to her said. "Don't I know you? You look awfully familiar.

Rena studied the woman. "You look familiar too. Do you live in Whitehaven?"

"No."

"Where do you work?" the stranger asked.

"Benjamin Hooks Library."

"I haven't been there, so that can't be it. I guess you just have one of those familiar faces," the lady grinned.

Rena extended her hand, "I'm Rena Graham," she said and the two of them shook hands.

"Graham? Hmmm. You wouldn't happen to be any kin to Patricia Graham, would you?"

"Patricia Graham?" Rena crinkled her eyes in thought. "Come to think of it, my husband has a cousin named Patricia."

"What's his name?"

"Stiles and he has a sister too. Her name is Francesca Graham."

"That's it," the woman's voice rose in surprise. "I don't know if you remember, but I used to come with Patricia to some of the Grahams' family functions, although it's been some time ago. Patricia and I were co-workers and friends. We both worked for the *Commercial Appeal*. My name is Teary Fullalove. Well, it's Teary Runsome now," the young woman blushed.

"Yea, that's right. I remember you now. It has been a long time. Didn't you get married or something and moved out of town?"

"Yes. I live in Colorado with my husband and kids. I'm here for a few days to finalize some things, and then I'm on my way back, and I can't wait either," Teary beamed with happiness.

"That's great." Rena hoped her envy stirring inside of her didn't show.

"Thank you. Now, tell me, what's your name?"

"It's Rena." The two ladies walked slowly as they engaged in conversation.

Listen," Rena said, and stopped in her tracks. "I was on my way to get something to eat. I don't know if you know this but Stiles is a pastor now. He's visiting some of the sick and shut-in this afternoon, so I thought I would come to the mall for a while."

"Oh, yeah, right. I keep forgetting that Stiles is a minister too. I didn't know he had gotten married."

"Yeah, he's the associate pastor at his father's church, Holy Rock. Did you know that his father had a stroke?"

"No, I don't have a chance to talk to Patricia that much since I moved. She doesn't know that I'm in Memphis. I planned on taking care of my business as quickly as possible and then flying back home. How is he?"

"He's improving. He was at church today, which is a miracle in itself."

"God is good like that. He's definitely worked miracles in my life."

"Hey, would you like to join me for lunch? I could use the company," Rena offered.

"Sure. I was going to grab something and take it back to the hotel, but I'd love to sit down and eat somewhere."

Rena and Teary left the mall and dined at J. Alexander's. The two ladies, who had never really known each other personally, enjoyed one another's company. Other than Francesca, Rena never had any other close women friends.

It felt good to be able to laugh and talk freely. In some ways, she imagined that many thought she lived a sheltered, reserved life, particularly the women at Holy Rock. Maybe they were right. Talking to Teary was a breath of fresh air.

They sat at J. Alexander's for well over an hour and a half before Teary announced she needed to get back to her hotel.

"Rena, it was nice seeing you again. I had a great time."

"The same here, Teary. I hope you have a safe trip."

"Thanks. And you be sure to take care of yourself. Oh, let me give you my card." Teary reached inside her purse and flipped through its contents until she ran across her business card holder. Opening the silver card holder, she pushed a card toward Rena. "Listen, I have to go. I need to go back to the hotel and pack. My flight leaves at seven. Feel free to give me a call sometime if you'd like to talk."

"I'll do that. Well, take care of yourself, Teary. It was nice seeing you again."

The ladies embraced before they parted ways: Teary to her perfect world, Rena to her nightmare.

32

"Look in the mirror. The face that pins you with its double gaze reveals a chastening secret."
—Diane Ackerman

The speech therapist worked with Pastor tirelessly over the months. Although he still slurred his words, Pastor was able to speak clearly enough for most people to understand. Physical therapy had been just as good because he no longer relied on a wheelchair, but could ambulate with the aid of a quad cane and a leg brace. Still unable to drive, Audrey, and sometimes Stiles, drove him wherever he needed and wanted to go. Pastor often asked to see Francesca, but was always told the same thing: no one knew where she was, and no one had heard from her.

"I want to see my daughter," Pastor told Stiles again, when Stiles had taken him for physical therapy.

"Pastor, I want to see her too, but how many times do I have to tell you, I don't know where she is."

"Rena?" His voice tremored.

Stiles looked at his father, somewhat confused. "Rena doesn't know where she is either, Pastor. I'm sorry."

Pastor's eyes grew large and liquid. "Th-they hurt my

Francesca," Pastor said slowly. The tensing of his jaw betrayed his deep frustration with speaking.

Stiles was caught off guard. Pulling into the driveway, he turned off the engine and met the pained look on Pastor's face. "But Audrey said Fonda didn't do anything to Frankie, and Minister Travis, well, he's not here to defend himself."

"Jail," he said.

Surprise siphoned the blood from Stiles' face. "Pastor, where is all of this coming from? You're going to get yourself all worked up. I don't know if Minister Travis is in jail, and Fonda, she's married with children. If these things happened, what can we do about it now?"

"Ask forgiveness . . ." his voice broke off in mid-sentence.

Pastor probably didn't realize the effect his words had on Stiles. It aroused old fears and suspicion so much that Stiles knew he had to find out the truth. "Father," he said after much thought. "I'm going to make you a promise right here and right now."

Pastor looked at his son with eyes that shimmered with a hope.

"I'm going to do what I can to find out what happened to Frankie." Stiles reached across the seat for his father's frail hands. "I don't know what the outcome will be, but whatever I find out, might tear this family even further apart. And if what she said about mother turns out to be true, we both have a lot to think about." A heaviness centered in his chest at the thought of what would be revealed.

"Thank you." A look of tired sadness passed over Pastor's face.

"Come on, let me take you inside," Stiles said. "It's been a long day. You need to get some rest, and I still have a class to teach this evening."

* * *

It was early evening when Stiles arrived home from the university. After his lecture, he dismissed the class early. It had been a long, exhausting, and eventful day. He sat in the car for a few minutes and thought back to what he promised Pastor, then went inside the house. The appealing aroma of soul food drifted through the air. His stomach growled in response. Rena was not in sight.

In the kitchen, Stiles saw that there were several pots on the stove. Walking over to where they were, he lifted the top off of one then another. Turnip greens, pot roast with gravy, fresh fried corn, corn bread muffins. What was Rena up to?

"Hello." He jerked his heard around when he heard her voice.

"Hey," you startled me. "Something I should know about?" he asked, pointing to the pots.

"Nope. I had a taste for a good home-cooked meal, that's all. You're welcome to eat," she offered. "That is, if you trust my cooking." Her words dripped with cynicism.

Stiles didn't address her smart comment. "I am hungry."

"Help yourself then." Rena turned and retreated to the den.

Stiles went to the guest bedroom, took a hot shower, put on his pajama pants and robe then went back to the kitchen to fix himself a plate.

With a plate of food in, he took off for the den. Rena was in there watching *Dancing With the Stars*. She had already fixed herself a plate of food and was obviously enjoying the taste of her own cooking.

Stiles thought of going back in the kitchen to eat alone, but decided against it. *No law against being civil. She's still my wife.* Sitting down in the chair across from her, he prayed and then hungrily dove into his food. "This is good."

"Thanks." Rena stood, picked up her almost empty plate and went into the kitchen. Moments later she returned. "You can put your plate in the sink when you finish. I'll clean the kitchen later," she said nonchalantly before she walked off.

Between bites, he replied. "No problem."

Rena went in the master bedroom and prepared to sleep alone, again. For some reason, her mind fell on Teary Runsome so she decided to give her a call.

When Teary answered, Rena was glad she made the call. Teary immediately made her feel better. They laughed and talked about some of everything. It was easy to talk to Teary, and Rena needed someone to confide in. Their conversation eventually became serious and when the subject of marriage and relationships came up, Rena admitted hers was falling apart.

"I understand more than you might think," Teary told her. "This is my second marriage and every day I feel like God gave me a second chance with Prodigal. But I didn't always feel this way, Rena."

"But Teary," Rena said. "Never in a million years would I have thought my life would turn out to be so disastrous. I'm in love with a man who no longer loves me, and it's my own fault. To make matters even worse, I don't know why I continue to remain in a lifeless marriage."

Teary readily identified with what Rena said. "Rena," Teary, said in exchange, "The things I could tell you about my first marriage would blow your mind. Like you, I was in love with a man who didn't love me. Looking back, I don't know if he ever did. It took years and I do mean years for me to let go of him. But God brought me through. I found the strength to move on, but only after he walked all over me and rushed to the arms of the woman he's married to now."

Listening to Teary helped Rena understand that she didn't deserve to be shunned by Stiles, Audrey, or anyone else. "Teary, but you're happily married with children, to a wonderful man, and I'm still miserable and stuck. I feel like I deserve everything that's happening in my life."

"Sometimes we can get ourselves in some mess," Teary chuckled lightly. "But girl, God can bring us out of the deepest of the deep. Yes, I'm happily married now. And one day, who knows, God is either going to fix the marriage you're in or he's going to give you the strength you need to let go and move on. If he wants someone else to come into your life after that, then fine. But you can't even think about that now. There's enough to deal with today without worrying about the future. I had to learn that the hard way," Teary confessed. "Pray, Rena. Ask God to show you what to do, and He will."

Rena felt more at peace after she finished talking to Teary. She knelt beside her bed and prayed. *Let the dishes wait.* She got in the bed and pulled the covers up to her waist.

Stiles took the liberty of cleaning the kitchen rather than leaving it for Rena. *She cooked a delicious meal. The least I can do is clean the kitchen.* He saw her door was closed when he passed by on his way to his room. Sitting at his desk, he turned on his laptop, signed into the university faculty page and pulled up the test he planned on giving his class at the end of the week. With that behind him, he proceeded to do some research on the name Travis Jones. His search revealed that there were literally tens of thousands of potential websites that had something about Travis Jones, but Stiles had to find the right one. For the next three hours he searched the Internet and his persistence paid off. He stumbled upon an old newspaper article from a couple of years ago that stunned him. The article was about the conviction of a young minister in Seattle sentenced to thirty years for the sexual assault of two young girls at a church where he was the youth minister. It was none other than Minister Travis Jones. Next Stiles went to the state jail's website and within seconds after putting in Travis D. Jones, his criminal record appeared with an icon of a camera next to it. Stiles' mouth dropped open when he clicked on the icon and an older, haggard, wild-haired version of the man who was once youth minister of Holy Rock appeared. He printed everything. Holding the printed sheets in hand, Stiles thought about Francesca. She was telling the truth. Stiles leaned forward in his chair, rubbed his hand over his face and sobbed.

He stood, went into the bathroom, and ran cold water on his face. Standing in front of the mirror he faced the man that stared back at him. "I'm sorry, Francesca. I'm sorry I wasn't there for you." Stiles cried like a baby before he lay prostrate on the bathroom floor and prayed to God. When he finally got in bed, he placed both hands behind his head. "Fonda, you're next," he said then turned on his side and went to sleep.

The six-and-a-half-hour drive to Chattanooga proved to be more than worth it for Stiles. When he called Fonda and told him he needed to talk to her, at first she was hesitant.

"What's it about?" she questioned.

"For one thing, shouldn't I get a better reception? Seems like you would want to see your cousin. It's been a few years, you know," said Stiles, hoping to hide the agitation in his voice.

"Of course, I'm glad to hear from you, but you know that growing up we were never close. You were always doing your thing," Fonda finally grinned into the receiver.

"True, but I really need to talk to you. And I need to do it in person."

"Sounds serious, so in that case, when do you plan on coming?"

"Today," he said.

"Today? Umm, okay, I guess that'll be fine. What time will you be leaving out?" she asked him.

He looked at his watch. "If I leave here in about an hour, I should make it there by two or three o'clock."

"All right." Fonda said hesitantly. "Do you need directions?"

"No, I've googled them already. I'll call you when I get there."

At 2:15, Stiles pulled up in front of a white house with blue shutters and a beautiful landscaped lawn. The wraparound porch added a sense of charm. He walked up the wooden steps and rang the doorbell. When she answered, Stiles recognized Fonda right away. Other than her hair being shorter and colored, and the scattered frown lines that surfaced when she greeted him, she looked practically the same.

"Oh my goodness, you are still Mr. Handsome," Fonda complimented.

"And you haven't changed a bit yourself," Stiles said before he hugged her.

"Come on in here. We have the house to ourselves. The kids won't be here until 4:30 and my husband, Marcus, usually gets here around six."

Stiles studied the house. It was nicely decorated and family pictures were everywhere. Fonda proudly showed him several pictures of Marcus and the kids.

"Would you like something to eat?" she offered. "I usually have finger sandwiches and snacks made for the kids when they get home. Marcus and I don't believe in them eating a lot of junk food."

"I understand. Finger sandwiches will be fine. I didn't stop to eat."

"Come on, let's go in the kitchen. We can talk in there."

Stiles followed her into the huge modern kitchen. She offered him a seat in the breakfast nook overlooking a spectacular backyard view. While she prepared mini ham and turkey sandwiches, he drank a glass of lemon iced tea. They exchanged small talk while Stiles ate.

"Thank you, Fonda. That was good," he said and picked up the napkin next to his plate to wipe his mouth.

"Tell me, what was so urgent that you had to drive up here today to talk to me, cousin? I can't help but be curious."

"Fonda." Suddenly his face went grim, and he raised his left hand, revealing his palm in an act of submission. "I'm not here to cause you any trouble; I just need you to tell me the truth."

"The truth?" her features remained deceptively composed. "The truth about what? I have no idea what you're talking about."

"About what happened between you and Francesca.

A look of discomfort crossed her face. "Francesca?" Fonda didn't deny that she knew what he meant. "Who dug that up after all these years?"

"Francesca. She even went so far as to tell us that my mother knew. Look, Fonda, I don't know how much you've heard over the years about my sister. But she's in pain, emotional torment, and if my mother has known about you and her all of these years, that makes matters worse."

Fidgeting in her chair, and licking her lips nervously,

she remained quiet for a moment, like she was trying to think of the words she wanted to say. "Stiles, we were kids. True enough," she spoke slowly, "I was a teenager, but I . . . didn't mean to harm her. I can't explain it. I guess I was going through my own mixture of emotional torment back then. I felt like I never quite fit in with my own family. I used to look at y'all as being the perfect family, and Francesca."

"Francesca, what?" he bent his head slightly forward.

"Francesca seemed like she had it all. I think back then I couldn't understand why her life seemed so perfect and mine wasn't. So I, I don't know, I just thought about how it would be to, you know," Fonda looked at him knowingly. "Experiment."

"Experiment! Fonda what on earth would make you do such a thing. She was a child. You were a teenager. Why couldn't you experiment," Stiles said and used his two fingers in a quote, "with someone your own age. God, I hate to say this, but if you felt such a need to experiment," he said with nasty emphasis, "it should have been with some teenage boy, not my twelve-year-old sister." He slammed the palm of his hand on the table and Fonda immediately jumped back in fear.

Stiles inhaled then exhaled. "I'm sorry. I didn't mean to do that. I just don't understand, is all. Did you tell Audrey? Did she know about this like Francesca said?" *God, please let her tell me no.*

Fonda nodded and Stiles dropped his head. "I told her after I saw her peeping in Francesca's bedroom. That night she saw us, I forced Francesca to do terrible things. I threatened to do something to her cat, Charlie, and to y'all too if she told anybody." Fonda eased her trembling hand toward his but he moved back and out of her reach. "Stiles, you don't know how many times I've regretted doing what I did. I've begged God for forgiveness. I've tried to be a model mother to my children. I felt guilty for such a long time. Stiles," Fonda pleaded, and tears cascaded down her cheeks. "I'm so sorry. Please, please forgive me." She sobbed this time, with her head in her hands.

Silence.

Stiles stood, walked to the other side of the table and laid his hand on her shoulder. Fonda lifted her head. A look of remorse and sadness covered her face. "Thank you, thank you for telling me the truth," he said.

Fonda stood in front of him. Stiles gently raised her tear streaked face until her eyes met his. "I'm a child of God; we both are. God forgave you a long time ago. It's time you forgave yourself." Stiles turned and left Fonda standing in the kitchen. He closed the door behind him and slowly walked to his car. Instead of leaving right away, he sat in the driveway, with his head against the steering wheel, and cried. He cried for his sister, for all the years of pain she had experienced; for the fear she must have felt from being violated and raped, but most of all he cried because they had a mother who had closed her eyes to it all.

33

Five months. Five months of not talking to her parents, her brother, or Rena. Five months of being down on her luck. Five months of living in holy torment—that's how Frankie described her life. Not only was her body jacked up, as she described it, from the accident, but for the past month and a half, she'd had at least five outbreaks; and as if that wasn't enough, she'd been feeling like crap for just as long. Her body ached, she was tired, depressed, listless, nauseated, and she was dealing with all of it at the same time.

Kansas entered the one-bedroom space they shared in Orange Mound. The place was actually a dump, but with sporadic income from Kansas' menial jobs and Frankie's food stamps, the women couldn't afford to complain.

"Dang, girl, when I left this mornin' you was in the bed and it's dang near five o'clock in the evening, and you still in the bed." Kansas commented coolly. "You need to see the doctor or something. It ain't like you to be lyin' round day afta day." Kansas pulled the worn brown comforter off the floor and spread it over Frankie.

"Yeah, I know. But I can't seem to muster up any energy. Maybe if I could get a part-time job or somethin' like you, I would feel better. Frankie pulled the comforter around her shoulders. "But I can't even think about cleaning some office building. This bum leg and arm of mine won't allow me to do hardly anything that's worth something."

"I don't know why you don't do like I told you and apply for disability. These food stamps ain't cuttin' it. And my penny-anny job definitely ain't hitting on nothing."

Frankie, pale and weak, threw the comforter back, got off the bed and moved to the shredded chair that was once a peach organza print recliner. Now all that remained of it were loose springs with cotton pieces peaking out.

"Tomorrow, I don't care whatcha say. You're going to get yoself checked. Maybe they can give you an antibiotic shot or something. Then you going to the Social Security Office and apply for your disability," insisted Kansas. "We could use that $600 a month they give if you get approved."

Too weak to protest, Frankie agreed.

The clinic, as everyone called it, was already packed with people when Frankie and Kansas walked in the following morning at seven o'clock. Kansas signed Frankie in at the front desk. They sat four hours before the stuck-up desk clerk called her name. A stocky, bearded man opened the heavy steel door for Frankie so she could go in the back to the clinic area. Just before the door closed completely, Frankie heard the same clerk call Kansas' name. Frankie turned and watched Kansas go to the window. *She didn't say nothin' about seeing the doctor too. Oh, well.* Frankie shrugged her shoulders and followed the nurse.

An appointment letter for Frankie arrived in the mail from the clinic eleven days after her visit. Sitting in the same old, dingy waiting room, Frankie wondered why she had been called to come back. The free meds she received had really made her feel better.

Too bad Kansas couldn't come with her today. She had been called to report to work early. After the long wait, first in the waiting room, and now in the patient room, the scrawny, scraggly haired doctor came in with her chart. Not bothering to speak, he opened the chart and began reading.

Should have already done that.

"Miss." He flipped the chart back over, in search of her name. "Miss Graham."

"That's me," Frankie flippantly remarked.

"As you know, we performed several tests during your last visit."

And? Get to the point.

"One of your tests came back positive for antibodies in your blood."

"Okay, and?" she remarked impatiently.

For the first time since entering the room, he looked at his patient.

"Not just any antibodies, I'm afraid. HIV antibodies."

Everything became blurry around her. *Did he say HIV?* She couldn't tell if she was falling or if her head was just spinning in motion.

Something latched onto her forearm and wouldn't let go. "Miss Graham. Miss Graham."

Slowly her eyesight came back into focus and the room stopped spinning. When it was all over, she was still sitting on the table. A nurse entered the room with a cold towel and placed it on her forehead.

"Are you all right, Miss Graham?" the doctor asked.

What do you think? "Yeah, I'm all right. But are you sure, doc? There has to be some kind of mix-up. You must have the wrong chart." Frankie leaned forward to read the name label on the chart.

"I'm afraid, everything is correct. I'm sorry."

Frankie shifted from hip to hip, hoping her constant movement would keep her from crying. "Can you tell me how long I've had it?"

"It's hard to pinpoint when a person acquires HIV. I can tell you that it takes some time for the body to develop HIV antibodies, but some people develop these antibodies within three months of being infected. For others, it can take as long as six months."

Frankie nervously chuckled. "This can't be happening. I already have herpes, and now you want to tell me that I'm HIV positive." Frankie extended her good arm out toward the doctor like she was pleading for help.

"Herpes can make the immune system even weaker, Miss Graham, which in turn can make you more susceptible to contracting HIV."

"This isn't real. It can't be," Frankie rebuffed in disbelief.

A gentler side of the doctor suddenly surfaced, and he sat down on the stool and began to patiently explain HIV.

"Look, Miss Graham." He gestured with his hands. "The important thing right now is to continue to get regular medical check-ups. I want to see you every three months. We need to watch you closely because of your herpes, which can be problematic for a person with HIV. You need to get plenty of rest, eat healthy, and if you smoke or do drugs, stop at once. Before you leave today, you'll get injections against Hepatitis B and bacterial pneumonia.

Taking out his prescription pad, he continued to talk. "I'm also going to start you on antiviral treatments and what we call, protease inhibitors. Take it as prescribed. It can help to slow down the progression of the disease.

Frankie sat deftly still as the doctor rattled on and on about what to do and what not to do.

On the bus ride home, her life replayed in her mind like a symphony band. So much wrong, so much hurt.

Frankie turned the key and glumly walked inside the sleazy apartment. Kansas was at home, and in the bed eating a bologna sandwich and drinking a soda.

"Where you been?" Kansas asked Frankie.

Frankie said nothing. Like a zombie, she walked over and sat down in the tore up chair. The springs boarded into her back but she didn't care.

Kansas watched her. "What's wrong with you?"

Shifting her teary eyes in the direction of Kansas, she tried to speak but nothing came out.

Kansas hopped off of the bed, and knelt down in front of Frankie. "What is it? What's got you crying?" Tenderness for the woman she loved was apparent on her face.

"One of my tests," Frankie could hardly speak, "came back positive."

"Frankie, what on earth are you talkin' bout?" Kansas' face was stricken with terror.

Frankie lifted her head and faced Kansas. What she was about to tell her could ruin her life and future too.

"I tested positive for *HIV*."

"You what?" Kansas jumped up. "*HIV?*" she yelled. Turning around with her head on her forehead, Kansas screamed. "You got *HIV?*" Kansas asked again to be sure she had heard right.

Kansas fell down on the filthy, worn carpet and cried. "I'm sorry. I'm so sorry. I didn't mean to do this to you. I didn't mean for this to happen."

Frankie stopped crying as quickly as she had started. "What are you talkin' about?"

Without any forewarning, Kansas picked up where Frankie left off and her tears flowed like the Nile River. "You gotta believe me when I tell you I didn't mean to give it to you. I didn't." Crawling on her knees, she stopped in front of Frankie and laid her head on Frankie's knees."

Frankie shoved Kansas away and stood up. "You, you did this to me? How? Why? Was this your sick way of tryin' to hold on to me? You knew all along that you had it and you didn't tell me, Kansas?" Frankie lashed out, and started striking Kansas repeatedly.

"No, I didn't know. I didn't mean to, Frankie. I swear I didn't." Kansas pitifully pleaded.

When she grew too exhausted to hit her anymore, Frankie stopped and started gathering the few items of clothing and toiletries she had. She walked out of the apartment with Kansas still begging and crying for her to stay. Without looking back, tuning the cries of Kansas out of her mind, Frankie stepped outside and into the unknown.

The tables had flipped over on Frankie once again. *No place to run. No place to hide. God, why do you hate me so much?*

34

*"Love is not enough. It must be the foundation, the
cornerstone—but not the complete structure. It is much
too pliable, too yielding."*
—Bette Davis

Thursday night Bible study was one of the few times
Stiles and Rena rode to church together. Their conversation was sporadic and proper. Tonight would be
different because Stiles made plans to settle things between himself and Rena once and for all.

Stiles turned on the lights inside the house, while Rena
lazily strolled back toward her bedroom. Her steps were
halted when he called her name.

"Rena, wait. We need to talk."

She blew through her lips. "Stiles, give me a break,
won't you? I'm tired of talking. I'm tired of listening to
you dictate my life and I refuse to argue with you anymore. I don't want to do anything but go to my room,
take a shower and go to bed."

"This isn't going to work."

"What isn't going to work now?" Rena stopped, inhaled then slowly exhaled.

"Us. I can't do this anymore. I've tried. I've prayed and
I've asked God to help me to move past all that's hap-

pened. But I just can't keep this up. I want a divorce, Rena."

"A divorce. I don't believe you, Stiles," Rena's voice began to shake. "Since when did God tell you, Mr. Man of God, to divorce your wife? And on what grounds?" her blurted loudly.

Stiles ignored the anger in her voice. "If you want me to go there, then I will. But I wouldn't have to tell you if you studied the word of God like you should. The word says that, "Marriage should be honored by all, and the marriage bed kept pure, for God will judge the adulterer and all the sexually immoral."

"The Bible also says, Pastor Graham," Rena spoke with nervousness and emphasis, "And be ye kind one to another, tenderhearted, forgiving one another, even as God for Christ's sake hath forgiven you. I thought we were going to try to work this out. I prayed that you would find it in your heart to forgive me and that we could start over."

"I do forgive you. But I can't be the husband I should be to you. It's time for me to admit that and to accept it. God has shown me that this marriage is done. You weren't the one for me, and that's my fault. I was caught up in you, the person, and didn't fully listen to God. When we go outside of His will and His way, God has a way to pull the reins back in on us. If you haven't asked him to, you should seek His forgiveness rather than concentrating on whether I forgive you or not. If I don't forgive you, that's between me and God." Stiles head went up in the air, evidently very pleased with himself.

"Don't you stand there and try to get all righteous and sanctimonious with me." This time Rena's voice rang out loud. "If you want out, fine with me. Enough is enough. There's no other way for me to prove how sorry I am for all that's happened between us. Let me ask you this though, Mr. Perfect." Rena's temper flared and she glared at him with burning reproachful eyes. "Haven't you ever made a mistake? Have you ever done something that you were sorry for? Said something you regretted?" She grew breathless with rage. "Answer me! Have you?"

"Yes, I have," admitted Stiles quietly. "But it didn't ruin any one's life. Don't get me wrong, I'm not trying to stand here and condemn you for what you've done. Believe it or not, I still love you, and I love my sister too. I didn't say anything about it to you before now, but I talked to Fonda and she admitted that everything Francesca said about what happened was true, unfortunately including how my mother treated her.

Rena placed her hands against her ears, like she was trying to drown out what Stiles said. "Stop your lying, you self-centered, selfish, arrogant son of a . . ." She pursed her lips before she said the unthinkable."

"It's true. As for Travis Jones, she was telling the truth about him too. But despite all of what she's gone through, it doesn't erase what happened between the two of you. It doesn't change the fact that you deceived me. And because of that, I can't have you as my wife."

"Oh, so what you're saying is that you had to go and investigate for yourself rather than believe the words of your own sister? It took someone else telling you the horror of what she went through. You know what, Stiles? Rena showed no sign of relenting. Sucking in her breath for a moment she glared at him. "You want to come out of this scotch free. Like you're so good and I'm so bad. I did wrong. How many times do I have to admit it? What Frankie and I did was wrong." Her voice escalated and both arms flew up in the air. "How many times must I be reminded of it? We committed sinful acts against God and against our own bodies. But you've committed your secret sins too. If you recall, you're no knight in shining armor yourself. Maybe you haven't slept with another man . . . I don't guess, who knows? But you've left your mark on many a woman in your day."

Stiles's jaw line jerked back and forth at the stone she'd thrown his way. Her words were vindictive and accusatory but true. At that moment, he felt his flesh taking over and he wanted to lunge out at her—he didn't. He stood still.

"Try to hurt me and attack me all you want, Rena. I'll pray for you.

Rena was on a roll and a flood of words kept spilling over. "That goes for Pastor, Audrey, and all of us. Nobody has lived a perfect life. Or don't you remember?" she continued angrily. "That's why God had to hang on that cross. For filthy sinners like you and me." Rena pointed to herself.

"I know the word of God, Rena." Stiles boldly met her eyes.

"Well act like it," she shouted, her voice becoming hoarse with frustration. "Stop being so darn hypocritical."

"Hypocritical?" He laughed out loud. "That's like the pot calling the kettle black, don't you think, when you're the biggest hypocrite of them all. You and that twisted-minded sister of mine. So, she was molested and raped. At some point, we have to move past the bad things that have happened in our lives, Rena, not wallow in them. Let me tell you what else I discovered recently. My sister is HIV positive! Do you know that, Rena? Oh, wait," Stiles said and palmed his own forehead. "What am I thinking? Of course you do. You probably are too. So who's the phony now?"

Rena swooned. Her mouth flew open.

"What do you have to say now?" Stiles retorted.

"Oh, my God. Oh, nooo," she screamed.

In between sobs, Rena's fury mounted again. "I'm not trying to make excuses for my actions. But I do know that sin is sin, Stiles. There's no little sin or big sin. All of it is the same. It leads to death and damnation. See, I know the Bible too, Pastor Stiles Graham," she chided. "I didn't know anything about Frankie having HIV. I feel sorry for her, for everything that she's had to endure, for people like you who are so darn condemning and judgmental toward her. I feel sorry for me too, but if it turns out that I have HIV too, then I'll pray for God to give me the strength to lean on Him. I'll pray that I won't be condescending and condemning like you and your self-righteous mother. You want a divorce? You've got it, baby! You're free to go on with your life, because," pointing a finger at Stiles, "I'm sure going to go on with mine." Rena promptly walked off. Sobbing, she ran down the hallway and into her bedroom. Slamming the door behind her, she threw herself across the bed and released a river of tears.

35

"You don't die from a broken heart—you only wish you did."
—*Unknown*

Frankie was ecstatic when she received notice that her disability benefits were approved. Through an advocacy agency for persons with disabilities, they helped her secure an affordable and accessible apartment in the small town of Newbern, Tennessee. It was far enough away from Memphis for Frankie to make a new start. With all that had happened in her life, she had a lot of soul searching to do. Living with HIV and genital herpes was a double death sentence for her, or so she believed.

Spending time with herself re-awakened an inner determination; she began to accept her illnesses and her physical challenges. Except for the one call she made to her family before leaving Memphis to tell them about her disease, Frankie cut off all ties with them. Stiles made it easier for Frankie to move on with her life, after he told her about his talk with Fonda. And now that he knew the truth about their mother too, Frankie determined he would have to deal with Audrey however he saw fit. As for Frankie, she hoped she could really let go of the past and start a new future.

Living alone, without contact with any of her old friends proved to be a big adjustment, but with each passing day, her life became easier. No more wild night partying, hanging out at clubs, or getting high. She still smoked cigarettes, but she'd managed to cut back on them too. Though her sexual preference had not changed, she had not been involved with a woman since moving to Newbern. She preferred, and rather enjoyed, the isolation and solitude, something she never liked before.

Lying in bed, she sometimes thought of Rena. Rena had stuck by her through thick and thin and Frankie told herself that she had no right to ruin the life of the one person she was sure once loved her. Thoughts of Pastor and his health invaded her thoughts too. How was he; did he miss her? As for Kansas, Frankie still had a hard time dealing with what she'd done. Yet, Frankie realized she and Kansas were alike in at least one way—they both had hurt people they cared about. As bad as Frankie would have liked to, there was no way she could turn back the hands of time and make things better. The flurry of life's events played over inside her mind like a scratched CD.

Turning on her side, she relived the moments when she was a happy, carefree young girl, before she was turned into damaged goods. The chain of tragic events that made her into the person she was today shook her and forced sobs to burst forth.

The love for God she had back then used to make her believe that she was someone special. "God, you promised that you would never leave me or forsake me. You promised that you would always love me. Tell me, Lord. What happened? Why did you turn away from me? Why has my life shipwrecked? I feel like a leper—cast aside, misused, misunderstood, broken, and beaten beyond repair." Francesca cried out to God like never before. When her eyes were swollen shut and her body was drained of tears, she slept peacefully for the first time in years.

Six days later, Frankie stepped outside of her apartment to retrieve her Sunday morning newspaper in the brisk mid-morning air. Closing her eyes, and taking a deep breath, she filled her lungs with the fresh air. Music coming from the complex's on-site church drifted past her ears. A larger church in the neighborhood held weekly Sunday morning and Wednesday evening worship services. Frankie stood on the porch and watched as a van filled with people drove in the complex on its way to the church within eyeshot of her apartment.

Some Sundays Frankie opened her window and listened to the music. A time or two she entertained the thought of going to see for herself what they were doing, but she dispelled that thought as quickly as it came to her. For some unexplainable reason, this particular Sunday morning proved to be different. Something drew her in the direction of the church and away from her apartment. She kept walking until she reached the entrance.

"Good morning," one of her neighbors said as they walked in front of her and opened the door to go inside.

Frankie responded politely. "Good morning."

"Are you coming inside?" the neighbor asked while holding the doors of the church open.

Frankie hesitated and then said, "Yes. I'm coming in."

"What can wipe away your sins?" the preacher asked and answered himself. "Nothing but the blood of Jesus. Someone in here needs the stench of sin wiped away from their life. Someone in here needs to know that God is a forgiving God." His voice escalated. "I tell you, someone in this very place needs to know that God is a habit breaker; that He is a healer and a deliverer. Someone, I tell you, needs to know that God is the God of second chances, third chances, and unlimited chances. Someone needs to know that God is a God of suddenty. He can suddenly turn your darkness into light. The God I serve can suddenly right your wrongs. He can suddenly save your sin-sick soul, and He can make a broken life whole. Oh, yes, God can."

The preacher stretched out his arms toward the gathering of people. "Come to, Jesus. All who are burdened and heavy-laden. He will give you rest. Surrender your all to Him. He will work it out."

From the back pew, Frankie listened to the preacher. At that moment, she felt like there was no one else around. He was speaking directly to her. She saw him. The spirit within that she had closed the door on so many years ago began to speak to her heart. She needed what she now had come to understand only God could give her—deliverance. Easing from her seat, she excused herself and moved past each person until she stood in the aisle. Walking slowly, limping and wounded in more than her physical body, she moved toward the front of the church and yielded her broken life and spirit to God.

36

"We must be willing to let go of the life we planned so as to have the life that is waiting for us."
—E. M. Forester

Mr. Bolden and Rena huddled in the corner of the library's meeting area.

"I hate to see you leave, Rena."

"I hate to leave behind dear friends like you too, Mr. Bolden. But it's time for me to step out and move forward. God has opened another door for me, and I'm going to walk through it."

"You're going to do great in Andover," he told her. "You'll be a great director at the new library up there."

"I hope so. Just a couple of months ago, right after my divorce was final; I couldn't imagine holding my head up ever again. I thought everyone hated me." Rena grinned. "Come to think about it, some people did hate me, and still do," she stated painfully. "But during these past months, I've learned how to stand up and be strong. I won't allow anyone to make me ashamed anymore."

"Good for you. You're a wonderful woman. You deserve good things in your life."

"Thank you, sir, and remember, we're going to keep in touch. Right?"

Mr. Bolden searched her face and saw peace and satisfaction there. "I wouldn't have it any other way. Come here." He embraced Rena. "May God bless you."

Rena said her final good-byes to her co-workers before she walked to her car. She opened the door and climbed inside, pausing for another minute to say good-bye to her past.

Driving along the stretch of highway, Rena prayed and asked God to guide her and direct her steps. She prayed for Frankie that wherever she was, that she was doing well and was safe. No more looking back; it was time to look forward to a new future, another chance and a closer relationship with the God who had loved her in spite of herself. With each twist and turn, each mile that led her further away from Memphis, Rena felt more confident, more at peace and full of joy. She was going home. Home to a new life, and a fresh beginning.

37

"People who are sensible about love are incapable of it."
—Douglas Yates

Audrey and several ladies from Holy Rock Women's Ministry met for their monthly luncheon meeting at Red Lobster in a private meeting room. Toward the end of the meeting, the ladies sat around and talked, rather they gossiped.

"First Lady, may I ask you something?" one of the ladies said.

"Certainly," Audrey replied.

"What really happened to your son's wife? It's like she disappeared off the face of the earth."

Audrey threw up one hand and waved it carelessly. "Honey, she left town after he divorced her. I tell you, it was the best thing she could have done. It was enough that she pretended to love my son, only to leave him heartbroken."

"I know she put him through a lot," another woman commented.

"Yes, I tell you, my son's wife was not all she pretended to be. All of the years I thought I knew that child and she turned out to be a deceitful little phony. And to think, we've known Rena and her family since they first moved to Memphis. Well, she sure had us fooled. Who would have thought that she was only using him? That's why you have to be careful these days."

A fair-skinned, older woman agreed with Audrey. "Yes, you sure have to be careful these days, First Lady."

This fueled Audrey's flame and she kept on talking. "You think you know somebody, and find out you don't know them at all."

"Lord, these women today are scandalous. I tell you, our men of God have to be *careful*," a short dark woman added.

"You're sure right," another commented. "We have to stay prayed up on their behalf."

"Is Pastor Stiles all right, First Lady, now that his divorce is final?"

"Yes, he'll be fine. Of course, the pain of divorce is something that takes time to heal. Even more so, for a man of God like my Stiles. He tried, but it was no way to mend their marriage. The girl was promiscuous, and she wasn't about to change. I tell you, I cried almost every night for months for my son. Thank God for Pastor; he keeps Pastor Stiles encouraged. And since he was appointed as the full-time pastor of Holy Rock, he doesn't have a lot of time to sit and feel sorry for himself."

The fair-skinned older woman was named Sister Jean. She readily agreed with Audrey. "Don't worry," she said and waved her hand. "He'll find another woman. That's for sure. A smart, intelligent, handsome man of God like him won't have a problem at all. This time, she'll be the kind of woman that will be worthy of being his wife and the First Lady of Holy Rock. We're going to keep praying that the next time he'll meet a fine Christian girl with true morals and respect. But we all know, that whoever it is, won't be half the First Lady you are, Sister Audrey."

Audrey blushed. "Thank you, Sister Jean."

"The truth is the truth." Sister Jean remarked and so did several of the other women were gathered in the room.

Audrey's face brightened like the morning sun. She was astonished at the sense of fulfillment she felt as she spoke. "I know one thing, whoever she is will have to be more than special. She's going to have to definitely prove that she's worthy if she ever plans on becoming, *my son's wife.*"

THE END

My Son's Wife—Readers' Guide

1. Why do you think Pastor Graham's family addresses him as "Pastor?"

2. What part, if any, does sexual molestation and abuse play in the way a person lives their life after having experienced such acts?

3. How do you feel about the relationship between Frankie and Rena when they were teenagers? When they became adults?

4. What do you think about the relationship between Pastor and Audrey? Do you believe she is a submissive spouse? Why or why not?

5. Do Christians and non-Christians alike frown on people who are different, especially those who practice homosexuality and lesbianism? Why? Are their beliefs justifiable? Why or why not?

6. Was Stiles justified in his reaction toward his sister? Toward Audrey? Toward Rena? Why or why not?

7. Why do you think Frankie held on to bitterness for so long?

8. Do you think Fonda suffered the consequences of what she did? How? Why Not?

9. How would you describe Audrey's personality?

10. Why did Audrey treat Francesca the way she did?

11. What do you think will happen to Stiles and Rena?

Words from the Author

Today we are bombarded with depravity of mind. Our people are dying not only physically, but spiritually as well. Something has to be done to stop the madness. Something has to be done to halt the senseless evil and hate that is spreading throughout our nation.

When I wrote *My Son's Wife*, it was not for the purpose of condemning or judging any group of people. It was, however, meant to show the destructive nature of sin. We become so caught up in what the next person is doing. Many of us go about pointing fingers at the next person without looking in the mirror and viewing our own faults. I hope that after reading *My Son's Wife*, that you will see the danger in condemnation of others and of yourself too. We all fall short in some shape, form, or fashion. But I am a believer that God is a deliverer. God is not a God of condemnation. He is a God of salvation, forgiveness and grace. His mercy endures forever. It never runs out!

In regard to acts of homosexuality and lesbianism, many so-called, uppity church folks don't want to read about it, or talk about it, unless it's in a judgmental way. They're quick to use the following words of God and twist it and make it work for their own advantage. The Bible does clearly address issues of homosexuality and lesbianism in the first chapter of Romans, starting with verse 18 and following (New International Version) However, these passages of scripture address much more. I've taken the liberty to underline some vital points throughout this passage that many Christians and religious people tend to conveniently leave off. *"The wrath of God is being revealed from heaven against all the godlessness and wickedness of men who suppress the truth by their wickedness, since what may be known about God is plain to them, because God has made it plain to them. For since the creation of the world God's invisible qualities—his eternal power and divine nature—have been clearly seen, being understood from what has been made, so that men are without excuse.*

For although they knew God, they neither glorified him as God nor gave thanks to him, but their thinking became futile and their foolish hearts were darkened. Although they claimed to be wise, they became fools and exchanged the glory of the immortal God for images made to look like mortal man and birds and animals and reptiles.

Therefore God gave them over in the sinful desires of their hearts to sexual impurity for the degrading of their bodies with one another. They exchanged the truth of God for a lie, and worshiped and served created things rather than the Creator— who is forever praised. Amen

Because of this, God gave them over to shameful lusts. Even their women exchanged natural relations for unnatural ones. In the same way the men also abandoned natural relations with women and were inflamed with lust for one another. Men committed indecent acts with other men, and received in themselves the due penalty for their perversion.

Furthermore, since they did not think it worthwhile to retain the knowledge of God, he gave them over to a depraved mind, to do what ought not to be done. They have become filled with every kind of wickedness, evil, greed and depravity. They are full of envy, murder, strife, deceit and malice. They are gossips, slanderers, God-haters, insolent, arrogant and boastful; they invent ways of doing evil; they disobey their parents; they are senseless, faithless, heartless, ruthless. Although they know God's righteous decree that those who do such things deserve

death, they not only continue to do these very things but also
approve of those who practice them."

So you see, Readers, God calls things like they are. We
all fall in one or more of these depraved ways of thinking. So what if you aren't a homosexual or a lesbian? If
you're a gossip, a slanderer, insolent, and faithless, you're
subject to the wrath of God too. If you don't believe me,
read the above passages of scripture in bold again.

Sometimes I believe we are so hard on those who practice homosexuality and lesbianism because it is something we can 'see.' It usually shows outwardly in a
person whereas, many of us practice secret sins; those
sins that nobody knows about. We lead double lives, and
keep our closets packed with skeletons.

The bottom line is that we should love one another, no
matter what our shortcomings are, no matter what our
choices are, no matter the color of our skin, our economic
status, no matter what our beliefs. Those, like myself,
who profess to be Christians, are supposed to love, to
welcome, to embrace, to draw all men, women, and children by displaying the same kind of unconditional love,
kindness and mercy of God. After all, I once was blind
but now I see, was lost but now I'm found. Who am I to
belittle any one when I am a sinner too, that just happens
to be saved by His grace.

Shelia E. Lipsey
shelialipsey@yahoo.com
www.shelialipsey.com

A Personal Invitation from the Author

If you have not made a decision to accept Jesus Christ as your personal Lord and Savior, God himself extends this invitation to you.

If you have not trusted him and believed him to be the giver of eternal life, you can do so right now. We do not know the second, the minute, the hour, the moment or day that God will come to claim us. Will you be ready?

The Word of God says,

"If you confess with your mouth, Jesus is Lord, and believe in your heart that God raised Jesus from the dead, you will be saved. For it is with your heart that you believe and are justified, and it is with your mouth that you confess and are SAVED." (Romans 10:9-10 NIV)

To arrange signings, book events, speaking engagements, or to send your comments to the author please contact:

www.shelialipsey.com

shelialipsey@yahoo.com

About the Author

Christian Novelist, Shelia E. Lipsey, is a native Tennessean, who continues to reside in the city of Memphis. She attended Belhaven College in Jackson, Mississippi, graduating magna cum laude with a BBA degree. She is a proud mother and grandmother. Among Lipsey's list of literary accomplishments and affiliations, she was awarded Conversations Book Club 2008 Author of the Year (thebestbookclub.info), Dallas Morning News Bestselling Author; Urban Knowledge Memphis Bestselling Author; Founding president Memphis African American Writers Group (MAAW), president UC His Glory Book Club (uchisglorybookclub.net) member of Memphis Rawsistaz Book Club, online member of Black Writers Christian Network, Booknibbler_Christian, Black, Copy Editor (www.thebestcopyeditor.com), Writers' Forum, and she is a staff writer for Sankofa Literary Society (sankofa literarysociety.org) columnist at Blogginginblack.com, as well as several other online literary groups. *My Son's Wife* is her third novel since signing with Urban Christian.

Beautiful Ugly

A Novel
By Shelia E. Lipsey

Envy Wilson, Layla Hobbs, Kacie Mayweather, three thirty-year old women, each with their own set of problems, situations, and secrets share a friendship bound together by their need for each other. One by one, they each try to play with the deck life deals them. After all, the alternative to living is dying, and who wants to go down that pathway? There is too much zest in living for them; too many things to see, places to go and an endless list of mistakes yet to be made.

Layla fights the battle of severe obesity, but her melodious voice can soothe the savage beast, but who can soothe her desire for love? Envy is Layla's backbone and is one of the few people in her life who doesn't beat up on her about being overweight. Kacie has six children and five baby daddies, but never a husband. She prays that Deacon, an older man she meets at church, will be the perfect man to love and care for her and her children. Envy has her own secrets that she refuses to share, not even with Layla and Kacie.

When life begins to change for each of these ladies, will their friendships hold up? When good things happen, can they cause bad reactions? Can a good man bring you down? Can a bad man bring you up? Can friendship last in the midst of joy and pain? Through it all, the three of them cling to each other – but the circumstances they face in life will hopefully teach them to cling to God.

Coming September 2009!